A Crime Through Time

John Anthony Miller

A Crime Through Time

ISBN: 978-1-950613-50-2

Taylor and Seale Publishing, LLC
2 Oceans West Blvd., Unit 406
Daytona Beach Shores, Florida 32118
marycpub1@gmail.com
386-481-0502 or 386-760-8987

Books can be bought at
amazon.com
Barnes and Noble
Books-A-Million
and wherever fine books are sold

To buy in bulk for schools, museums, and organizations, please contact Taylor and Seale Publishing for special discounts.

Printed in the U.S.A.

Dedication

For Bobcat—gone but never forgotten.

Acknowledgements

Special thanks to Donna Eastman at Parkeast Literary

and Dr. Mary Custureri

and Dr. Melissa Shaddix

at Taylor and Seale.

Thank you to Chris Homes for the cover art.

Prologue

Montmartre, Paris
April 9, 1874

A cobblestone street crawled up the hill that led to the artist's studio. Narrow and winding, made of mismatched brick of brown and gray, people, horses, and wagon wheels traveled upon it, passing from one boulevard to the next. Defined by stone walls, tall at the bottom where the incline began and narrow at the top where it ended, they wrapped the road with a mother's hand to suggest a security that might not exist. Trees sprouted behind the walls, branches spilling over the capstones, leaves rustling in breaths of wind that bathed the street and city sprawling beyond. The ancient wall and crumbling mortar that glued it together created an illusion of a country lane—not an alley tying bustling boulevards together. But then, Paris had always been a land of illusions, a city where you saw only what you wanted to see and pretended the rest did not exist.

It was almost dark when the artist's model stepped from the studio on top of the hill at the end of a crooked road that wound its way to the boulevard. Her blonde hair spilled onto a green dress that flowed to leather shoes, the cloth mended with a subtle stitch just below the breast. She peered down the hill as she closed the door behind her, a gas streetlight on the distant corner casting a muted glow on passing carriages, horses hooves clicking in cadence on the cobblestone street. The sun had faded, leaving an auburn stripe at the base of the western sky, fading into the horizon as darkness stole the day.

At the top of the hill, a jumbled row of townhouses stretched in a line from the studio, flickering candles in their windows flinging shadows on the street below. On the incline, where the walls rimmed the road, a dark tunnel carved through trees, light from the boulevard shimmering at the opposite end. Branches hung over the road and swayed like monsters' limbs about to grab their prey.

The model paused and eyed the lane. The street was bare—no coaches, bicycles, or passersby—only branches soughing in the wind. Children played in their houses, mothers made their suppers, fathers drank beer at nearby taverns after long tiresome days in factories and shops. Convinced she had nothing to fear, even as eerie as the road might seem, she started down the incline. She stayed close to the street, intimidated by the wall and all she imagined was behind it—shadows of those who would never be known, plotting deeds too evil to fathom. At its shortest elevation, where the capstone kissed the pavement, lavender spilled over the top, and she smelled the sweetness as she passed. But as the walkway descended and the wall spread higher, whatever it hid was veiled in mystery—if, indeed, anything even lurked there at all.

She took a dozen steps and glimpsed a shadow. She paused, her pulse starting to race as she peered into blackness, studying silhouettes from dancing branches, amused that shadows seemed so daunting. After walking a few feet farther, a faint noise marred the night, and she turned, eyes wide.

An auburn cat near the base of the wall scurried to brush her leg.

She gasped. "You scared me, little kitty!" she exclaimed, laughing as she bent to pet it.

The cat rested on its hindquarters, purring loudly, king of the road and all its domains. The woman caressed its head and neck when an unexpected noise, like a shoe scuffing stone, scared the cat, and it darted down the alley.

The model rose, eyes wide, muscles tense. She scanned the road, listening intently, but saw nothing nearby, no one behind her, only silence tainted by the bustling boulevard below—a lone carriage pulled by a tired mare rolling down the road. She quickened her pace, hurrying down the hillside, almost half her journey completed.

The sound repeated, the scuff of a shoe, and she looked in both directions, her heart thumping against her chest. She examined each crack and crevasse in the uneven stone that made the wall, studied windows in houses high on the hill, and searched for a face that might peer from within. But none did. She listened intently for anything that might make a noise—people, animals, or branches that moved and scraped stone. But all was still, save for the faint chatter of leaves as the breeze disturbed them.

As she turned to go, she suddenly gasped, eyes bulging, as calloused hands wrapped around her neck, squeezing tightly. She screamed, or tried to, but only a whisper escaped, the grasp too tight and confining. Her muffled gasp, followed by the faintest cough, barely disrupted the night and was heard by no one at all.

"Don't move," a voice hissed with breath stinking of beer. "It'll be easier. You won't suffer."

Her arms flailed in weak defense, and she kicked the man behind her, the sole of her shoe banging his shins. But the more she struggled, the tighter the grasp, his fingernails digging deeper, ripping the fragile skin on her throat. He pulled closer, his hold tighter.

She tried to scream again, looked wildly up the hill, but found a deserted lane. Her assailant chose the darkest recess, midway between the boulevard below and the houses on top of the hill. She squirmed, growing weaker, clawing at hands that clasped her neck, tearing his flesh with her fingernails. Her tongue swelled, her mouth agape, as she gasped for breath that escaped her, no matter how hard she fought. She yanked the hands that held her, trying to loosen their grasp, and swung her arms wildly, battering his torso with her elbows, each blow fainter than the last until they barely landed at all. She kicked his shins with the heel of her shoe, but he ignored her, squeezing tighter.

"There now," he said in a raspy voice. "Sleep, little angel."

Chapter One

Deauville, France, on the Normandy coast
March 25, 1956

Zélie Girard sat in a high-backed leather chair, her forearms leaning on cushioned armrests. Barely five feet tall, with black hair in a soft bob, her brown eyes showed sadness as she gazed around the empty room, waiting for the closed door to open. Eight chairs surrounded an Art Nouveau table, two wide legs at each end, the rectangular top a series of inlaid hardwoods. The floors were maple, glossy and unmarred, the baseboards and crown moldings a shade darker. Honey gold walls were accented by evenly-spaced seascapes, scenes of waves attacking the Normandy coast, so expertly painted she felt the spray. The room reeked of wealth, money inherited, newly made, and sometimes even stolen—but always in accordance with the law. It was here that decisions were made that few could fathom; thousands of francs routinely changed hands. Zélie was uncomfortable. She didn't belong. It was a world in which she'd never walked and had never expected to visit.

The door opened abruptly, and a man entered, tall and slender, faint lines spreading from his eyes, his gray hair immaculately trimmed. He wore a dark blue suit, hand-tailored and nicely cut, with a blue silk shirt. His tie was anchored by a gold clip, matching cufflinks that glinted on his shirt. He looked like he'd stepped from a magazine, his nails perfectly clipped, his black leather shoes reflecting the light that spilled upon them. He belonged in the room, another fixture to complement the crystal light, lavish moldings, and pricey paintings. He smiled, showing perfect teeth, as he did when it was necessary, but it wasn't genuine. He only smiled to calm her as she sat alone, trembling slightly, waiting for his arrival.

He sat in his usual chair at the head of the table and set down a folder filled with papers beside two black pens with silver tips and a small manilla envelope. He opened the folder and shuffled the papers, rearranged a few, and then looked up at Zélie.

"Good morning, Mme. Girard. I am Gabriel Bissett. How are you today?"

Zélie was nervous, not sure what to expect. "My name is pronounced Zee-lee," she said, smiling. "And I am well. Thank you for asking."

He nodded politely. "Zélie," he repeated, although it seemed he preferred formal address. "On behalf of myself and the law firm of Delacroix and Bisset, I would like to extend our sincere condolences for your loss."

"Thank you, M. Bisset. Your kind words are much appreciated."

He sat back in the chair. "I first met your mother-in-law almost forty years ago. But then, everyone knows each other in a small town. Were you close to her, Mme. Girard?"

Zélie sighed, reliving years that passed too quickly, memories that were best forgotten. "At one time I was," she said. "But it got harder after my husband, Samuel, died."

"At Dien Bien Phu, I was told."

She nodded, her heart still heavy almost two years later. "A senseless war in Indochina."

"I assure you, Mme. Girard, that the entire country mourns with you."

She forced a smile. It was an empty phrase she had heard before. "Thank you, M. Bissett."

Zélie watched him for a moment, wondering if he wanted to know more. "I did keep in close contact with Eva, my mother-in-law, after we lost Samuel. Mainly for my son Luc. He needed her. And I suppose she needed us. We were all she had."

"Life can be lonely, at times," Bissett said, his face a compassionate mask. "Luc is six years old?"

"Yes," she replied, her sadness fading to find a smile. "A good child, he really is. Lost without his father, as can be expected. Now to lose his grand-mère so soon after."

"It must be difficult," Bissett said with just the right amount of sympathy. "If we, at the firm, can ever be of any assistance, please do not hesitate to ask."

She smiled, understanding that the pleasantries had ended, and it was time to conduct the business for which she had come. She nodded to the papers before him. "Shall we begin?"

"Yes, of course," he said, acting as if he didn't want to, even though he obviously did. "I'm sure you're anxious to finalize everything."

"I am," she said softly, although nothing was more final than death. It was a lesson she had learned and would never forget.

"Did you visit Eva in Deauville at all?" he asked. "Or did she usually go to Paris?"

"No, we came to Deauville often. Luc and I moved to a small flat after his father died—it was all I could afford—and it was difficult to have visitors."

"I understand," he said.

Zélie realized that he really didn't. And he never would. He didn't have to worry if he had money for groceries or to buy shoes for a child who had outgrown what he had. Gabriel Bissett would never understand. "Luc stayed with Eva often—usually just for the weekend, but longer in the summer."

"Then you are familiar with the property?"

"Yes, very much so."

"It is a wonderful location," he said. "A few blocks from the beach, but far enough away from the race track and casinos. It's a quiet street, a main house and three cottages, designed as holiday lets, although two currently have year-round tenants. The property suffered no damage during the war, unlike so many other buildings in Deauville."

She briefly thought of the world war and the many lives impacted, including her own. "If nothing else, the income from the cottages will allow me to spend more time with Luc," she said, grateful to inherit the property. "He's a troubled child, as I'm sure you can imagine. I'm hoping the relocation helps him."

"I'm sure it will," he said. "It's much different from Paris—a slower pace, lower expenses, little crime. You were employed as a teacher?"

"I was," she replied. "Piano and music theory at a conservatory."

"The cottages should provide enough income to support the property," he said. He looked up from the papers, his gaze meeting hers. "But it is heavily mortgaged, through two liens, one somewhat recent. The banks agreed to transfer the debt to you, given the inheritance."

Zélie was quiet for a moment. "I was quite surprised, when you told me on the telephone, by the debt my mother-in-law incurred. The house has been in my husband's family for many years. I assumed any mortgage had been paid in full."

"No, I'm afraid not," Bisset said with a frown. "It seems Eva had some financial difficulties, but I didn't explore what caused them. If all three cottages are rented, the income will pay the mortgages and most of the upkeep, with a little left over."

Zélie felt like she was sinking in quicksand. "I want to keep the house in the family and someday pass it on to Luc. He has so little of his father. But it might be difficult with all the debt. I'm hoping to teach music to earn additional income—if a demand exists."

"I'm sure it does," he mumbled, glancing at the papers and not paying much attention. "Eva left some money with her estate. Not much, but enough for a few months' expenses."

Zélie nodded, a bit relieved. She had little money, most of which had been used to relocate.

Bissett handed her a pen. "We have some papers to sign, and, when we're finished, I'll give you the keys to the property and a check for the remainder of the estate."

Zélie smiled and looked at the stack of papers, suddenly feeling weary. "Thank you," she said as she took the pen. "I do appreciate your assistance."

Chapter Two

Montmartre, Paris
May 9, 1874, one month after the murder

Elise Lyon stepped from a handsome black carriage with gilt trim pulled by a chestnut mare with white socks.

"Shall I wait here, Madame?" the coachman asked as he helped her. "Or shall I come to the top of the hill?"

"No, this is fine," she replied. She paused, gazing up the incline at a cluster of disjointed houses past stone walls that rimmed the road.

She was attractive, her brown hair pinned above her head, her face marred only by a freckle or two, a slight scar above her left eye. Her brown eyes twinkled with mystery, inviting most who noticed to want to know more. She wore a sleek blue blouse and pleated skirt, hand-tailored, accented by a string of genuine pearls that matched her earrings.

The heels of her shoes clicked on the pavement as she slowly walked the incline. She stopped to admire a rare bed of blue iris pallida. A perfect match to her pleated skirt, she plucked a few to form a bunch and lifted them to her nose, drinking the scent of spring.

Elise continued, the walls shrinking as she approached the top of the hill, lavender spilling over the capstone. She looked at the mismatched collection of houses ahead, strung in a row and splashed in lavender, beige, and blue. They were in various states of disrepair, stucco was cracked, paint chipped, doors and windows weathered and worn. They sat close to the road, a meter away, with broad windows and narrow balconies, chimneys poking through sagging roofs that were covered with crooked slabs of slate. A salmon-colored house stood at the end of the lane, and Elise suspected it was her destination. Defined by long narrow twelve-paned windows that faced the road, it was likely a former shop of some sort. On the building's side, an oval window peeked from beneath an arch of stone protruding from the wall to form the base of a corbelled chimney for a second-floor fireplace.

When she reached the house, no sign announced an artist's presence, but the number eight affixed under a glass lamp that displayed a half-melted candle matched the address on her scrap of paper. The door molding was wide and fluted, built in sections of aged marble, a thin line of mortar barely visible. The green paint on the planked door was scarred and fading, matching the molding around the windows.

She knocked timidly, a few minutes early. As she waited, a group of boys approached, seven or eight years old, and she smiled as they passed, eyeing the strange woman in expensive clothes. Seconds later, a middle-aged woman, her black hair tinged with gray, her face long and narrow, emerged from the neighboring house, watching her curiously and scolding the boys.

"Are you looking for Jean-Pierre, Madame?" the woman asked.

"I am," Elise replied. "I'm having my portrait done."

The woman came closer, her gaze shifting from Elise's clothes to her face. "It'll be a beautiful painting, I'm sure."

Elise smiled, nodding slightly. "Thank you so much," she said. "What a kind thing to say." She handed the bunch of iris to the stranger. "For you."

The woman's eyes widened. "Thank you, Madame," she said, taking the flowers. "But don't you need these for your portrait?"

"No," Elise said, still smiling. "I just picked them along the road."

The door to the studio opened, and a man emerged, lean and handsome, his brown hair unfashionably long, his face blemished by a two or three-day growth of beard. He nodded to his neighbor and smiled at Elise. "Mme. Lyon?"

"Yes, Monsieur," she said sweetly, as much for the neighbor's benefit as his.

"I am Jean-Pierre, commissioned by your husband to paint your portrait, and this is my neighbor, Mme. Michel." He turned to the middle-aged woman. "May I present Mme. Elise Lyon?"

"We've met," Mme. Michel said, nodding politely. "And she's a delightful woman. Her portrait shall be your finest, I'm sure."

"It will be, Mme. Michel, I promise," Jean-Pierre said as he guided Elise inside.

The studio was sparsely furnished, more for function than comfort. A couch leaned against the wall, the white cloth smudged with splatters of paint. A faded full-length curtain covered an opening, likely a closet that housed supplies. The stairs to the second floor were beside it, the exposed steps dark but worn in the center from many years of footsteps.

The remainder of the room, and much of the space along the walls, was cluttered with canvases and frames. Some were completed paintings, others were half-finished, and some were completely naked, waiting for the brush to dress them. A large easel was centered in the room, flanked by two that were smaller, a chair before them.

A few meters from the door a single chair had been placed to catch the sunlight as it streamed in the studio. The center window was half opened, a butterfly perched on the sill, orange with black speckles, unable to decide whether to enter or fly out to the vast unknown.

Mme. Michel stood just beyond the open window, eavesdropping, while she spoke to a friend. Elise caught Jean-Pierre's attention and nodded toward them. Jean-Pierre smiled subtly, knowing whatever he said or did was for their benefit, also.

"You're welcome to watch the session, Mme. Michel," Jean-Pierre called.

"Thank you, Jean-Pierre," Mme. Michel replied and then whispered to her friend. "We might. Just from the window for a bit."

Jean-Pierre turned to Elise. "What will your husband do with your portrait?"

"He will hang it over the fireplace in his study," she said, still gazing around the room. The clutter was annoying but also fascinating, offering an unguarded glimpse into the artist's mind. She wondered why the gifted struggled with simple things in life—like tidiness.

"I hope you find my efforts comparable to other portraits you may have seen," he said as he started to arrange his supplies.

"I have no doubt that it will."

"You'll be quite pleased, Madame," Mme. Michel said through the window. "He's a marvelous artist."

"Thank you," Elise said, glancing at Jean-Pierre. "My husband made the right choice."

"It will take several weeks," Jean-Pierre warned. "An imposition, perhaps?"

Elise shrugged. "I'll manage. I'm looking forward to it."

"Please," he said, motioning to the straight-backed chair in front of the window.

Elise sat upright, her hands in her lap, while he fussed behind the easel, fixing the canvas just the way he wanted, getting his pencils and charcoal and paints properly placed. She was amused, seeing the perfectionist in the man that he might not see in himself.

"I've never been a model before," she admitted.

"Most haven't," he muttered, preoccupied, sorting through stubs of charcoal.

She gazed at the partially finished paintings scattered around the room. Many showed the Normandy coast, imposing cliffs and an angry sea that slowly wore them away. A few depicted villages and towns that dotted the shore, most unchanged for centuries. Almost all were in the Impressionist style, a bold approach initially criticized by experts. She didn't recognize any of the portraits, although she suspected one woman was the wife of a government official. All were in various stages of completion. A few were nudes, all of the same woman, a young blond with blue eyes.

"Who is she?" Elise asked, pointing. She glanced to the window where Mme. Michele still stood, wondering if she might reply.

Jean-Pierre looked up, his expression showing that his thoughts were disturbed. "Giselle," he said simply.

"A model?" Elise asked. "Or more?"

"She was here many times," Mme. Michel interjected with a knowing nod, as if she were too polite to provide the answer to Elise's question.

Jean-Pierre shrugged. "Both, perhaps," he said, implying the relationship was complex.

Elise focused on Giselle, naked and exposed, almost intruding upon her privacy as she studied the swell of her breasts, the curve of her buttocks. She was attractive, and, given the number of paintings in which she was featured, Elise suspected she had a generous benefactor.

"I'll start with faint charcoal outlines of different poses," Jean-Pierre explained. "And when I select the one I like the best, I will start to paint. You'll be here for an hour today, maybe a bit more, but our sessions will never be more than ninety minutes. And we will meet at various times." He motioned to the window. "To capture different light and shadows."

"Whatever is needed," she said, eyeing Mme. Michel at the window. She found it amusing that the woman was so nosy.

When Jean-Pierre finished arranging his tools, he looked up to study the position of her face, subtle shadows the light formed as it streamed through the window. He frowned, looked at her more closely, stepped from behind the easel, and walked toward her.

"Is something wrong?" she asked.

"No, you just need to move a bit," he said as he gently tilted her head to the left. "That's better."

She looked in his eyes, big and brown, and studied the chiseled leanness of his face. His hands were soft, but he was an artist, not a bricklayer.

He returned to the easel and studied her a moment more. Then he smiled. "We begin," he said, holding a piece of charcoal between his thumb and index finger.

She stayed still, not moving her head, although her gaze still wandered the room. As he formed a faint outline of her face with his slender stick of charcoal, she studied the paintings, counting a half dozen sketches and two portraits of Giselle. With Jean-Pierre immersed in his work and Mme. Michel watching from the window, Elise avoided asking the question that plagued her since she arrived.

Why were the works of Giselle all unfinished?

Chapter Three

Deauville, 1956

It took Zélie just over an hour to conduct her business, and, after politely thanking M. Bissett, she left the conference room and approached the receptionist, a middle-aged woman with her hair in a bun.

"He was very well behaved," the receptionist said, glancing at a young boy sitting alone in the waiting room.

Zélie was relieved. Luc could sometimes be difficult. "I'm not surprised," she said, more for Luc's benefit than the secretary's. He sat quietly, holding a small firetruck, looking very bored. "Are you ready to go, Luc?"

He nodded and went to stand beside his mother. Shy but curious, slight with dark hair and eyes like his mother, he was coping with so many changes—none of which were good.

"Thank you for watching him," Zélie said.

"No trouble at all," the woman said as she resumed her typing.

"Come on, Luc," Zélie said, taking him by the hand. "We're going to our new home. Where grand-mère used to live."

"When will I see my new school?" he asked.

"Tomorrow," Zélie said. "Today, we'll get settled."

They left the office and went out on the street, one of the busier boulevards in Deauville. Zélie unlocked the door of her older black Citroën. It was a reliable automobile, although the rear fender was dented, and some rust showed on the grille. She'd used it very little in Paris where most of what she needed had been nearby and whatever wasn't could be reached by bus or train. Now it was her primary mode of transportation. She hoped it posed no problems. She wasn't prepared for unexpected expenses.

Their new home sat on a quiet street several blocks from the center of town, and it only took a few minutes to get there. Zélie parked along the curb. Mature trees were spaced along the pavement, their limbs spilling over the road. A three-foot high brick wall ran along the front, a short white railing with thick balusters on top. A long driveway led to a cramped garage at the rear of the property, the paint on the wood panel doors chipped and fading. Three identical cottages sat with their entrances facing a side street. The end units were occupied, the center cottage vacant.

Zélie realized that, as soon as she was settled, she should contact the estate agent to arrange for holiday lets. Hopefully, the empty cottage could be rented quickly—maybe Eva had much of the summer already booked. Deauville was more than a beach resort for the well-to-do from Paris. It was a world-renowned equestrian center boasting yearling sales that brought buyers from around the globe and a racecourse that ranked among the best in Europe. The village swelled with tourists every season, which stretched from spring's end through early fall.

She paused to study the brick house with its marble moldings, unable to believe it belonged to her. The arched entryway was on the left, two arched windows with spider-web mullions beside it. The second floor wasn't as grand—three square windows, evenly spaced, diagonal mullions dressing the panes. And finally, a smaller third floor, a lone window facing the street. It was a beautiful house that fit in a fairy tale, and Zélie had always loved it.

"Come on, Luc," she said, taking the boy's hand and leading him up a curved walkway bordered by dormant flower beds and overgrown shrubs. "This is our home now."

"I miss grand-mère," Luc said softly, grief written on his face.

"I know," Zélie said, her hand moving the hair away from his forehead. "I miss her, too. But she's with papa now."

"I don't want to be a grown-up."

She knelt beside him, gazing into his sad eyes. "Everyone becomes a grownup."

"But grownups die," he said softly. "Like papa and grand-mère. You'll die, too, and I don't want that to happen."

"Oh, Luc," she said, hugging him tightly, her heart heavy. "I'm not going to die. I promise you."

"I don't want to be alone," he said, starting to sob. "I won't know what to do."

"You won't be alone," she assured him, wiping his tears away. "I'll be with you. Today, tomorrow, forever. I promise."

He nodded, tears subsiding, but a troubled look stayed fixed to his face.

"Come on," she urged, acting excited. "Let's go see our home."

She opened the door, her new life about to begin, and led Luc inside. They were met with an eerie silence, disturbed only by the ticking of a grandfather's clock on the foyer's far wall. Stairs began against the left wall and curved upward in a sweeping quarter circle to meet the second-floor hallway; an arched opening under the stairs led to the dining room. The decor throughout the house was Art Nouveau, defined by bright colors and sweeping curves. An arched doorway to the right led to a parlor, light green wallpaper with swirling flowers, the molding dark green, a white couch in front of a marble fireplace, a set of barrel chairs with a table between them.

"It's quiet," Luc said.

"It is," Zélie agreed, almost feeling like she had to whisper. She had seen these rooms a hundred times, but now she saw them differently.

Another archway led to a second parlor furnished much like the first, a chaise lounge instead of the couch, an upright piano against the wall by the window. Sheet music sat in the holder, untouched for months, a song by Edith Piaf in the key of A flat. A stand-up radio stood against the near wall with two parlor chairs beside it.

"Can I listen to the radio?" Luc asked. "Grand-mère always let me."

"In a minute," Zélie said. "Let's walk through the house first."

Behind the foyer was the dining room, with a curio cabinet against the far wall, a web-like mullion accenting the glass. A large table, legs curving to join at the center, chairs matching, consumed much of the room. The kitchen was functional, recently updated, red and white checkerboard tiles on the floor, white cabinets with four-paned glass doors. Red and white ruffled cafe curtains hung in the windows, a bread box sat on the countertop—a set of tin canisters for flour, sugar, coffee, and tea beside it. An oval wrought-iron table with four chairs occupied the far corner where she and Luc would take their meals.

Zélie could feel her mother-in-law's presence, a sad emptiness that overwhelmed the room. She opened the cabinet doors, smiling faintly at familiar dishes, but found no food in cupboards or cabinets. She checked the refrigerator. It, too, was empty. The law firm had arranged for thorough cleaning, since the property had been vacant while the estate was being settled.

"Let's go upstairs," Zélie said. "Then you can listen to the radio."

She took him by the hand and led him up the sweeping staircase. They walked down the corridor, master bedroom to the right, the headboard a large oval, the sides curving down to the footboard, a crimson bedcover. The bureau and wardrobe had waterfall fronts, and a vanity sat against the far wall, a large oval mirror anchored to it.

"Will you sleep in grand-mère's room?" Luc asked.

"Yes, I will," she said, looking at his little face, so afraid of the unknown. "Is that all right?"

"I suppose so," he said.

"Let's go see your bedroom."

They went across the hall into his room, unchanged since their last visit—a single bed, wardrobe, bureau, and desk. It was what he had always known, an anchor to some stability. The spare bedroom beside it was filled with their belongings, boxes shipped from Paris. The bathroom was across the hall, next to the master bedroom, with pale blue tile and dark blue trim, a pedestal sink, and a large curving bath.

"All right, Luc," she said. "Let's find a radio program for you. I'm going to wash the bed linens and do some cleaning. Then we'll go to the market."

"Aren't we going up in the attic?" he asked.

Zélie had only been in the attic once that she could remember. Crammed with old furniture, lamps, boxes, and crates, it was a mystery that must be explored. But not now.

"Maybe later," she said, her gaze fixed on the door.

Chapter Four

Montmartre, 1874

The modeling session lasted just over an hour, and when it ended Jean-Pierre led Elise to the door. "Not too uncomfortable posing, I hope."

"Not at all," she replied. "But difficult, sometimes, to remain still."

"We can pause when you need to rest or move about," he said. "It's just the light. We must capture the light when it's at its best."

They stepped onto the pavement. Mme. Michel was sitting on her stoop, watching the boys play ball, keeping a wary eye on artist and model while pretending she did not.

"She was at the window the entire time," Elise whispered. "But now she watches the boys play ball."

"She observes many of my sessions. More interested in what is said than what is painted."

"Do you think she approves of me?"

He shrugged and leaned closer. "Everyone on the street will know what Mme. Michel thinks a few minutes after you've gone."

She smiled. "It was an innocent session between model and artist. Nothing more. So how much can she say?"

"I'm sure she'll be watching closely. At least for a while."

"She heard every word. Not a single sentence was missed."

"And answered questions not even posed to her," he added, chuckling.

"Will she be at every session?"

"She'll soon lose interest," he said as he surveyed the street, noticing how the light was perfectly framed by the trees. "Where is your carriage?"

"Waiting down the hill," she said. "I wanted to walk. It looked so pleasant, the flowers, tree limbs dangling over the street."

"It is beautiful," he agreed, seeing it with an artist's eye. It was the light that held his attention and how it impacted the view. "Another scene to paint. But only when the light is right."

She paused to observe, trying to see what he did. But it didn't seem that she could. "Your landscapes are breathtaking. I feel like I could walk right into them."

"I will paint this crooked lane," he decided, studying a limb that stretched over the wall and hung above the street. He walked with her for a few more steps. "Shall I escort you to your carriage?"

"No, that's not necessary," she said. She turned and smiled. "Until we meet again."

Jean-Pierre watched her for a moment walking down the hill, the boys shouting and playing ball, birds singing songs he had heard before. Paris was so beautiful in the spring, especially for those who could appreciate it—fading paint on hundred-year-old buildings, branches spilling over crooked lanes that twisted from one broad boulevard to the next, flowers flaunting the rainbow's colors, sprouting from beds beside pavements and boxes beneath windows.

He turned to enter the studio, nodding to his neighbor as he did so.

"She's a beautiful model," Mme. Michel called over to him.

"Yes, she is. I'm looking forward to painting her portrait."

Mme. Michel smiled coyly. "Yes, I bet you are."

Jean-Pierre nodded politely.

"Expensive clothes," Mme. Michel commented. "The skirt and blouse were lovely. Must come from wealth."

"Yes, she dresses nicely," he said and offered no more.

Once inside, he closed the window—it had served its purpose. It had stayed open for Mme. Michel, so she could observe an innocent session, see what was in the studio, overhear a conversation that might never have happened had she not been listening. But soon she would lose interest in both him and his model, like she had with those before, and he could do what he wanted when he painted.

He eyed the studio and decided to remove some of the paintings lying askew, staged for the eyes of others—like Mme. Michel. They were no longer needed. He took two nude sketches of Giselle, admired them for a moment, and put them in the storage room, followed by two more. It was cramped—a few shelves, a bench with a basin of water, a cot with mussed sheets, boxes of paints and supplies. He stacked the sketches in one corner.

He returned to the studio and set an easel outside on the pavement. He placed a chair in front of it, splashed blotches of paint on his palette, and took up a few of his brushes. Then he sat quietly for a moment, studying the lane as it wandered down the incline, the sunlight streaming perfectly through the tunnel the trees created, bathing the boulevard below. Lavender spilled over the capstone, the crooked wall, weaved down the road defined by mismatched cobblestone worn by wagon wheels as the birds leaped from limb to limb, whistling and warbling, singing their songs. But the light would not last, so he had to paint quickly.

As the brush danced along the canvas, the narrow lane coming to life, he thought of his session with Elise Lyon. She symbolized Paris—beauty, poise and intellect—and he would have to portray her in many different ways to capture all that she was, what she represented, and all she could be, whether she realized it or not. But he knew that, above all else, she was only an illusion. Just like the city and everyone in it.

Chapter Five

Deauville, 1956

Zélie spent most of the day getting the house ready. She cleaned the bathrooms and kitchen, did a few loads of wash, and ran the vacuum. Luc was settled in the parlor, playing on the floor. He listened to his favorite programs on the radio, briefly practiced his piano lesson, and played with his toys—a small collection of trucks and bulldozers that he drove around the carpet. Zélie checked on him periodically, and, when she had almost finished cleaning, she found him kneeling on the chaise lounge, curtain drawn, gazing out the window.

"What are you looking at?" she asked as she walked into the parlor.

"The men outside."

She went to the window. "Who are they?"

"M. Rayne," he said. "And M. LaRue."

"The men that live in the cottages?" she asked, the names familiar.

"Yes," he replied. "M. Rayne played soldier with me when I came to see grand-mère."

Zélie peeked around the curtain so she wouldn't be seen. Behind the building farthest from the road, an older man was repairing a bicycle, different parts lying on the ground around him. She knew it was Marc Rayne, a retired policeman. She had met him while visiting her mother-in-law.

"I only see M. Rayne," she said, scanning the property.

"M. LaRue went back inside."

She turned away. "I never met M. LaRue."

"There he is," Luc said, pointing. "He came back out."

Zélie returned to the window and saw what seemed to be a boy, a teenager maybe, small framed. "Are you sure that's a man?"

"Yes, Maman," Luc said. "He's nice, too. But he doesn't play like M. Rayne does."

Zélie kept looking, wondering why an old man had been playing with a child, and who M. LaRue might be. "Why don't I invite them over for dinner on Sunday?" she suggested. "We can get to know them better."

"That'll be fun," Luc said. "We can play with my trucks."

Zélie smiled. "I'm sure they'll be very excited."

After she finished cleaning, Zélie took Luc to the market, buying a week's supply of food along with personal items and more cleaning supplies. When they returned home, she made dinner, onion soup with croissants, a salad, and some sliced cheese.

"Tomorrow, I'll take you to your new school," Zélie said as they enjoyed their meal.

"Will it be the same as my old school?"

Zélie hesitated. "I think you'll like it better," she said, more optimistic than she felt. Luc was a loner, impacted by his father's death and now the loss of his grand-mère. She hoped Deauville would be a new beginning but feared it might be harder—a constant reminder of those he loved and lost.

When they'd finished eating and Zélie had cleaned up, they went into the parlor. Luc played with his trucks while she sat on the piano stool, looking at the sheet music on the stand.

"Can we go into the attic?" Luc asked.

"I'm so tired," she said, lightly playing the melody of "La Vie En Rose," by Edith Piaf with her right hand. "Can we go tomorrow?"

"Please, Maman," he said. "I want to see what's up there."

She sighed and stood, smiling weakly. "Just for a few minutes."

He ran up the stairs and was waiting at the attic door when she got there.

"You really do want to explore, don't you?"

"I think there's toys up there."

She smiled and opened the door, turned on the light, and they climbed the steps, finding two finished rooms, bedrooms when the house had been built. But now the wallpaper was faded, the paint chipped and dull, the spaces likely used as storage for many years. Her husband had never mentioned the attic—or what was in it—and he'd spent much of his life in the house.

"I'm going to look through everything," Luc said, running through the attic and taking the tops off cardboard boxes.

Zélie sighed, gazing about the room, studying the dust and clutter. Boxes were stacked everywhere, a few wooden chests, wingback chairs that pre-dated the house, end tables with the sweeping curves of Art Nouveau design, thirty years old at most. Brass lamps, paintings, stacks of books, a few maps—all in frames that had once hung on walls—were scattered about the rooms.

Then she saw the portrait.

Chapter Six

Montmartre, 1874

Lyon and Son, established in 1701, was a Parisian investment firm that lurked in the shadows of legitimacy. It was managed by Elise's husband Henri Lyon who had inherited the business at the age of thirty-three. He made tremendous amounts of money, not all of it legally, and supposedly bribed politicians to pretend not to see what most others did. Rumored to have funded both sides of the recent Franco-Prussian War, a humiliating defeat for France, some said Henri Lyon had no soul, at least when it came to making money. He was a portly man, his brown hair showing strands of gray, his beard immaculately trimmed, who liked his shirts ironed and starched.

His office was in a Neoclassical building in the second arrondissement, a block from the Paris Bourse. It was a warm room with built-in bookcases, a marble fireplace of Italianate design, and comfortable leather chairs. His mahogany desk displayed only his prized possessions: a teak box from the Congo containing his finest cigars, a brass clock, and a marble bust of Napoleon. A rack behind his desk held maps of French colonies that spanned the globe where his holdings were gradually increasing.

Like many in his social class, Henri Lyon had married late, his wife much younger, an ornament to hang on his arm, a faux expression of youth and virility, a possession more than a partner, a symbol more than spouse. Much like other men of his status, he did what he wanted, paid little attention to his wife, and ran his household with a strict discipline that lent little room for compromise. A bully in the business world, he found the same behavior worked just as well at home.

As Henri sat in his office reading *La France*, the financial newspaper, he was interrupted by a timid knock on the door. "Yes?" he called, not looking up.

The door opened slightly, and his clerk peeked in. "M. Sinclair is here to see you."

"Show him in."

A man entered, almost thirty, with black hair and dark eyes. Polite and respectful, he could also be callous and cold when needed. As the owner of Normandy Mines, a global conglomerate, he knew that managing assets was serious business, and there was little room for warmth or emotion.

"Andre," Henri said without rising, his eyes fixed on the paper. "You're very punctual."

"I wouldn't want to keep you waiting," Sinclair said, unable to hide a hint of disdain. "May I sit?"

"Yes, of course," Henri said, motioning to the chair in front of his desk. He had never liked Sinclair and suspected he never would. But he enjoyed their meetings immensely. He had caught Sinclair in a cage, a financial disaster of the younger man's own making.

Sinclair sat down, collected his thoughts, and began an unpleasant discussion. "I was surprised to learn that you purchased one of my loans."

"At a discount, I might add," Henri muttered, ensuring Sinclair realized his finances were in shambles. "It seems you're overextended."

Sinclair sat back, eyeing Henri warily. "Temporarily overextended," he clarified. "Pending planned asset sales."

"But the loan I purchased is almost due, Andre. No time exists to sell assets."

"The bank that held the lien was amenable to a two-year extension," Sinclair explained. "So the need for cash was not as pressing."

Henri sighed, pleased that Sinclair was so uncomfortable, and feigned an innocent reply. "Apparently, they had little faith in your ability to pay, regardless of the terms. They were quite anxious to sell it."

Sinclair's face firmed. "And you were quite willing to accommodate them."

Henri shrugged. "At significant risk, I might add. But I suspected you would attempt to fix your finances, so I thought it acceptable."

Sinclair hesitated, as if beginning to realize he might be outmatched. "I have some alternatives in lieu of payment."

Henri Lyon loved the jousting that went with negotiations. Especially when he held such a dominant position. And he almost always did. "I'm willing to entertain your proposal," he said, even though he wasn't. He already knew what he wanted.

"Are you willing to extend the loan duration?"

Henri hesitated, but gave it his consideration. Extending the loan would earn additional interest plus an upfront fee. But if Normandy Mines failed, he could lose his entire investment. "I could be persuaded for the right opportunity. How long of an extension?"

"I think two or three years, under the same terms, would be adequate."

"What are you offering in return?"

Sinclair paused and considered his portfolio. "I have a ten percent interest in a coal mine near the German border. I'll transfer profits for a two-year period."

Henri studied Andre Sinclair, pretending to be proud and confident while his business collapsed around him. "That's a start, Andre. Something I'll consider. But coal is so dependent on supply and demand."

Sinclair's eyes widened, surprised his offer hadn't been accepted. Maybe Henri's reaction was part of the dance such negotiations demanded. "Can you extend my loan for thirty days? You can assess the coal's value, and I'll continue to pursue alternatives."

Henri turned the page of his newspaper, showing no interest at all. "I'm afraid that's out of the question. I need the capital."

Sinclair pursed his lips. "Would you consider real estate? I'll transfer ownership of the right property, in lieu of cash, to satisfy the debt in full."

Henri yawned and looked up. "I might, but only if the holdings compliment my own."

Sinclair sat back in the chair, folding his arms across his chest. "I've offered two alternatives—coal or one of my real estate holdings."

Henri was quiet, adjusting his approach. He didn't need Andre Sinclair. But Andre Sinclair needed him. "What's my incentive?"

"You'll make a nice profit," Sinclair said. "Any swap would be steeply discounted."

"Assuming your evaluations are correct. But I'm afraid I need more."

Sinclair studied Henri cautiously, a man he didn't want to underestimate. "I'll give it my consideration," he said tartly and rose to leave.

"Please be expedient. The loan is due the end of the month."

Sinclair started for the door but stopped and turned. “Why play this game, Henri? This negotiation that neither of us has time for?” he asked. “If coal or buildings don’t interest you, and I can’t pay in cash, tell me what you want. I need time. What will it take to extend the due date of the loan for at least two years?”

Henri smiled slyly. Sinclair had walked into his trap. He hesitated, allowing the tension to mount, acting as if he’d considered all possible alternatives before he spoke. “I want the yearling.”

Sinclair’s eyes widened. “Absolutely not,” he declared, his anger melting in devastation. “You can take anything else. But not the yearling.”

Henri tried not to smile. He knew the yearling was Andre Sinclair’s most prized possession. That’s exactly why he wanted it. He shrugged. “It’s your decision, of course, Andre. But if you want an extension, I’ll only accept the yearling as payment.”

Sinclair glared at him. “Someday you will lose something that’s dear to you, Henri. And no one in Paris will care.”

Chapter Seven

Deauville, 1956

At 5:45 p.m., there was a knock on Zélie's front door. "I'll get it, Maman," Luc called, running into the foyer.

Zélie came from the kitchen, a white apron wrapped around her floral dress. She wanted dinner for her tenants to be just right, a sign that their relationship would be a good one. It had been a long time since she cooked for a man, let alone two, but she enjoyed making a nice meal, especially when it was appreciated.

Luc opened the door and admitted Marc Rayne, the retired policeman. He was average height and build with blue eyes, his hair black and gray, maybe sixty years old. He limped badly, although Zélie had never asked why. She assumed it was related to the war, which had crippled and maimed so many, or maybe his police work. He held flowers, white roses sprinkled with lavender, and a bottle of chardonnay.

"Mme. Girard," he said as he handed her the flowers. "Thank you for the invitation to dine."

Zélie couldn't resist lifting the flowers close and enjoying their scent. "M. Rayne, thank you so much. You're too kind. You didn't have to bring anything."

"Please, call me Marc," he said. "Flowers and wine are the least I can offer."

"Thank you, it's much appreciated. Please, make yourself comfortable while I put these in some water."

"How are you doing, little Luc?" Marc Rayne asked, walking into the parlor and sitting on the couch next to the boy.

"I'm going to a new school."

"You are?" Marc asked. "That must be fun."

Luc frowned. "I don't like it," he whispered. "But don't tell, Maman."

"It'll get better," Marc assured him. "You'll see. Just give it a chance."

Luc eyed him thoughtfully, and his face brightened. "Do you want to play with my trucks?"

"Luc, do not torment M. Rayne," Zélie called from the kitchen. "Would you like a glass of wine, Marc?"

"Yes, that would be nice."

They were interrupted by another knock on the door. Zélie went into the foyer and opened it.

A man about her height stood before her—just a shade over five feet tall. He was slender, with brown hair and eyes, mid-twenties at most, dressed in gray slacks and a blue shirt.

"Please, come in," she said.

"I'm Anton LaRue," he said, smiling. He handed her a small box. "Macarons for dessert."

"Oh, thank you, M. LaRue. I'm Zélie Girard."

"Please call me Anton."

"Of course," she said. "Come make yourself comfortable. I'll get you something to drink."

They gathered in the parlor, sharing a bottle of wine, getting to know each other. Zélie had met Marc a few times, just in passing. He was quiet, looked as if he felt uncomfortable, but was very polite. Anton was the opposite, handsome, smiling and talkative. As the two men talked to Luc about his schoolwork, Zélie returned to the kitchen and finished preparing dinner. A few minutes later she came back in the parlor.

"Dinner is ready," she announced.

They gathered in the dining room, one of the few times Zélie expected to use the Art Nouveau furniture that painted such a beautiful portrait of a passing era. She poured chardonnay for everyone and filled their bowls with vegetable soup. A pitcher of water sat in the center of the table.

"You're a retired policeman?" she asked Marc once they'd started the first course.

"I am," Marc replied. "From Calais."

Zélie hesitated. She wanted to know more but was afraid to pry. "I saw you repairing a bicycle."

Marc nodded. "A hobby, only to keep busy. I restore abandoned bicycles and donate them to charity."

"What a nice hobby to have," she said, her question answered. She knew he couldn't ride a bicycle. Not with his injured leg. "What made you settle in Deauville?"

He poured a glass of water. "I was traveling the coast and thought this might be a nice place to stay. My son lives not far, so it's convenient. I wanted to get away from the city. Deauville is quiet all winter and offers some excitement in the summer—the best of both worlds."

"I'm a jockey," Anton said, as if expecting to be questioned next. "I've lived in Deauville my entire life, as has my father and his father before him."

"How exciting," she said, recognizing what an asset his size was. "Did they all work with horses?"

Anton nodded and laughed. "A family passion. It must be in our blood."

"Can I ride your horse?" Luc asked, eyes wide.

Anton chuckled. "Yes, of course you can. But only after all your schoolwork is done."

"And your chores, too," Zélie added.

"Do you like Deauville?" Marc asked, looking at Zélie.

She paused to consider her answer. "It's a lovely town. So different from Paris. I suppose I'm still getting used to it."

Marc hesitated as if he wanted to speak but wasn't sure he should. "Will you be keeping the property?" he asked, watching Luc to see how closely he listened.

"I hope to," she replied. "If I can manage the expenses."

"We're sorry about your mother-in-law," Marc said, glancing at Anton, who nodded. "She was a good woman."

"Yes, she was," Zélie agreed, eyeing Luc closely. "It's hard. For both of us."

"She was a friend to me," Anton said. "And she knew her horses."

Zélie set her spoon in her bowl. "Eva?" she asked in disbelief, referring to her mother-in-law. "She knew her horses?"

"Oh, yes," Anton said. "She was a huge racing fan. Sometimes we talked for hours."

Zélie was surprised, feeling like she might know less about her mother-in-law than she thought she did. "Did she bet on the races?"

Anton laughed. "Constantly," he said. "She loved it. Sometimes she shared her picks with me, but I don't gamble."

"I would have never guessed," she muttered, pensive. She now knew the cause of the heavy debts her mother-in-law had incurred. "Her love for horse-racing might answer some questions."

Anton looked at her, his head cocked. "What questions are they?"

She hesitated, not sure whether or not to discuss her personal problems. But they would find out sooner or later. "Eva was deeply in debt. Shortly before her death, she heavily mortgaged the property to pay them."

Marc glanced at Anton. "We had no idea. Are the costs excessive?"

Zélie smiled weakly. "Yes, more than I can manage," she admitted. "It's imperative that I rent the third cottage as quickly as possible. A year-round tenant would be best, as opposed to holiday lets."

"Maybe we can help," Anton said. "I'll ask around the stables."

"Yes, we should be able to find someone," Marc added, his face etched with concern.

"Thank you so much. I appreciate it." She paused, her thoughts drifting from her mother-in-law's secret to a recent discovery in the attic.

Marc eyed her closely. "Is something wrong?"

"No, not really," Zélie said, shaking her head. "But Eva's love of horses might explain something else."

Anton glanced at Marc, confused. "What might that be?"

"There's a portrait of a horse in the attic along with a few other paintings," she said. "Maybe you can help me find out what it is. It's well done, definitely painted by a master."

"I would love to," Anton said. "We can look after dinner."

"It's old," she continued. "I think it's dated 1874."

Anton sipped his wine. "The track at Deauville was only a few years old at that time."

"I may be able to help, too," Marc offered. "I can use some of my detective skills."

Zélie smiled. "It'll be a nice mystery to solve."

"Maman, maybe we can find out who the lady is," Luc added.

The two men looked at each other. "What lady is that?" Marc asked.

"There's a portrait of a woman, too," Zélie said. "She's beautiful, with a twinkle in her eyes that hints at a secret she doesn't dare tell. Someone very talented painted it. But I have no idea who she is or why Eva had it."

Chapter Eight

Montmartre, 1874

Henri Lyon sat behind a broad desk in his study, a loose, half-turned pile of papers before him. A Bordeaux bank was failing, ripe for acquisition, and he evaluated risk versus potential reward. A tap on the door interrupted him.

"I'm not disturbing you, am I?" Elise asked as she peeked in.

"No, of course not," he said, even though she was.

She entered, walked to a window, and opened the drapes, allowing light to spill in. "That's better," she said. "It was much too dark."

Henri watched with some amusement and returned to his papers.

"How was your day, darling?" she asked.

"Busy," he muttered. He knew financial reports masked the most important nuggets. He had to dig for them, like a miner searching for gold. But fool's gold had to be avoided.

She sat in a leather chair in front of his desk, quietly waiting for his attention. When she didn't get it, she spoke. "What are you reading?"

"A financial report. A bank faces difficulties from turmoil in African colonies."

"Nothing serious, I hope."

He glanced up. "Turmoil breeds opportunity. I intend to exploit it."

She smiled. "No one is better suited for that than you."

He looked at her, eyebrows arched. "Compliment or insult?"

"Perhaps both," she teased.

He knew she was there for a reason since she rarely disturbed him while he worked. He suspected he knew what it was. "How is the orphanage?"

She hesitated, reluctant to share a situation that never seemed to improve. "Funds are always needed," she said meekly.

He moved his papers aside and gave her his full attention. He always did when money was involved. "If you weren't on the oversight board, the orphanage would fail."

"It would," she agreed. "And many little children would have no home."

"It's been neglected for years," he said, frowning.

"An impact from the war, I suppose. Much like many businesses."

He opened the top drawer of his desk and removed a leather binder containing checks drawn on Lyon and Son. He picked up a pen, writing quickly. "I'm feeling generous today."

"Thank you, Henri," she said as he offered a donation. He had many faults, as he was the first to admit. But he was generous to those less fortunate, a trait few ever saw and less knew. "It's for a good cause, caring for the children."

He signed the check and handed it to her. "How was your portrait session?"

"It wasn't quite what I expected. Although there was much to learn."

"Is the painting finished?" he asked, glancing at the fireplace across the room and the empty wall above it. "I'm anxious to see it in place."

"No, we've just begun. Jean-Pierre said it takes many sittings, a dozen or more."

His gaze returned to the papers on his desk, a table of financial figures that caught his attention.

She paused, watching him. "I had no idea it would take so long. Several weeks."

"Why is that?" he muttered. He looked up as he turned the page, his gaze shifting between her and the report.

"It's part of the process," she explained. "Something to do with the light at different times of day. I saw several portraits in various stages of completion."

"What other portraits?" he asked, not listening or caring.

She shrugged. "I don't know who they are, although I did recognize one woman. I think she's the wife of a government official."

His eyes widened. Jeannette Richelieu, wife of a finance minister, had recommended the artist to him. Jeanette was a woman he was close to—closer than Elise needed to know. "What government official?"

"Richelieu?" she wondered aloud, not quite sure. "I've seen her photograph in the newspapers."

He watched her warily, trying to determine if she knew more than a name. It didn't seem that she did. And it didn't really matter anyway. "What did you do all morning, if the portrait isn't done?"

"I posed."

"For what?" he asked, suddenly suspicious. "If the process takes weeks, what did he do?"

"Charcoal sketches," she said. "All from different angles."

"But I commissioned a portrait, not sketches."

"I think he draws initially," she explained. "He then selects his favorite and abandons the remainder."

"It had better not cost more money," he grumbled.

"I'm sure it won't," she assured him. "He seems an honest man."

"He came highly recommended," Henri said. "Supposed to be the next Monet."

"Who is Monet?"

"An Impressionist," he said. "It's a new style of painting. I financed their exhibit. At a hefty interest rate."

"I don't know if he'll become the next Monet, but he is very good. His coastal scenes are breathtaking—very dramatic."

"Yes, I'm sure," he mumbled, returning to his report. He finished the page he was reading and turned to the next.

She waited a moment more and then rose to go. "I'll let you get back to your work. Thank you for the donation. It helps the children. You're very kind."

"Yes," he said, scanning the page. Just as she reached the door, he was struck with a thought. "Was the coachman with you?"

She looked at him curiously. "No, he wasn't. The studio is on top of a charming hill in Montmartre. I had the carriage wait at the bottom so I could walk."

His eyes widened. "Why did you do that? You can't be left alone. Not even to walk a single block."

"But why?" she asked curiously. "It was a beautiful day, and I wanted to enjoy it."

His face flushed, angry that she was so naive. "Because there's a maniac among us."

"What are you talking about?"

"The woman who was murdered last month," he declared, his voice louder.

"But that has nothing to do with me," she said. "And besides, my coachman was fifty meters away."

Henri frowned, eyes flashing with anger. "A killer prowls the city," he warned. "And you must never forget it."

Chapter Nine

Deauville, 1956

Dinner at Zélie's lasted almost two hours and consisted of several courses: soup, cheese, pasta, salmon, and salad, complimented by an oak-aged chardonnay. Coffee and dessert followed, chocolate mousse and the box of macarons that Anton had brought. After it ended, they retired to the parlor with glasses of chardonnay.

"How is your school work coming, Luc?" Anton asked.

Luc pushed a small firetruck across the Persian carpet. "It's good."

Marc smiled as he watched him. "Is that your favorite truck?"

Luc nodded. "It has a ladder and everything."

"What do you want to be when you grow up?" Marc asked.

"A fireman."

Marc laughed. "A fireman? I thought so. That's an exciting job. I used to be a policeman."

Luc stopped playing and looked at Marc curiously. "How come you're not a policeman anymore? Is it because you can't walk right?"

"That's enough, Luc," Zélie said. "M. Rayne doesn't want to talk about being a policeman."

"No, it's all right," Marc said, motioning to Zélie. "Yes, Luc. It's because I have trouble walking."

"What happened to you?" the little boy asked, gazing at him curiously.

Marc looked at Zélie as if to signal that a gunshot wound might be too sensitive to discuss—especially given the death of Luc's father.

Zélie gently shook her head. "Come on, Luc. Enough playing. It's time for bed,"

"Maman," Luc groaned. "I don't want to go to bed. I want to play with M. Rayne and M. LaRue."

"You can play another time," Zélie promised. "You have to go to sleep. You have school tomorrow. Say good night to our guests."

Luc reluctantly stood. "Good night."

"Good night, Luc," Anton said. "Maybe after school I can take you to see the horses. If your maman agrees."

Luc's eyes got wide. "Can I, Maman?"

Zélie smiled. "We'll see. We don't want to bother M. LaRue."

"It's no bother," Anton assured her. "You can join us if you like. You too, Marc."

Zélie took Luc up to bed and returned a few moments later. "Thank you both for being so good to him. It's been hard. He lost his father and now his grand-mère."

"We'll look after him," Anton said. "I'll teach him about horses."

"And I'll teach him about everything else," Marc joked.

They all laughed. "He is a good boy," Zélie said. "I'm so blessed to have him."

"We all are," Marc said. "He brightens our day."

"Has the transition been difficult?" Anton asked. "Moving from Paris?"

Zélie shrugged. "It's gone smoother than I thought. Deauville is a nice town for Luc to grow up in. I think it'll be good for both of us."

"What type of work do you do, Zélie?" Marc asked.

"I taught music theory and piano in Paris," she said, a worried expression crossing her face. "I'll have to give private lessons here. But I have to find some students quickly."

"I'll ask my son," Marc said. "He has two children who might be interested." He laughed lightly. "I may have an interest, too."

"Thank you so much," Zélie said. "It's better to get students through referrals than advertising. I suppose I can check with the school, too."

"I'll post a notice at the stables," Anton said. "Many of the workers have children."

"Everything will work out," Marc assured her.

Zélie smiled. "I sure hope so. Unless Eva had another vice I don't know about."

Marc and Anton laughed. "Many love horse-racing," Anton said. "And Deauville is the horse-racing capital of France."

"I know," she replied. "I just had no idea she bet on the races. But it explains her debts."

Anton nodded as if to confirm what she said. "Eva knew all the local horses, champions or not."

"I'm surprised," Zélie said. "I never would have guessed. But it might explain the portraits in the attic."

"May we see them?" Anton asked.

"Maman!" Luc screamed.

Zélie bolted from the chair, eyes wide, and raced up the stairs.

Chapter Ten

Montmartre, 1874

Three days later, Henri's warning had been long forgotten, and Elise sat upright in the straight-backed chair by the open studio window, a light breeze bathing her face. She watched Jean-Pierre as he studied the canvas, focused on his palette, and then squinted, eyeing her closely.

"Tilt your head a little to the left," he asked.

"Like that?" she asked, moving as directed. She had tried not to move, but it was difficult to remain still for an entire session though he was very patient when she didn't.

"Yes, that's perfect." With eyebrows knitted and face firm, he turned his attention to the canvas, muttering inaudibly, chasing a perfection that always seemed to elude him.

She glanced at the opened window, the narrow lane beyond quiet and still. "Where's Mme. Michel today?"

He did not reply at first, his hand moving in broad strokes. "Minding her children, perhaps," he said. "But never far away, I assure you. If the window is open, assume she can hear."

She glanced at the cluttered studio, canvas and frames, portraits and landscapes. She inadvertently moved.

"Tilt your chin up."

She did as he asked, determined to concentrate.

"That's good," he said. "Perfect. The light is just the way I want it."

"Is that why you wanted me to pose at twilight?"

"Yes, just as blackness appears," he replied. "When the sun's remnants are just an angry sliver on the horizon. I wanted the light to be weak, the shadows mysterious, the darkness dominant."

She had never thought about the sunrise or sunset or the shadows the sun creates. But Jean-Pierre was obsessed with it. This was her first visit near dusk, and her next, she had been told, would be late morning. "Is light that important?"

"Ah, but it is," he exclaimed, pausing to look at her in disbelief. "Light is everything."

She tried not to smile. His passion for painting sometimes amused her.

"You do not agree?" he asked, cocking his head.

She laughed lightly. "I don't understand."

"I will explain," he said simply. "Light, or the lack of light, creates the shadow your nose casts on your cheek, or it darkens the color of your dress just below the collar."

"The shadows are important?"

"Yes, of course," he said. "Without light there is nothing—only blackness. With some light, there is mystery, shadows that hint of something more. And with bright light, you're exposed. You hide nothing."

"I never realized," she admitted.

He smiled. "And now you will never forget."

She would also never forget his smile—warm and inviting. He returned to the canvas and she gazed at the paintings and sketches leaning against the walls or stacked around the room. Many of the coastal images were gone, sold perhaps, and Jean-Pierre's current theme was Paris—its streets, buildings, and people. The paintings were beautiful, all in the new Impressionist style, brush strokes so vivid and rich that they made her feel like she'd walked into the scene. As she continued to scan the room, careful not to move her head, she saw an image of the road outside the artist's studio—the cobblestone incline that she'd walked on her way to the studio, leaving her coachman at the boulevard so she could admire the stone walls that hemmed the road, flowers that spilled over the capstone, charming houses with peeling paint.

"I love the paintings of Paris," she said softly. "They're so vibrant."

"The city is alive," he stated, as if she'd understand. He studied her just like he did the canvas, searching for perfection in each. "I'll share a secret."

She smiled. "The first of many, I suspect."

"The buildings talk to me," he claimed. "So do trees and flowers and cobblestones."

She laughed. "They never talk to me."

"You think I'm crazy," he said, smiling. "A lunatic."

"No, I don't. I just don't understand."

"You will in time, because I will show you."

"You'll teach me to hear buildings and flowers and trees?"

"I will teach you to listen. And much more."

She hesitated, not sure she understood. "I already know how to listen."

"Ah, but you don't," he said, his painting paused. "Few people know how to listen. They're too busy thinking about what they will say. They think they listen, but they don't really hear."

She considered his comment. Henri rarely listened to her. It seemed others didn't, either. But she wasn't sure if she did. "Is it hard to learn?"

"No," he scoffed. "It's not hard at all. You must use what God gave you. Not just your ears, but your eyes and nose and touch—how your feet feel when they walk on uneven stone that makes the streets, or the leaf that flutters against you on its journey to the ground. Or the smell of a flower or the sound of a bird—not his chirps, anyone can do that. But the hummingbird's wings as they flap beside you."

She was quiet, thinking of all he said. "You're passionate about life."

"We all should be," he said simply. "Or we shouldn't bother to live it."

She smiled. "Philosopher and artist joined as one. A unique combination."

He shrugged. "Not so much a philosopher."

"How would you describe it?"

He paused as his hand moved delicately, the brush caressing the canvas. "A lover of beauty in all forms."

"I will enjoy learning about beauty," she said playfully.

"I think you will, also. And I will enjoy teaching you."

It was quiet as he worked, glancing up to study the features of her face, concentrating on the canvas, dabbing at the palette to mix his paints and create the colors he needed most.

"If you love to paint landscapes and scenes of the city, why do you do so many portraits?"

"Portraits pay my bills," he said simply. "Nature quenches my thirst for beauty."

She hesitated. "If you don't like portraits, is it difficult to do mine?"

"I didn't say that I don't like to do portraits," he replied. "I said nature quenches my thirst for beauty. But beauty can be found in many places."

"But not in portraits?"

He smiled, started to speak, paused, and then continued. “By painting you, my thirst for beauty is quenched in ways even nature cannot provide.”

Chapter Eleven

Deauville, 1956

It was fifteen minutes later when Zélie returned downstairs and joined Marc and Anton in the parlor. "I'm so sorry," she said. "He has nightmares."

"Should we go?" Marc asked, starting to rise.

"No, it's fine," she said, motioning for him to sit. "I got him back to sleep."

"Is he afraid in his new home?" Anton asked.

She hesitated, not sure how much to share. "No, it's not that. Luc has problems coping. He has nightmares about me dying."

Anton cringed. "Oh, how terrible."

"But it is understandable," Marc said. "He lost his father. He lost his grand-mère. You're all he has."

"I know," Zélie said, and sighed. "He's afraid to grow up because he thinks he'll die."

"Oh, that's so sad," Marc said. "Poor little guy."

Anton glanced at Marc. "Maybe if we can keep him occupied, he won't dwell on what he's lost."

"I think that would help," Zélie said. "I'm trying to give him my constant attention to help him get through this."

Anton was quiet, almost as if he was afraid to pry. "Have you considered a psychiatrist?"

"I have," Zélie replied. "But I don't know who to use. I don't want to scare him and make it worse."

"Is it the same nightmare?" Marc asked.

Zélie nodded. "He dreams that I'm in danger, or close to dying. But then he wakes up before anything bad happens."

Marc winced. “That’s a horrible dream.”

Zélie nodded. “And it stems from more than losing loved ones. When we lived in Paris, just before Luc’s father died, we were standing on a corner at Rue de Rivoli—Luc used to like to go and look in the shop windows—waiting for the streetlight to change. A man lost control of his automobile and crashed onto the sidewalk. My husband yanked Luc out of the way, but the car brushed me, knocking me to the ground. I was dazed, roughed up a bit, but not seriously hurt. Luc never forgot that. Now he dreams variations of what happened but with much worse outcomes.”

“No wonder he can’t sleep!” Anton exclaimed.

“We later learned the driver had suffered a heart attack,” Zélie explained. “It really wasn’t his fault. But Luc doesn’t understand.”

“Maybe once he’s settled in Deauville, his fears will ease,” Marc said.

“I hope so,” Zélie said grimly. “I think once he realizes that I’m not going anywhere, he’ll feel better.”

Anton was quiet for a moment. “I’ve seen children calm considerably when introduced to horses. I’ll take him to the stables, and we can see how he responds.”

“Thank you so much,” Zélie said. “I’m willing to try anything.”

“I’ll spend some time with him, too,” Marc offered. “I’ve nothing to do all day anyway.”

“I so appreciate it,” she said. “I think being in his grand-mère’s house might make it worse. He’s reminded of her constantly.”

Marc looked at his watch. “It’s getting late. We should probably go.”

Zélie glanced at the Art Deco clock on the piano. "Let me show you the paintings first. It'll only take a minute."

They followed her up the stairs. Zélie held a finger to her lips as they quietly passed Luc's bedroom and went to the attic door. "There's actually two rooms," she whispered. "They must have been bedrooms at one time."

"Is much stored up here?" Anton asked as they quietly climbed the steps.

Zélie rolled her eyes. "Oh yes. It's packed. Families have put junk up here for a hundred years. Furniture, collectibles, books, paintings. You'll see."

When they reached the top of the stairs, she took them across the room to the first painting. It was a horse, majestic and muscled, chestnut brown with three white stockings and a white blaze marred by a marking.

"Golden Cross," Anton said as soon as he saw the portrait.

Chapter Twelve

Montmartre, 1874

It was dark when Elise left Jean-Pierre's studio, the sun falling behind the jagged rooftops of Paris. As she closed the door behind her, she peered down the hill, a gas streetlight lit on the main boulevard beyond. The back wheels of her carriage poked from behind the wall, parked on the street where she had left it.

She walked into shadows, the road growing darker as it began its decline, the faint glow from flickering candles in house windows dying before it reached her. No gaslights were installed in the alley, and with tree limbs reaching over imposing walls, the narrow lane was draped in blackness.

Elise paused, remembering Henri's warning: a lunatic was loose in the city. But she could see her coach, not more than fifty meters away, and even though she traveled through a tunnel of darkness to reach it, she shouldn't be afraid.

A couple strolled the boulevard beyond, the man in a tweed suit with top hat, carrying a cane more for show than support, the woman's green dress billowing down to her shoes. But no one else walked the streets, not behind her or before her, and only an occasional carriage passed, destined for parts unknown. As she moved farther down the incline, branches whistled in the wind, ominous whispers in an unknown tongue.

She quickened her pace, walking on the right-hand side of the road and staying close to the curb, somehow feeling safer, the wall threatening for reasons she couldn't explain. And as the stone mass stretched higher, branches sprawling over its top smothered the moon so no light could pass.

With less than half her journey completed, a racket rose behind her, rattling and disjointed, loud and unidentifiable. She turned abruptly, eyes wide and heart racing, to find a silhouette atop the hill. It grew larger, bearing down on her. She froze. A bicycle whizzed past, a teenage boy upon it. She laughed, amused she had been afraid. The boy rode down the hill, turning left when he reached the bottom.

Just as she was about to continue, a faint footstep fell, a twig snapped. Elise hesitated, about to turn, when calloused hands grasped her neck and started to squeeze. She tried to scream but could only gasp, choking for breath she couldn't find. She kicked, swung her arms wildly, and started to pull away. But the more she struggled, the tighter his hold became.

She turned and twisted, trying to scream, fighting to loosen his grasp, her efforts in vain. She glanced wildly in all directions, hoping for help, but saw no one approaching. Her assailant had chosen the darkest recess on the entire lane, and she suspected most would avoid it—just as she should have done. She summoned all her strength, bent her right leg at the knee, and drove her foot downward, the heel of her shoe smashing her assailant's toe.

He loosened his hold, moved his foot, then held her even tighter.

People passed on the boulevard below, not looking up the hill, oblivious to the danger only meters away. Elise spun, flinging her elbows into his stomach. When he flinched, she again slammed her heel on his toe, choking, fighting to breathe.

He let go of her throat, not making a sound.

She ran, sobbing, struggling in her skirt. Just as escape seemed assured, she tripped and fell, her face hitting the curb, smashing her lips and nose.

Her assailant leaped on top of her, fighting to cover her mouth.

"What's going on up there?" a voice called from the street.

The weight upon her eased. Her attacker climbed off and hurried away, his footsteps growing dimmer. Elise spun as a figure in black fled toward the houses. Just as he reached the end of the wall, he jumped over the stone and vanished.

"Are you all right, Madame?" asked an elderly man with bushy whiskers.

Elise started crying, both from pain and relief. "No, I don't think I am."

"Try to sit up," the man suggested. "And let's have a look."

Blood dripped from her lips and nose; her cheek was scratched and swollen.

"You're hurt," he said. "We need to get help."

"I thought he was going to kill me," she wailed.

"Police!" the man yelled. "Police!"

Another man came to their aid, followed by a woman, and then a policeman scrambled up the hill. They gathered around Elise while she held a kerchief to her nose, struggling not to cry.

"What happened, Madame?" the policeman asked.

"I was walking down the street, looking for my coachman, when someone attacked me."

The policeman looked up and down the tranquil lane. "Whoever it was has escaped," he said. "Are you all right?"

"He was choking me," she sobbed. "His hands clutched my throat, and I couldn't breathe."

The policeman tenderly touched her throat, found no marks or bruises, and examined the scratches on her face. "We'll get assistance, Madame. And everything will be fine."

Chapter Thirteen

Deauville, 1956

"Who is Golden Cross?" Zélie asked as she stood in her attic with Marc and Anton, looking at a large painting in a molded walnut frame.

"A famous race horse," Anton replied. "His portrait hangs in the race track clubhouse."

Marc glanced at Zélie. "I never heard of him. Did he win a lot of races?"

"He must have," Anton said, chuckling. "Or his portrait wouldn't be there."

"Why Golden Cross?" Zélie asked. "That's a strange name."

Anton bent over and pointed at the portrait. "This white mark above his nose is called a blaze. There's a chestnut marking, almost a perfect cross, at the top of the blaze, just above his eyes."

"He was named for the marking?" Marc asked.

"Yes, I think so," Anton replied. "I can find out more at the racetrack."

"Do they have paintings of all the famous horses?" Zélie asked.

"No, not all," Anton said. "Only a dozen or so, the best of the best, the greatest horses in the history of France —maybe even the entire world."

Zélie looked at the portrait with new appreciation. "I had no idea," she muttered. "Do you think Eva knew?"

Anton thought for a moment. "No, I don't think so. She never mentioned it, if she did."

"When did Golden Cross race?" Zélie asked.

Anton shrugged. "I'm not sure. But I'll find out."

"Is there a date or artist's signature on the painting?" Marc asked.

Zélie looked in the lower right corner. "There is," she said. "1874."

"Eighty years ago," Marc said. "An artist's name?"

Zélie bent down to look closer. "No, not a name. But initials—JP."

Marc shrugged. "I can't think of a famous artist with those initials. But I can do some research."

"It is a fabulous painting," Anton said. "Look how the artist captured the horse's strength, the taut tendons, the muscle definition."

"He was very good," Marc agreed, studying the portrait. He glanced around the room. "Are there more paintings up here?"

"I haven't sorted through everything," Zélie said, "but there is a portrait of a woman, also brilliantly painted."

"Show it to us," Marc urged.

Zélie led them around a chaise lounge, likely as old as the portrait of Golden Cross. Another painting, just as large and housed in an elaborate gilt frame, leaned against the back of the couch. It featured a woman of breathtaking beauty, her brown hair pinned above her head, exposing a face marred only by a freckle or two and a small scar above her left eye. Her brown eyes twinkled with mischief and mystery. She wore a sleek blue blouse and long skirt clinging to a shapely frame. A string of pearls on a thin silver chain wrapped around her neck, matching her earrings.

Anton whistled softly. "She is beautiful."

"The painting is wonderfully done," Zélie said. "It looks like she's alive."

"It does," Marc agreed. He leaned closer, looked at the portrait and then at Zélie. "There's a resemblance."

"To me?" Zélie asked with surprise.

"Yes, there is," Anton agreed. "I see it too. Slight, but still there—around the eyes."

Zélie laughed. "Thank you both. But she's an absolute beauty."

"Yes, she is," Marc said. "And so are you."

She smiled and felt herself blush. "Thank you."

"Is there a date on it?" Anton asked.

Zélie looked in the right corner. "1874."

"Signature?" Marc asked.

"Jean-Pierre," she said, turning to face them.

"Hmm," Anton said. "Probably the same artist that painted Golden Cross."

"I'll see what I can find out about Jean-Pierre," Marc said, studying the painting closely. "I'm a retired policeman. It gives me something to do."

Chapter Fourteen

Montmartre, 1874

The black carriage with gilt trim stopped before the Lyon townhouse, and the coachman helped Elise climb out. "I'll summon Sebastian," he offered, referring to her servant. "Should we get a doctor, too?"

"No, I'm all right," she said weakly as he opened the front door.

"Sebastian," the coachman called. "Please, come quickly! Mme. Lyon has been injured."

A man hurried into the foyer, well dressed in a clipped beard and moustache. "Mme. Lyon, what happened?" Sebastian asked, eyes wide, as he hurried to her side.

She smiled, his concern comforting. "I was attacked," she said softly. "And almost killed."

"Where were you?" Sebastian asked, glaring at the coachman as he led Elise into the parlor, guiding her to the couch.

"I waited at the bottom of the hill, as instructed," the coachman protested. "The artist's studio is at the top."

"I wanted to walk," Elise said, coming to the coachman's defense. "I'm to blame. No one else."

"What can I get you?" Sebastian asked, still annoyed with the coachman. "Are you in pain?"

She shook her head. "No, but I'm shaken. Just let me sit for a moment."

"Did the police find the culprit?" Sebastian asked.

"Not yet," Elise replied. "But they are conducting an investigation."

The coachman watched as Sebastian cared for Mme. Lyon. "If I'm not needed for anything else, I'll take my leave," he said, making more of a request than a statement.

"Yes, of course," Elise replied. "Thank you for your kindness. It's much appreciated."

"I'll summon M. Lyon," Sebastian said, leaving the parlor with the coachman. "He just came home a few minutes ago."

As they left the room, Elise tenderly touched the bruises on her face. The pain was subsiding and would likely be gone by morning. She glanced at the grandfather's clock against the wall. It was mid-evening, well past dinner. Where had Henri been?

"What happened?" Henri asked as he rushed into the parlor.

"I was attacked," Elise said, dabbing her battered lip with a kerchief.

"Attacked?" he exclaimed as he sat beside her. He leaned close, lightly touching her face to check her bruises.

"While leaving the studio," she explained, trying to be brave. But she broke down and started crying. "He tried to kill me!"

"Where was the coachman?" Henri demanded, glaring at Sebastian. "I want the man fired."

"No," Elise protested, touching Henri's arm. "It wasn't him. I wanted to walk."

Henri's face reddened, his anger not subsiding. "I told you I did not want you left alone. Not ever. There's a lunatic on the loose!"

"I know, it's my fault," she said. "I should have had the carriage wait outside the studio."

"Where are the police?" Henri asked, rising from the couch and pacing the floor.

"They came right away," Elise replied. "Only a few minutes—"

"Did they catch the man?"

"No, he got away," she said. "The police think it was a robbery."

"It was that madman who murdered the woman last month!" Henri shouted. "Why would they ever think it was a robbery?"

"The police thought anyone who looked at my clothes would think I was a wealthy woman."

"And so are many other Parisians," he scoffed. "What are they going to do about it?"

"They're searching for the man. And they asked me questions. The inspector is coming in the morning to get more information."

Henri returned to the couch, paused a moment to calm himself, and eyed Elise's injuries. "Are you all right?"

She nodded, her face pale. "Perhaps if I lie down a bit," she said. "I do feel faint."

"I'll have the housemaid get some ointment for your bruises," Sebastian offered. "She'll bring it to your room."

"Thank you, Sebastian," she said, gently touching her face. "It does hurt."

Henri sighed, shook his head, and stood. "I'll be here in the morning when the inspector arrives. I'll make sure he finds this maniac."

"Oh, thank you, Henri," she said. "I want the man caught, too."

"He will be," he declared. "I have one simple question for the police. How do they intend to solve this crime?"

"I'm sure they'll do everything they can."

He paused, reflecting on the next day. "I must review some papers in my study if I hope to leave later tomorrow."

Elise frowned, but tried to hide it. "Go and attend to them," she said, forcing a smile. "Sebastian will ensure I'm cared for."

"Yes, of course," Henri muttered, his thoughts elsewhere. "Is there anything else?"

She hesitated, trying not to sob. "I don't know why anyone would want to kill me."

Chapter Fifteen

Deauville, 1956

Marc Rayne had been a police officer in Calais for almost forty years—except for periods of military service. But a recent robbery arrest gone wrong had ended with three bullets in his left leg and back. Several surgeries were followed by a long, painful rehabilitation. He'd recovered but limped badly, barely a day passing without pain wracking his crippled body. A widower nearing sixty, he retired from the Prefecture of Police, no longer able to perform his duties.

While he decided what came next in life, he rented a cottage from Eva Girard, a quiet woman who rarely discussed her past. But few did. The war had left too many painful memories, touching the survivors in ways none could have ever imagined, and most did all they could to forget it.

Deauville had been hurt badly; the coast was inundated with German soldiers waiting for an Allied invasion, and many buildings in the town had been damaged or destroyed in the fighting. If a global cataclysm wasn't enough, France now fought in its colonies, in far-away places like Indochina where men came home in caskets, just as Luc's father had done. But while the world war was a struggle against fascism, a battle of good versus evil, the war in Indochina knew no beginning or end, offered no justification. It merely existed without many knowing the reason why.

Now Zélie was his landlord, and he saw pain in her eyes and the damage done to little Luc after losing his father and grand-mère. He enjoyed having dinner with them. Zélie was a fabulous cook and a great host. He would like to return the favor, but he had few talents in the kitchen. He wanted to help—she reminded him of the daughter he had never had—and somehow get her through the mourning that seemed like it would never end. But he knew that he couldn't. Their sorrow would fade, but never disappear, always holding a piece of their hearts. He could lend an ear, be a friend when they needed one, look after Luc when asked. But not much else. They had to find their own way, just as he had when darkness hid the light and tomorrow offered nothing more than a broken yesterday.

The portraits in Zélie's attic were intriguing. He had seen several scattered about the two rooms, but the woman and the thoroughbred were among the best. He intended to solve the mystery the paintings presented. It was the only way he could help her. He was a former investigator. He would investigate.

He made phone calls to friends and former coworkers and found an art historian who lived in Deauville, a former professor at the Sorbonne. He arranged a visit and went the same day. Mme. Marie Dufour and her husband lived in a cottage outside of town. Marc drove his red Renault down the road that led out of Deauville and found her house sitting a few miles north, isolated on a dirt lane that looked down on the beach.

The front door opened as Marc came up a brick walkway, and an elderly man stepped out. "Hello," he said. "Are you M. Rayne?"

"Yes, I am," Marc replied. "I'm here to see the professor."

"I'm Jacques, her husband," he said, glancing at Marc's leg. "War wound?"

Marc nodded. "Something like that."

"We've all been scarred," Jacques muttered. "Damn Germans. But it's nice to meet you, M. Rayne. Come with me. Marie is waiting for you."

He led Marc to the opposite side of the house where a covered terrace stretched to the north, offering a generous view of the sea. Shielded from neighbors by reeds and a few scattered trees, the terrace offered a sanctuary, an oasis hidden from the world's prying eyes.

Professor Dufour sat at a wrought iron table, gazing out at the sea, an empty mug and a Regency romance novel with a worn dust jacket on the table before her.

"The policeman is here," Jacques announced as they rounded the corner.

"Hello, M. Rayne," she said, rising to greet him.

"Professor, thank you so much for seeing me," Marc said. "Especially on such short notice."

"I'm surprised you found me," she said. "But I'll use any excuse to discuss art. Please, sit down. And call me Marie."

"Thank you, Marie," Marc said as he sat.

"I'll leave you two to chat," Jacques said. "Can I get you anything, M. Rayne?"

"No, thank you. I'm fine."

As Jacques left, Marc smiled at Marie. "What an enchanting cottage you have," he said, a slight breeze blowing off the water. "Such a beautiful view of the sea. Have you lived here long?"

"We left Paris a year ago," she said. "But we've owned the house almost twenty years and used to spend our summers here. It was so secluded when we bought it. Now it seems everyone wants to live on the coast."

Marc glanced at the stone house and timber rafters that defined the terrace. "You're fortunate it survived the war."

"It almost didn't," she said. "The Germans confiscated the house, and it was badly damaged during the Allied invasion. But we managed to restore it. We're among the fortunate, I suppose. Belongings can be repaired or replaced."

Marc nodded. He knew what she meant. Belongings can be replaced. Loved ones cannot. The war had touched everyone, leaving bruises that never healed. "It's a property worth saving. A wonderful sanctuary."

Marie smiled. "It is," she agreed. "How about you, Marc? What brought you to Deauville?"

He shrugged. "I suppose I'm just trying to find my way."

"Aren't we all," she said, chuckling.

"I came here to retire, after spending my life in Calais."

"Maybe we seek the serenity of the sea," she said. "After life in a bustling metropolis."

"I suppose you're right," he agreed. "It soothes the soul."

"What brings you to see me?" she asked and then smiled. "I suspect a mystery needs to be unraveled."

Marc laughed. "A minor mystery, perhaps. I was wondering if you ever heard of an artist named Jean-Pierre. He would have painted in the 1870s, maybe a bit beyond."

"Yes, of course," she said. "Jean-Pierre was an Impressionist painter of some note. Never famous, like Monet or Van Gogh, but still gifted."

"Was he an artistic genius, like Monet?"

She hesitated. "He was extremely talented but never reached the ranks of the masters. But he did come close. He was most known for his brilliant use of light, using shadows to create a sense of mystery—a unique approach."

Marc nodded. Art was never one of his strong points. But he suspected it would be soon. "Do you know much about him?"

Marie collected her thoughts. "Jean-Pierre made a living by painting portraits, some of which survive. His portrait of Mme. Jeanette Richelieu, the wife of the finance minister, hangs in the Louvre."

Marc's eyes widened. "Oh, then he must have been very good."

"Yes, he was. His portraits are excellent, very life-like. And some of his landscapes are breathtaking."

"Was he famous during his time?"

"In Paris he was, primarily because his portraits were in such demand. But landscapes were his passion."

"A friend of mine inherited a house and found two of his paintings, maybe a few others, stored in her attic. The first painting depicts a horse called Golden Cross. I'm told he was a famous thoroughbred, perhaps the best of the best."

She paused, pensive. "I didn't know he did any animal paintings. But he was probably commissioned to do it, just as any other portrait."

Marc nodded, suspecting she was right. "My friend has another painting of a beautiful young woman, born to wealth judging by her clothes, and dated 1874. Do you have any idea who that might be?"

She shook her head. "No, not really. As I said, he did many portraits. Maybe if I saw it, I could tell. Some of his portraits are very well-known, like Mme. Richelieu."

"Is there a catalogue of his works?"

"Not that I know of. But some of his paintings are featured in different reference books. The problem I think you may face is that Jean-Pierre was a bit of a recluse. Not much is known about him or his works. I may be able to do some research and find out more."

Marc hesitated. He wasn't sure if a cost was involved or if Zélie had any desire to know about the artist. "Let me talk to my friend and see what she wants to do."

"Of course," she said. "But tell her I would be happy to help. Art is my passion."

Marc smiled and rose to leave. "Thank you for your time, Professor."

"You're very welcome. If you have any other questions, don't hesitate to ask."

Marc turned to go when he thought of something else. "Are Jean-Pierre's paintings valuable?"

"Oh, yes," she said. "Very much so. Not like the famous Impressionists, but he's still highly collectable. Not many of his works are available—either lost in the world wars, destroyed, or secretly held in private collections. But the rarity only adds to their value."

Chapter Sixteen

Montmartre, 1874

Inspector Nicolas Babin was a veteran investigator for the Paris Prefecture of Police, pompous and condescending, typical of some who achieve great success. He was stout, a lover of fine foods, his hair white, and he boasted an immaculately waxed moustache, each end curved upward into a slender semi-circle.

Babin's assistant, Lieutenant Claude Dumont, was younger, a pensive man with brown hair and dark eyes. More intellectual than most assumed, he obeyed orders without complaint, voicing no concerns even when he wasn't in agreement. His collar patch displayed one white stripe, a trainee under the tutelage of Inspector Babin.

"This will be a good learning opportunity for you, Dumont," Inspector Babin said as their carriage stopped in front of the Lyon household. "A wealthy woman attacked on a dark street. An attempted robbery, no doubt, thwarted by an innocent passerby."

"A woman was just murdered in the same location," Dumont said. "Maybe the two are related."

"Perhaps or perhaps not," Babin said. He raised a finger, signaling caution. "We must gather evidence and see where it leads. Not leap to conclusions without facts."

"It seems more than coincidence," Dumont suggested.

"The murdered woman was poor, rumored to be a prostitute. Someone's mistress, most likely. Quite the opposite of Mme. Lyon. But they could be related. In time, we will know."

"I understand," Dumont replied. "A proper investigation must be conducted."

"I've decided to let you oversee the questioning of Mme. Lyon," Babin continued. "I shall remain in the background, like a shadow, only to intervene if needed."

"Thank you, Inspector. Your continued support is greatly appreciated."

"I'll transcribe the session," Babin continued. "You must focus on the task at hand. Keep your thoughts clear and speak with authority."

"I will, sir. I won't disappoint you."

They left the carriage, the driver remaining, and went to the door, tapping a bronze lion's head doorknocker to announce their presence.

Sebastian admitted them, directing them to the foyer while the family was summoned. A moment later, Henri Lyon led Elise in from the dining room. He looked at the detectives suspiciously, and Babin assumed he was protective of his wife—or perhaps even himself.

"Good morning," Babin said, nodding politely. "I am Inspector Babin, and this is my assistant Lieutenant Dumont."

"Henri Lyon and my wife Elise," Henri replied. "Let's sit in the parlor. We'll be more comfortable there."

The parlor was a luxurious room painted pale yellow with white trim. A fireplace filled much of the interior wall, marble columns supporting a mantel with carved vines sprawling across it. A mirror with gold trim hung above the hearth, its reflection making the room seem larger than it actually was. Two built-in bookshelves flanked the fireplace, arched tops with fluted moldings, the shelves filled with leather volumes, all in mint condition. A Chantelle sofa with matching armchairs was spaced before the fireplace, wrought iron tables beside them. The ceiling was contoured, decorative plaster along the edges, a crystal chandelier hanging from a flower medallion.

Lieutenant Dumont paused as he entered, admiring the room and the wealth it displayed. Inspector Babin brushed past him, having been exposed to the most luxurious homes Paris had to offer and not impressed by this one.

"Please, sit down," Henri said, motioning to two armchairs while he and Elise sat on the sofa.

"A beautiful room," the lieutenant said, his gaze fixed on the leather volumes.

"Yes, we enjoy it," Henri said tersely, glancing at his pocket watch.

Inspector Babin eyed Henri Lyon warily. He did not like him, but he wasn't sure why. He assumed he would know shortly. His gaze shifted to Elise Lyon. "You are not badly hurt, Mme. Lyon?"

"No," she said, smiling weakly. "I think the bruises will fade in a day or two."

Babin nodded respectfully, paused for a moment, and then began. "Lieutenant Dumont will conduct the questioning," he announced. "I will assist as needed."

"I'm hoping you catch the culprit," Elise said. "I won't feel safe until you do."

"Who would?" Henri interjected. "You were almost murdered."

Dumont withdrew a notebook from his pocket, scanned through the pages for a moment, and then began. "Mme. Lyon, I reviewed the policeman's statement from the scene of the crime and spoke with your coachman and those who came to your aid. But I do have a few questions, if you'll be so kind."

"Yes, of course," she said softly.

"Mme. Lyon," Dumont began, "can you describe your injuries?"

"Her mouth and nose were bruised," Henri said, gruffly answering for her. "Can't you see her lip is swollen?"

Dumont looked directly at Elise. "Does that describe your injuries?"

She nodded. "Yes," she said. "And the man's hands were—"

"Does this have anything to do with the maniac that's on the loose?" Henri interrupted brusquely.

"And what maniac is that?" Babin asked with a hint of distaste.

"A woman was murdered last month," Henri said. "A killer is roaming the city. I would expect you to be quite familiar with the case, Inspector."

"You are correct," Dumont said, eyeing Henri cautiously. He hadn't expected anyone so confrontational. "A woman was murdered last month. But we don't know if that's related to the attack on Mme. Lyon."

"My wife was the victim of a violent assault," Henri growled. "She's frightened, and so are the citizens of Paris."

"We understand that, I assure you," Dumont replied. "Mme. Lyon, can you please describe the minutes leading up to the attack, just so I ensure our notes are correct?"

"She was having her portrait painted by a local artist," Henri intervened. "The attack occurred after the session."

"Jean-Pierre?" Babin asked, writing in his small notebook.

"Yes," Henri replied. "He's been working on her portrait for a week or so."

Dumont shared a guarded glance with Babin. "And the attack occurred as you left the studio, Mme. Lyon?"

"Her coachman waited at the foot of the hill, on the corner," Henri interjected. He stood and started pacing, a scowl on his face. "He wasn't in a position to see what happened."

"Yes, I was attacked just after I left," Elise confirmed, her eyes glassy as if still dazed. "And, as Henri said, the coachman was too far away to assist."

"Do you think you were being watched prior to the attack?" Dumont asked.

Henri looked at him sharply. "What other conclusion can be drawn?"

Babin was losing his patience with Henri. "Mme. Lyon is a wealthy woman," he said. "The perpetrator may have seen her enter the studio and planned to rob her when she left."

"Except nothing was taken," Henri countered. "Or did you fail to note that?"

"But it might have been," Babin argued, "had the attack been successful."

"Mme. Lyon," Dumont continued, "was anyone watching you?"

"No, not that I noticed."

"Other than a boy on his bicycle," Dumont said, scanning his notes, "you saw no one. Is that correct?"

"How many times does she have to answer the same questions?" Henri asked. "Is this how you conduct an investigation?"

Dumont glanced at Babin, who discreetly nodded. "Mme. Lyon?"

"Yes" she replied. "I thought it strange. No people, not even stray cats or dogs."

"And the attack occurred near dusk?" Dumont asked.

"Just after," she said. "The street was dark."

Henri marched across the floor, seething, and stood directly in front of Babin and Dumont. "You don't even know when the crime occurred?"

"We visited the crime scene before we came here," Dumont said, looking past Henri at Elise. "The attack occurred midway down the incline, where the stone walls edge the street?"

Elise's eyes widened as if she relived the trauma. "Yes," she said quietly, her body trembling slightly.

"How many more questions do you have?" Henri asked, glancing at his wife. "Can't you see that she's upset?"

"Only a few more," Babin said, not intimidated by the boisterous Henri Lyon.

"You never saw the assailant?" Dumont questioned.

"If she saw her assailant, he would be in your custody," Henri bellowed, eyes wide. "Even an incompetent inspector could find a suspect whose identity is known."

Dumont kept his gaze fixed on Elise, waiting for a reply.

Elise shook her head. "No, I didn't see him."

"Could he have been waiting atop the wall, or in a tree branch hanging over the street?" Babin asked.

"Maybe he dropped from the sky," Henri said with disgust. "Or was shot from a cannon."

Elise looked at Dumont and nodded.

"What is the first thing that happened?" Dumont asked.

"I heard noises, a footstep, a twig snapping," she said, "and I turned to see if anyone was there."

"Turned to face the top of the hill?" Babin asked, taking notes.

"Yes," she confirmed. "I felt someone's hands around my neck. He squeezed very tightly, and I couldn't breathe."

"Did you attempt to fight him?" Babin probed.

Elise nodded. "I stomped his toes with the heel of my shoe. And I started swinging my elbows, hitting his torso."

"And he loosened his grasp?" Dumont asked.

"Of course, he did," Henri smirked, shaking his head with disbelief. "She got away, didn't she?"

"I pulled away and started to run," she said. "But I tripped. That's when I bruised my face. He climbed on top of me."

"How did you get away?" Dumont asked.

"Someone at the bottom of the hill started yelling," she said. "My attacker rose and fled, leaping over the wall."

"Are we almost through here, Lieutenant?" Henri asked, looking at his watch. "I do have a business to run."

"You are free to go, M. Lyon," Babin said, surprised by Henri's callousness, galled that his focus had so quickly shifted from his wife to his business. "I think Mme. Lyon is capable of answering the questions."

Henri frowned, but remained. "I'm here for my wife. She needs me."

"Yes, I understand," Babin said, although he really didn't. He turned to Elise. "How big was the assailant?"

Elise thought for a moment. She glanced at Henri hovering over her. "He was about the same height as my husband."

"Did the assailant talk at any time, Mme. Lyon?" Dumont asked.

"No, he did not," Elise said.

"And you're absolutely certain it was a man?" Dumont asked.

Elise paused, unsure. "It never occurred to me that it wasn't."

Chapter Seventeen

Deauville, 1956

Zélie stood at her kitchen stove and looked out the window while she prepared garlic soup for dinner. Luc was playing in the yard with Marc Rayne, throwing a ball back and forth. She knew it was painful for Marc, his stiff leg and bad back hampering movement so natural to most. She watched warily, and, when she saw Marc wince as he bent over to pick up the ball, she thought they had played long enough. She turned the stove down, letting the soup simmer, and went outside. She was about to turn the corner into the back yard when she heard Luc talking.

"Did you know my papa?" he asked.

Zélie paused, wondering whether or not to intervene. She peeked around the corner as Marc walked toward Luc, his back to her.

"Did I know your père?" Marc asked, feigning disbelief as he repeated the question. "Of course, I did."

"You did?" Luc asked, excited.

"Yes, everyone knew your père," Marc continued. "He was a hero. One of the bravest men that France has ever known. The entire country is grateful to him for all he did for us."

"Really? My papa is a hero?"

"Absolutely," Marc insisted. "He was a great man. You should be proud. He's admired by all, just as he should be."

Zélie wiped a tear from her eye and waited a moment more. She didn't want them to know she was eavesdropping. Then she turned the corner and walked into the yard. "How's the ball game going?"

"Oh, hello, Zélie," Marc said. "How are you?"

"Hi, Maman," Luc said. "I thought you were playing the piano."

"I was," she said, smiling. "But I stopped to get dinner ready."

"My maman is the best piano player in the world," Luc said to Marc.

Marc's eyes widened. "She is?" he asked, looking at Zélie. "You'll have to play for me sometime."

Zélie laughed. "I will," she promised. "Luc plays piano, too."

"Do you want to play ball with us?" Luc asked, ignoring her piano comment.

"No, but thank you," she said with an adoring look. "Maybe next time."

Luc tossed the ball to Marc who caught it and threw it back.

"But I'm afraid it's time to stop," Zélie said. "I came out to get you for dinner."

"Aww, but we're playing," Luc complained.

"We can play again tomorrow," Marc said, intervening. "Or any time you want. But we had best mind your maman."

"All right," Luc moaned.

Zélie smiled at Marc. He was such a good man, kind and compassionate. "Would you like to join us, Marc? It isn't much. Just some garlic soup with ham and cheese baguettes."

Marc seemed appreciative he'd been asked. "No, but thank you," he said. "I wouldn't impose."

She laughed. "You're not imposing at all."

"Please, M. Rayne," Luc urged. "Will you have dinner with us?"

Marc smiled, hesitating. “If it’s not too much trouble, I would like that.”

“You’re never any trouble,” Zélie assured him. “Come on in. It’s ready now.”

They crossed the yard and started up the steps to the back door. “I do have something to tell you,” Marc said, as he leaned heavily on the railing to pull himself up the steps. “I did some research on our artist friend, Jean-Pierre.”

Zélie’s eyes widened. “Really?” she asked. “That was fast. You must have been a great investigator.”

Marc laughed. “I’m not so sure about that.”

“I can’t wait to hear what you found.”

“I think you’ll find it interesting,” he said. “I was certainly surprised. I also met a valuable resource if we want to know more.”

Zélie wanted to help as he fought to get up the last step, but she was afraid to offend him. She waited, pretending not to notice his struggle, and held the door open. “You can tell me all about it over dinner.”

Chapter Eighteen

Montmartre, 1874

Two days later, Elise Lyon's coach stopped in front of Jean-Pierre's studio. The driver got down from his perch and helped her from the carriage. Mme. Michel was sitting on her stoop, and she walked over to greet Elise.

"Was it you?" Mme. Michel asked, studying the bruises on Elise's face.

Elise smiled faintly. "Yes, just as I was leaving my last session."

"The police questioned me," Mme. Michel said. "Inspector Babin and another man. I forget his name."

"They're very thorough," Elise said. She didn't want this nosy woman prying into her affairs, but she realized she was a witness. Whatever she'd seen or heard was valuable.

The door to the studio opened, and Jean-Pierre stepped out. "How terrible," he said, cringing, as he tenderly touched her face near her swollen lip. "Does it hurt?"

"It's starting to heal," Elise said. "Still tender."

"Did the police question you, also?" Mme. Michel said.

"Yes, they did," Jean-Pierre replied. "I'm still shocked this occurred. And just outside my door."

"The police think it may have been a burglar," Elise said.

"A thief who randomly chose the first beautiful woman he saw?" Jean-Pierre asked. "Somehow that doesn't make sense."

Elise smiled at his unintentional compliment. "But it does seem the best explanation."

Mme. Michel studied her warily. "It's identical to —"

"Come inside," Jean-Pierre said, interrupting her mid-sentence. "We must begin."

They entered the studio, and Elise sat in the chair beside the window while Jean-Pierre went behind the canvas, scraping blotches of paint onto his palette with a knife.

Mme. Michel's face appeared at the window. "It's become a dangerous neighborhood. All sorts of crime. It never used to be like that. It was quiet once, a good place to raise children."

Jean-Pierre shrugged. "Only temporary, I'm sure, Mme. Michel."

"I'm not so certain," Mme. Michel replied. "Not with what happened last month."

"Do the police have any clues, Mme. Lyon?" Jean-Pierre asked, ignoring his neighbor.

"I don't think so," she said. "But they seem determined to catch the man."

"Such a horrible tragedy," he said, slowly shaking his head. He left the canvas and walked toward her, looking at her closely. He paused, his fingers caressing her face, the smoothness of her cheeks. "Do you feel well enough to pose?"

"With my face bruised?" she asked. "Can you work around it?"

"Yes, it's all right. Today, I'll focus on your eyes."

"My eyes?" she asked. "Can you do that, just pick a body part and paint it?"

"Of course, I can," he said. "But your eyes will be the most difficult."

"Why is that?"

"I have to capture them perfectly."

"Dark brown," she said. "It shouldn't be too hard."

"Oh, no, no, no," he said. "There's so much more."

She laughed. "I suppose you don't see what I do."

"Apparently not," he said, feigning offense. "But after I finish your portrait, you will see what I see. And the rest of the world will, too."

"I'm sure your portrait will be every bit as beautiful as you," Mme. Michel interjected. "Jean-Pierre's the best artist in Paris. Just look at some of his work."

"It would be impossible for a painting to capture Mme. Lyon's beauty," Jean-Pierre said. "But I'll try. It won't be easy."

"Why is that?" Elise asked, smiling, even though her lip hurt when she did so.

"Because your eyes show a love of life that few will ever know. They speak to me, asking questions. And they sometimes show mischief, teasing, as if a trick were about to be played. But to those who see them for the first time, they show beauty blended with innocence."

Elise laughed lightly. "You should have been a poet."

"You won't be disappointed when he's done," Mme. Michel called. "I've watched him paint many portraits, some of the most powerful women in Paris. And all were amazed at how well he captured their likeness."

"Yes, I'm sure they were," Elise replied to Mme. Michel.

"Many portraits," Jean-Pierre mumbled. "But today it is the eyes."

"And what do you see in my eyes today?" Elise asked, amused by both his behavior and Mme. Michel's attention.

"I see the child in the woman," he continued, back behind the easel, his brush on the canvas. "The student in the teacher. A mystery with no clues."

She started laughing. "I see an artist who speaks nonsense."

He laughed with her. "And what do you see?"

She studied him for a moment, not sure of what to say. "I see a complex man," she said softly. "Simple on the outside, complicated on the inside."

"And what else do you see?" he asked, leaning closer to the canvas.

"I see a man who laughs when the world is watching but who cries with pain when they are not. I see someone vulnerable, afraid to be hurt. Or maybe afraid to be hurt again, is a better description."

"You're observant," he said. "But perhaps not correct."

"I think he's a lonely man," Mme. Michel said, still part of their conversation. "He doesn't have a lady friend. And none on our street can understand why."

"I agree," Elise said, enjoying the way they teased him. "Maybe I see a man who doesn't want to see what I may see. Or what others, like Mme. Michel, might also see."

"Maybe," he said, the brush still moving. "Or perhaps the past is best forgotten, the memories vague and uncertain, twisted to what we wish could have been."

"Or maybe we twist the memories to ease the pain?" she asked, probing.

"Could it be that the future offers much more than the past?" he asked. He turned, pointing to an unframed canvas, a painting of a Parisian café. "What do you see?"

"A beautiful painting by a true genius," Mme. Michel said. "That's what I see."

Elise studied the canvas and the bold brush strokes that made the painting. "I can taste the man's pastry as he sits at the outdoor table and reads the newspaper or smell the fragrance from the flowers in the boxes. I can feel the sunshine bathing the street, hear the two women talking as they enjoy their espressos. I see Paris and all it represents."

"And the flaws are hidden?" he asked.

Elise paused, studying the painting closer. "Yes, perhaps."

"Or maybe there are no flaws?"

"Everything has flaws."

"Yes, everything has flaws," he agreed. "Some are minor, some are not. But the finished portrait reveals how well the artist copes with flaws. It is the same for us. How we cope with flaws determines who we are."

"Yes, we all have flaws," she said, thinking of her own. "In our person and in our lives. I suppose we have to accept them."

Jean-Pierre shrugged. "Or turn them into strengths."

Chapter Nineteen

Deauville, 1956

Marc Rayne struggled up the back steps, pausing to rest when he reached the door. "I'm sorry," he said. "Sometimes my muscles spasm if I'm too active. I'll be fine in a minute."

Luc watched him, wide-eyed. "How come your leg doesn't work?"

"Stop it, Luc," Zélie scolded. "That's not nice."

"No, it's all right," Marc said. "I don't mind."

Zélie waited, holding the door open. "Are you sure?"

"Yes, it's fine," he said and turned to Luc. "I had a bad injury, and it took a long time to get better. But I still can't walk very well."

"Do you want me to help you?" Luc asked, reaching out to take Marc's hand.

Marc smiled and grasped the little boy's hand. "Thank you, Luc, I appreciate that."

They walked into the kitchen, the boy guiding the man. Zélie watched them, smiling, and added another setting to the table. "What would you like to drink?" she asked Marc.

"Whatever you have is fine with me," he said as Luc led him to a chair.

Zélie poured two glasses of red wine, a pinot noir, and filled Luc's glass with cider. She added garlic soup to each of their bowls. Fresh bread was already on the table.

Marc sampled the soup. "Hmm, this is very good. You're a wonderful cook. Thank you so much for inviting me."

"We're glad to have you," she said. She thought about what she had overheard in the yard, the kind words Marc had said to her son about his father. "We appreciate your friendship."

"As I do yours," he replied, blushing slightly. He seemed genuinely touched.

They were quiet for a moment, enjoying their soup.

Zélie set her spoon down and sat back in her chair. "What did you find out about the paintings?" she asked.

Marc glanced at Luc, smiled for a moment, and turned to Zélie. "How many portraits are in the attic?"

She shrugged. "I will have to look," she replied. "The two that I showed you. I know there are more, but I didn't pay much attention to them. I'm not sure if they're by the same artist."

"Can we go up and look?" Luc asked. "I think some of the boxes are filled with toys. I looked the other day, but I couldn't find any."

"I bet we find some this time," Marc said. "Maybe we'll see some firetrucks."

"Oh, please," Zélie said, laughing lightly. "Don't encourage him."

Marc held his hand to his mouth as if he shouldn't have spoken. "Maybe your maman can help you look for toys."

"Why did you ask how many paintings we have?" Zélie asked.

"I visited a retired art professor this morning," he said. "She lives just outside of town. A fabulous resource, and she's willing to help us if we want."

"Did she have good information?"

"Yes, she did. It was incredible, actually." He paused, ate a spoonful of soup, Zélie watching anxiously.

He took a sip of wine and then continued. "She's extremely knowledgeable, taught at the Sorbonne. Such a delightful person. I enjoyed talking to her. She lives a few miles north of town, in a cottage beside the—"

"Are you teasing me?" Zélie interrupted, laughing. "Or just building the suspense?"

Marc chuckled. "I was toying with you."

"I deserve it, I suppose."

"Anyway," he said, ready to tell the story. "She told me that Jean-Pierre was a very accomplished painter."

"Really?" she asked, eyebrows arched. She took a sip of wine.

"He even has works in the Louvre."

Her eyes grew wide. "Seriously?"

Marc nodded, sipping some water. "More important for you, she suggested his paintings could be quite valuable."

Zélie froze, her glass in mid-air. "I never expected that."

"Neither did I," he admitted. "But you know what it might mean."

"Yes, I do," she said, feeling relieved, as if a burden she carried had been taken away. "Is there a chance my financial problems may soon be solved?"

"They could be," he said. "Although she needs more information and would have to check the paintings to ensure they're authentic."

"Did she know who the woman in the portrait was?"

"No, she didn't. But she said she'll help us find out."

Zélie hesitated, not sure who to involve or what the expense might be. "I don't know how to proceed," she said softly. "I can't afford to pay her. Or you for that matter. Unless I sell a painting."

"I suggest we make a list of all the paintings and visit her. She told me she could get some reference books on Jean-Pierre, if we wanted."

She hesitated, wanting to know more, but afraid she might not be able to proceed. "How much does she charge for her services?"

He shrugged. "She may not want money. Maybe she would enjoy doing the research. But we'll never know until we ask her."

Zélie was quiet for a moment, thinking. "I suppose that's what we should do. Make the list, go visit her, and see what she says."

"I agree," Marc said. "Who knows what we'll learn? You could be in for a huge surprise."

She sighed. "It seems too good to be true. I could pay off Eva's debts, maybe even send Luc to a private school."

Marc eyed Luc to see if he was listening. He wasn't. "Find a good doctor to help him cope."

"And address his nightmares," she said hopefully.

"Then that's what we'll do," he declared. "First, we'll make the list. And I'll call her to see if there's any fee."

"Oh, Marc, I don't know how to thank you," Zélie said, seeing a solution she never dreamed existed.

"We can check the attic after dinner if you like," he said, finishing his soup. "It shouldn't take long."

She looked at him, such a kind man. They were alike in some ways—Marc hurt physically, forced to give up a job he loved, just as she hurt emotionally; they both knew pain. “But I can’t pay you, either,” she said softly. “At least not now.”

“I don’t want any money,” he said and then looked at her with feigned surprise. “I thought we had agreed on a fee, anyway.”

She looked at him curiously. “We did?” she asked. “What was that?”

“Piano lessons.”

Chapter Twenty

Montmartre, 1874

Andre Sinclair knew his company was overextended. He walked a tightrope, risking bankruptcy for what he hoped would be a lucrative reward. He only had to survive the next few years without drowning in debt. So many opportunities had been available after the Franco-Prussian War that he had borrowed heavily to purchase anything that complimented his existing portfolio. He was confident it had been a risk worth taking, and if he ever found himself in the same situation, he would do it again. His investments would grow, and, after weathering the near term, increased returns would justify his boldness. But he hadn't anticipated all possibilities. He hadn't considered Henri Lyon.

When the loan's due date approached, he had planned to renegotiate the terms with the bank, extending the payment as required. The institution stood to make a tidy profit, more money than originally projected, while avoiding an unwelcome default. But now Henri Lyon held the loan. A tidy profit wasn't enough for him—it never had been. Lyon sought total destruction, preying on vulnerable men, or the businesses they owned, and taking what only weeks before they never would have been willing to give. Lyon demanded payment in full. But Sinclair didn't have the necessary cash—not even a fraction of it. His only hope was to extend the end date for at least two years. And Henri Lyon would make him pay dearly to do that.

Sinclair wondered why the bank had decided to sell his loan, especially with no warning. It wasn't typical; he had worked with them before. So had his father before turning the business over to him. It made him suspicious. Maybe Lyon had researched Normandy Mines and found its vulnerabilities. Then he'd pressured the bank to sell the loan, leveraging whatever dealings they shared or spreading sordid secrets he knew or invented. Sinclair would never know the truth, and he wouldn't attempt to find it. But he did know he was in a dangerous position, and so did Henri Lyon.

Sinclair had few alternatives. Only a complex deal with a third party could save him—financing from another bank, or a firm willing to take stakes in businesses he already owned. But it all would take time. Enterprises had to be examined, assets evaluated, books reviewed. He had to stall, convince Lyon he was negotiating in good faith when in reality he was not. And if all else failed Sinclair would have to part with the yearling.

Lyon was a nasty man, his thirst for the kill not easy to quench. And his desire to compromise didn't exist. It wasn't about money for Lyon. It was about inflicting pain. Sinclair really had only one viable option, a plan he had already begun to put in place.

He had to destroy Henri Lyon before Henri Lyon destroyed him.

Chapter Twenty-One

Deauville, 1956

After finishing dinner and enjoying crepes for dessert, Zélie brought Luc up to bed, leaving Marc alone in the parlor. When she returned, she found him looking through her sheet music.

"You are serious about playing the piano, aren't you?" she teased.

"I am," he said, laughing lightly. "I can play a little. But I'm anxious to get better."

She smiled. Maybe he would be her first pupil. "I'm sorry I kept you waiting. Luc finally fell asleep. At least for now."

"Is he still having nightmares?"

She nodded. "A few times a week."

Marc's eyes narrowed. "The same dream?"

"For the most part but with some variations."

He was quiet for a moment. "Maybe they'll fade with time."

"I sure hope so," she said. "I'm starting to worry."

"You're doing the best you can," he assured her as he put the sheet music back in the holder.

"If they don't stop soon, I'll have to get professional help."

"I'm sure he'll do better once he's settled," Marc said. "Just give it a little more time."

Zélie sighed, not sure he was right. "Maybe I need to sell those paintings," she said. "Then I can get him all the help he needs."

He smiled. "That may be easier than you think. Shall we go in the attic and take a look?"

"Yes, of course," she said. "Let's see what we find."

Marc followed Zélie up the stairs, moving much better than he had earlier.

"Are you feeling all right?" she asked, watching his progress.

"Yes, I'm fine now. No spasms."

They quietly passed Luc's bedroom and approached the attic.

"I'll leave the door ajar," she said softly. "Then I can hear Luc if he calls me."

They climbed the stairs, and Marc paused, eyeing all the boxes and furniture crammed in the rooms. "I never expected this much."

"Both rooms are full," she said. "Some of the stuff is beautiful—glassware, lace, furniture. But I don't know where it all came from."

"How should we approach this?"

"Let's clear a space against the wall, and we'll stage the portraits there."

"That should work," he said. "Although we have to be careful. They might be valuable."

She laughed. "I can only hope."

Zélie cleared a space, moving two Art Deco end tables, pushing them against a back wall. Boxes of books and old photographs followed. Once the floor area was clear, they took the portraits of the woman and the racehorse, Golden Cross, and put them against the freed wall.

"I'll search over here," Zélie said. "Why don't you look through the other room?"

For the next thirty minutes, they moved boxes and crates, tables and chairs, a chaise lounge, several posters from the turn of the century, some military artifacts from the First World War, a collection of brightly colored rocks from Madagascar, women's clothes, probably belonging to Eva, and an assortment of toys: balls, toy soldiers, a chess set missing some pieces, metal cars and trucks. Mingled among the varied assortment were several paintings, all as large as the first two. Zélie and Marc removed them from the piles and brought them to the staging location, propping them up against the wall.

"Are you finished?" Marc asked, admiring the portraits.

"Yes, I think so," she said, glancing back at all she had searched through. "There might be some smaller paintings in the boxes."

"This should work for now."

"How many do we have?"

"Eight," he replied, rearranging them so they all faced the room. "Including the first two you had found, Golden Cross and the woman's portrait."

"Here's a portrait of the same woman, sitting with a man on the beach, but it's not dated."

He studied the painting for a moment. "It's Deauville," he said. "That's the promenade behind them."

"I wonder who he is?" she asked.

"I've no idea, but I'm sure we'll find out."

She studied the portrait. "He's attractive—brown hair, a bit long, a two-or three-day growth of beard, brown eyes."

"This one is interesting," he said. "A blond woman, very attractive."

She laughed. "And naked."

He smiled. "I wonder how she relates to the others."

"Here's an odd one. Two policemen in front of a Paris police precinct."

Marc laughed. “That’s quite a moustache on the older gentleman.”

“I bet he spent more time grooming it than I do with my hair,” she joked.

“What else do we have?” Marc asked, scanning the remainder.

She looked at the next portrait. “A Parisian café.”

Marc checked it closely. “Normandy Mines,” he said, pointing to the building at the edge of a portrait dominated by the café and its patrons. “It will be interesting to see if that business still exists.”

“This one is titled *Montmartre,*” she said. “A charming lane enclosed with stone walls.”

“The last one is an artist’s studio in Paris,” he said. He stepped back, studying the portraits. “And they’re all signed by JP or Jean-Pierre.”

Chapter Twenty-Two

Montmartre, 1874

A quaint café, owned by the same family for generations, sat on a corner in Montmartre. Oval tables spread along the pavement allowed patrons to enjoy the spring day while drinking coffee and reading newspapers. A narrow lane across the street climbed a hill, walls enclosing the road, a string of houses at the top where it wound to another busy boulevard.

Inspector Babin and Lieutenant Dumont enjoyed their coffee—along with a raspberry tart for the inspector—and scanned a newspaper while warily watching the lane and the artist's studio at its peak. A black carriage with gilt trim waited just outside the door, the driver perched upon it, a newspaper opened before him.

"She's coming out now," Claude Dumont observed as Elise Lyon stepped from the studio. Her coachman climbed from his perch to open the carriage door.

Babin looked at his pocket watch. "Just over an hour," he said. "At least the carriage waits by the studio. The attack never would have occurred if he had been there during the last session."

Dumont eyed the coach as it started down the incline. "I thought Lyon might delay work on the portrait," he said. "For his wife's protection."

"You do not understand Henri Lyon," Babin scoffed. "Elise Lyon is more a prized possession than a wife. No doubt, a rich and powerful friend has had his wife's portrait painted by Jean-Pierre. Henri Lyon must do the same. Her safety is secondary."

Dumont raised the newspaper as the carriage approached, helping to hide their presence. The coach turned the corner at the bottom of the hill and rattled down the road, joining the collection of wagons and carriages that passed along the busy boulevard.

"We'll watch more of her sessions," Babin said, "while we learn her routine. Come, I want to once more examine the scene of the crime."

"Do you think her assailant also watches?" Dumont asked as they left the café and crossed the street.

"Perhaps he does," Babin said as they started up the incline. "We must watch everything, not just the studio but also who comes up and down the lane or lingers on the corners. I suspect we soon will see the same face more than once."

They walked in silence, pausing midway up the incline. "This is where the attack occurred," Dumont said. "Almost the same location where the prostitute was killed."

Babin held up his finger to signal silence. "But we do not know where the prostitute was killed. We only know where her body was found."

Dumont eyed the lonely lane stretching between busy boulevards, a few houses on the top of the hill. "I presume the killing took place here. Why would the killer move the body?"

"Presume?" Babin asked incredulously. "We do not presume, Lieutenant. We prove."

"Yes, of course," Dumont muttered, turning to study the stone wall, growing shorter as it climbed the hill.

Babin scanned the cobblestone street from the bottom at the boulevard to the top of the hill where the mismatched houses were joined in a row. "Definitely the darkest location," he observed. "And far enough away from both the street and the houses, so he might not be seen."

Dumont studied the branches spilling over the top of the wall. "This limb is strong enough to support a man," he said, pointing to a stout branch.

They looked at the majestic plane tree, its limbs stretching in many directions. "A man could easily climb the tree and wait until an unsuspecting victim happened along," Babin suggested. "Then drop down beside her."

"It seems that the attack was planned."

"Planned for minutes or planned for days, we do not know," Babin concluded. "But in either scenario, the attacker was watching Elise Lyon. They knew she was visiting the artist's studio." He paused to cast a knowing glance at Dumont. "For whatever purpose."

"They may have known how long she would be there," Dumont said. "Perhaps from observing earlier visits."

Babin nodded, fingering the curve of his moustache. "They knew her carriage and coachman and made sure he couldn't see what was about to occur."

"The attack did mirror that of the prostitute. She was strangled to death."

"But with no apparent motive," Babin countered. "Whereas the attack on Mme. Lyon suggests a robbery."

Dumont looked at his superior, daring to question. "But we don't know that for sure. It could be the same man."

"It's clear that Elise Lyon's life is in danger, regardless of the assailant and his motive. Although I'm not sure why."

Dumont was doubtful. "She isn't the type to make enemies. She seems to be liked by all."

"Yes, so it appears. But in Paris the world is never as it seems."

"But we've seen nothing to the contrary," Dumont said, not fully understanding.

Babin ignored him. "Maybe the artist does more than paint portraits," he suggested. "Maybe they're lovers."

Dumont pursed his lips. "We've seen no indication that they are."

"Not yet," Babin said. "But I suspect, in time, we will."

The two men were quiet, studying the scene of the crime, the houses on the hill, where no one had seen what had happened, the boulevard below, where bystanders intervened.

"And we have Henri Lyon," Babin continued. "Not a popular man, except to those who invest in his company, a bit callous, perhaps."

"I'm sure he has enemies," Dumont said. "But what successful businessman doesn't?"

"Yes, but do any of his enemies fear him or hate him enough to harm his wife for revenge?"

Dumont shrugged. "I suppose we have to find that out."

"I want to talk to Mme. Michel again," Babin said, starting up the hill. "She had valuable information on our last visit. Maybe she'll remember more."

"Should I talk to the other residents?" Dumont asked.

"I see no reason why," Babin replied. "No one saw anything. But another visit to the artist might be revealing."

They walked up the hill, and Babin went to the stoop of Mme. Michel and tapped on her door. Dumont stopped at the artist's studio and looked at some of the portraits and landscapes displayed in the window, advertisements for his services. The painter was very skilled, bringing landscapes to life, making you feel as if you could walk right into them. He wondered what other skills the artist possessed.

He knocked on the door, patiently waiting. A moment later the door opened, and a man looked at him strangely.

"Hello Jean-Pierre," Dumont said with a wry smile, nodding toward Babin at the adjacent doorway. "It seems we meet again."

Chapter Twenty-Three

Deauville, 1956

It was just after ten a.m. the following morning when Zélie's telephone rang. It was the estate agent, providing details on the cottage rental for the summer. "I'm so sorry," he said. "But we haven't had much interest in letting the cottage on a weekly basis or even for the season."

Zélie's heart sunk. Without the rental income, she was in serious financial trouble. "Can you try to find a yearly tenant?"

"Yes, of course," he said. "I'll update the listing. I'm sure you understand. Every year, it gets harder to compete with the big hotels."

Zélie sighed, knowing she was in for difficult times. "Did my mother-in-law have any issues?"

"At times, yes," he said. "Last year was particularly bad."

"Thank you for your efforts," Zélie said as she ended the call. "Please keep me updated."

She hung up the phone and closed her eyes. She had to find out if the paintings had any value. It might be her only hope.

Marc Rayne arrived at eleven a.m. for his first piano lesson, part of their agreement for the investigative services he was providing. Zélie led him to the piano where she had a chair arranged beside the stool. She had some instruction booklets that she had used in Paris, and, as soon as she evaluated Marc's musical ability, she would start the lesson.

"I think I'll enjoy this arrangement," he said once he was settled at the piano.

"Do you know anything at all about music?"

"I do," he said. "I once took lessons but only briefly. Although I still remember the basics. I thought piano playing would act as a good stress reducer."

"I'm sure it is," Zélie said. "Most find it relaxing."

"I'm sure I will, too."

"We'll have our lesson weekly, every Tuesday at eleven," she said. "But you'll have to come daily to practice. When would you like to do that?"

"Eleven should be fine, if not too inconvenient. But I do insist on paying you."

"No," she said, shaking her head. "That wasn't our agreement. The lesson is in exchange for helping me."

"No, not anymore," he said. He turned to face her. "Zélie, I need to keep busy—more than fixing old bicycles. Doing a little detective work helps me do that."

She hesitated, not interested in charity—if that's what he was proposing. "Are you sure you won't reconsider?"

He shook his head. "No, I insist. No other arrangement works for me. Eleven a.m.?"

She paused, considered another protest, but relented. He seemed genuinely interested in playing the piano—as any other student would. "Eleven should be fine," she said. "Now, let's find out how much you know, so we can start your lessons at the appropriate level."

They spent the next thirty minutes discussing key signatures, scales, time signatures, and tempos. Zélie chose the appropriate lesson plan and gave Marc his initial instruction. Time passed quickly, the pupil very attentive, and the lesson soon came to a close.

"I enjoyed that very much," he said.

"Good, I'm glad," Zélie said, pleased he liked the lesson. "I'll leave your instruction book on the piano, ready for you when you practice. You may come over whenever you like. But we'll target eleven a.m."

"How soon before I can play this?" he asked, pointing to sheet music for Mozart's Piano Concerto No. 21.

She smiled. "I think you'll need a few more lessons."

"Can you play it?"

"Yes, of course," she said. "Would you like to hear it?"

"Please, I would love to," he requested. "Just for a few moments."

They switched seats, and Zélie opened the sheet music. Seconds later her fingers caressed the keys, bringing the pleasing movement to life. She played for several minutes and then stopped, smiling.

Marc started clapping. "Fabulous," he said. "Absolutely beautiful."

"Thank you," she said humbly. "I don't normally have an audience."

He rose to go. "Such talent. You're very good."

"Thank you so much," she said, beaming as she followed him to the door. "It won't be long before you're playing just as well."

He opened the door to leave but hesitated a moment. "I don't want to intrude or make the neighbors talk because I spend so much time with you."

She laughed. "I'm not worried about the neighbors' gossip. They'll find something to talk about, whether it's me or not."

He seemed to relax. "I didn't call the art professor last night when I got home—it was a little too late. I'll call her now and see when she's available. I'll find out about the fees, too."

"I really do appreciate your help," she said. "I think I would be lost without you."

He laughed. "I think you might be lost with me. But we'll see what we can find."

She smiled. "I hope all of this works out. I talked to the estate agent before you came."

"What did he say?"

She slowly shook her head. "Renting the cottage as a seasonal let doesn't look promising."

"Too much competition from the hotels, I assume."

She nodded. "I hope the professor can help."

"I'll arrange a visit, and we'll find out," he said. "Do you want to come with me?"

Chapter Twenty-Four

Montmartre, 1874

Henri Lyon sat in the Stohrer Restaurant, eating salmon, roasted potatoes, and broccoli for lunch. A bottle of white wine, an oak aged chardonnay, sat beside him. He dined alone every Wednesday, sitting at the same secluded table, enjoying a superb meal worthy of his ample frame. He had just finished eating, eyed the crepe on the plate before him, and poured the last of the contents of his wine bottle into his glass, when two men approached his table, pointing to empty chairs.

"May we?" asked Inspector Babin as he stood with Lieutenant Dumont.

Henri was surprised, not expecting visitors, especially policemen, and having so routinely dined alone every Wednesday afternoon. "Yes, of course, please join me," he said as he summoned a waiter.

"No, nothing for us," the Inspector said, waving the waiter away. "Although the crepe looks inviting."

"Would you like one?" Henri asked, eyebrows arched.

Babin, no stranger to fine food and pastries, studied it a moment more. "Perhaps, I shall."

"Lieutenant?" Henri asked.

"No, thank you," Dumont replied.

Henri summoned the waiter, and a moment later a crepe was served to Inspector Babin. No one kept Henri Lyon waiting—or his guests.

"M. Lyon, may we ask a few questions?" Dumont asked.

"Yes, of course."

Dumont glanced at Babin and then began. “Do you have any reason to believe that someone might try to kill your wife?”

Henri’s eyes widened. He thought for a moment, started to speak, but hesitated. “No, of course not,” he said. “Everyone adores Elise. Why would you even ask that question?”

“We’re conducting an investigation,” Dumont offered. “We want to consider all possibilities.”

Henri was confused. “But you said it was a random robbery.”

“It most likely was,” Babin interjected between mouthfuls of crepe. “But suppose it wasn’t?”

Henri’s face firmed. “But you said most likely.”

“Still the strongest possibility,” Dumont assured him. “But we need to evaluate every possibility.”

Henri assessed the men before him. He hadn’t been impressed initially, reputation or not, and he wasn’t impressed now. It was difficult not to get aggravated. “I can’t imagine anyone wanting to harm her. She’s delicate, like fragile glassware that’s handled with care. Everyone loves her. I’ve never heard anyone speak ill of her.”

“Yes, of course,” Dumont said. “But we must consider it.”

Henri shrugged, not convinced. “I do want all avenues explored. And I want the culprit found. As quickly as possible.”

“We agree,” Babin said, licking the tips of his finger where some cream from his crepe still lingered. “And we do apologize for the imposition. But when we saw you in the restaurant, we took the liberty of interrupting your lunch to ask a few questions.”

"Ask whatever you like," Henri said, lifting his glass to his lips. "I'm concerned for my wife's welfare."

Babin motioned to Dumont. "A good opportunity for you, Lieutenant," he said. "Please, ask M. Lyon what we discussed."

Dumont smiled faintly, collecting his thoughts. "How long have you been married?"

"Almost a year."

"Newlyweds," Babin said.

"Yes, we're very happy," Henry replied, his eyes narrowing.

"How did you and Elise meet?" Dumont asked.

"I have a cottage on the Normandy coast, in Deauville," Henri explained. "One of my greatest passions is horseracing. Elise's father is involved with the racetrack. I know him well."

"Was it an arranged marriage?" Babin asked.

Henri shrugged. "An arranged introduction, I suppose. I helped Elise's father extricate himself from a precarious financial situation. During the course of the negotiations, I became a frequent visitor to their home."

"What type of financial difficulties?" Dumont asked.

"You should probably ask him, although I will say they were severe."

"You paid his debts?" Babin asked, glancing at Dumont.

Henri paused, sipping his wine. "It's none of your business, Inspector."

"But you fell in love with his daughter?" Babin asked.

Henri eyed them warily. "I was ready to marry."

"You're such a wealthy man," Babin continued. "You could have married anyone."

"I'm not sure what you're trying to say," Henri said, his face firm. He was tiring of the pompous inspector.

"Many wealthy women would be honored to be your wife," Dumont noted.

Henri shrugged. "I could have married anyone. But I didn't want to. I've met most of the eligible woman in Paris."

"None interested you?" Dumont asked.

Henri hesitated, eyeing each man carefully. He wondered why they were focused on him. He tensed, suspecting a trap was about to be sprung. "Not as a wife," he said evasively.

"As a mistress, perhaps?" Babin probed.

Henri said nothing and then sipped his wine. When the glass rested once more on the table, he spoke. "What are you trying to say?"

"Nothing," Babin replied innocently. "Nothing at all. It just seems strange that such a wealthy man would marry so far beneath his social standing—a woman whose father works at the racetrack."

"I don't care what other people think," Henri said curtly. "People care what I think."

Dumont and Babin shared a glance and shifted uncomfortably. "Do you have much in common?" Dumont asked.

"She has a love for horses, something we share," Henri replied. "We also support several charities, one of Elise's passions. She's on an oversight board at the orphanage."

"Does her lack of sophistication, at least by Parisian standards, bother you at all?" Dumont asked.

Henri laughed. “Not in the least. Elise is very intelligent—far more than most of our civil servants, police inspectors included.”

Babin gasped, offended by the insinuation, and looked at Dumont. They were quiet for a moment, eyeing Henri warily.

“Does omission from the Parisian society bother her at all?” Dumont asked.

Henri sat back in the chair and folded his arms across his chest. His patience was exhausted. “I never thought to ask,” he said gruffly. “I don’t care, and I suspect that neither does she.”

The policemen shared furtive glances, none of which went unnoticed by Henri Lyon. He finished his wine and lit a cigar. “Do you have more questions?”

Babin nodded politely. “I assume Mme. Lyon is considerably younger than you.”

“She is.”

“Twelve years, maybe?” Babin asked.

“Fifteen,” Henri said. “But hardly unusual.”

“No, not unusual,” Babin replied, although his expression showed he didn’t agree.

“Is it a happy marriage?” Dumont probed.

Henri struggled to maintain his composure. “I don’t know what you’re implying, but I think this interview is over.”

“Please,” Dumont said, raising his hand. “Don’t be offended. They are only questions that have to be asked.”

Henri puffed his cigar, gazed around the restaurant, and then nodded. “Continue.”

“Do you have any enemies, M. Lyon?” Babin asked.

"I have many enemies, Inspector, men that despise me. But I'm sure you already know that."

"Who is your greatest enemy, the man who hates you above all others?" Babin asked.

"Andre Sinclair."

Chapter Twenty-Five

Deauville, 1956

Anton LaRue was twenty when he won his first race. As the son and grandson of horse trainers, he had spent his entire life in the shadows of the Deauville track. He was expected to be a winner. But in the six years that followed his initial triumph, he'd won only a handful of races, all with different horses. He eked out a living, riding for Stepping Stone Stables, which was known for the slender stream that crossed its pastures, flat stones spaced across it.

He was an inch or two over five feet tall, barely a hundred pounds. With the size, ambition, and love for horses that successful jockeys possessed, most predicted a promising career. But he never raced a horse that matched his ability or passion—at least until now. Stepping Stone Stables was home to a stunning stallion named Silver Shadow with an impeccable pedigree. The thoroughbred had won his first race by five lengths with Anton LaRue stretched over the horse's neck, pushing him past the competition. Owned by an industrialist from Paris, a man as committed to Anton LaRue as he was to Silver Shadow, the horse would soon become the most watched thoroughbred in all of France. Silver Shadow was Anton LaRue's future—he knew it, and so did his father, the owner, and anyone familiar with horses.

Anton had enjoyed dinner with Zélie and Luc. He had known Luc from when he'd visited his grand-mère. Anton felt his pain, losing so much at such a tender age, because he, too, lost a parent while very young. His mother died in an automobile accident when he was only eight years old. Anton was determined to help Luc Girard get through the darkest days of his young life, to ease his suffering, to help him adjust, and to make a man from the timid boy that always seemed so sad.

The clubhouse at the Deauville racetrack displayed paintings and photographs of famous horses, undefeated champions, the best in racing history: Golden Cross, Callistrate, Kincsem, and a dozen more, their images spread down a hallway in chronological order. Anton walked down the corridor, found the portrait of Golden Cross, and studied it closely.

The painting wasn't as crisp as the portrait in Zélie's attic, the muscles not as defined. It was still well-done, even if it did pale in comparison. He looked at a brass plate on the wall beside the portrait and read the narrative: *Golden Cross, named for his distinctive blaze. Born in 1873, sold to Andre Sinclair at the 1874 yearling sale for 6000 francs. Won the Grande Poule des Produits in 1876. Total races: 37. Total wins: 37. Sired Chantilly, Avalanche, Brown Biscuit—all future champions.*

Anton studied both the painting and the placard for several minutes. What a remarkable horse Golden Cross must have been, born shortly after Deauville became established as a racing hub, the land surrounding the town home to many stables. He wondered what it had been like, eighty years before. He took a small notepad from his pocket and copied down the information. He then sought the manager for groundskeeping, Philippe Armand, known for his knowledge of racing history.

"Hello, Philippe," he said, finding the man on his way to his office. "May I ask you a few questions?"

Armand paused, glanced at his wristwatch, and turned to Anton. "Yes, of course," he said. "Is there a problem with the grounds?"

Anton smiled. "No, of course not. The grounds are impeccable—as they always are."

Armand relaxed. "Thank you," he said. "Coming from you, that's quite a compliment."

"I was hoping I could ask you a few history questions," Anton said. "I'm conducting some research for a friend."

Armand brightened, pleased he was acknowledged as an expert. "Yes, of course," he said. "I hope I can help."

"Can you tell me anything about Golden Cross?"

Armand arched his eyebrows. "He was a great one," he said. "The first true champion at Deauville."

Anton took out his notebook. "I copied the information from the placard by his portrait," he said, showing Armand. "Is there anything else you can tell me?"

Armand scanned his notes. "Undefeated, as you've noted. And fetched a record price at the yearling sale—I think the equivalent of several hundred thousand francs in today's currency. It was the early 1890s before a yearling commanded a comparable price."

"Do you have a list of the races won by Golden Cross?"

Armand thought for a moment. "Yes, I'm sure I do. I have reference books in my office. I'll look for you. Although some of the tracks no longer exist."

"Do you know anything about the owner?"

Armand hesitated. "His name was Andre Sinclair, but I don't know much more. I'll have to research him, as well. As I recall, the buyer at the yearling sale no longer owned Golden Cross when he raced. Give me a few days to check. I'll find out for sure."

"Thank you so much, Philippe," Anton said with a slight bow. "I really appreciate your help."

Before Anton left the clubhouse, he went to a bulletin board just outside the race track cafeteria. Many of those who worked at the track and the stables that surrounded it frequented the dining room. He removed a note from his pocket. He'd written an advertisement for a vacant cottage for rent. He posted it on the board. He was trying to help Zélie Girard—in more ways than one.

Chapter Twenty-Six

Montmartre, 1874

Henri Lyon was wary of the investigators' questions, which focused more on his relationship with Elise than solving the crime. And although Babin and Dumont probed into his personal life, he suspected for good reason, they found nothing different from other men of his status. Yes, he was older than his wife. And the marriage was based on a financial arrangement. Many were; it wasn't uncommon among the elite. Elise's father owed Henri a tremendous debt of gratitude. By offering his daughter's hand in marriage, he had bettered all of their lives. The detectives had also hinted that Elise might be uncomfortable in a world in which she didn't belong and could have already grown tired of a life she'd never chose. Henri didn't know their objective, but he suspected they were trying to plant doubt where it didn't exist. He didn't know why.

"Inspector Babin and Lieutenant Dumont came to see me today," Henri said as he and Elise ate dinner, chicken stewed with wine, mushrooms, and bacon.

She sipped her wine. "What did they want?"

"They asked a lot of questions," he said. "None of which made sense."

"Are they close to finding my attacker?" she asked. "I'm afraid it'll happen again."

He ate a forkful of chicken, savoring the taste. It had been superbly prepared. "I have little faith in them. I'm tempted to hire a private concern to protect you and investigate the crime."

"I don't need protection," she said. "Not now. The coachman is always with me."

"Yes, see that he is," he muttered, still not convinced.

Elise hesitated, eyeing him curiously. "What questions did they ask?"

He looked up from his dinner. "Do you miss Normandy?" he asked without answering. "We can spend more time there if you like."

"Sometimes, I do," she admitted.

"Paris must be difficult," he continued. "Such a large city, everything happening so quickly."

She laughed. "Not at all. It's exciting. I like it."

"You don't miss the countryside, life in a charming village by the sea?"

She shrugged. "We don't visit as often as I would like, but I do enjoy dividing my time."

He studied her closely, searching for sincerity but not sure he found it. "Babin and Dumont have several different theories about the attack. Part of any investigation, I suppose."

She looked confused. "Why would they care if I liked Paris or not?"

"Because they hinted that you're unhappy, and it may have something to do with the crime." He paused, studying his wine glass, and then looked at her. "And because they're incompetent fools."

She frowned. "If Babin and Dumont have questions, why don't they ask me?"

"I'm sure they will," he said. "Sooner or later."

"What else did they want to know?"

Henri chewed thoughtfully for a moment. "They wanted to know if I had enemies."

She shook her head. "You don't, do you?"

"Of course, I do," he said. "All successful businessmen have enemies. A man can't please everyone. Not when money is involved."

"I don't know why they asked you that," Elise said. "What does it have to do with the man who attacked me?"

"They suspect someone seeks revenge," he said. "Babin wanted to know who I feared most—as if they'd committed the crime."

"Who do you fear most?"

"No one," he said, chuckling. "Others fear me. But I had to give them a name, so I offered Andre Sinclair."

"Andre Sinclair?" she asked. "No one will believe that. He's such a nice man. You have no reason to fear him."

"But I do," he insisted. "At least if I had to choose someone. His business is collapsing, and he blames me."

Elise was taken aback. "Why does he blame you?"

"Because I hold a sizable loan of his that's about to come due."

"What will happen?"

Henri sighed, wiping his face with a cloth napkin. "I haven't decided yet," he admitted. "Normandy Mines is overextended because Sinclair made bad financial decisions. My investment in his business is at risk."

"But that sounds like a financial issue," she said. "Why would you fear him because of that?"

"I only fear him because he fears me."

She hesitated, trying to put the pieces together. "Why would Babin and Dumont ever ask you that?"

"Because they think the man who assaulted you may have done it for revenge against me. They suspect it was not a random robbery."

Her eyes widened. “If it wasn’t a robbery, what was it?”

“They seem convinced that someone is trying to kill you.”

Chapter Twenty-Seven

Deauville, 1956

Zélie pulled weeds from flower beds in her quest to restore the gardens to the beauty they had known under Eva's loving care. She glanced at her watch, waiting for Luc to get home from school. She was worried about him. He seemed to be getting worse, not better.

Luc had awakened near 3 a.m., screaming hysterically. It had been his worst nightmare yet, another dream that she was about to die, this time from a terminal illness—just like his grand-mère. Zélie had assured him it was only a dream, that she had no illness, and he had nothing to fear, but he hadn't listened and insisted she kept secrets. After twenty minutes of sobbing, his anxiety had eased, and she was able to get him back to sleep. When he woke up for school, he refused to discuss it. She didn't know what she could do to help him. Was it only a phase, something that would slowly go away? Or was it much worse, something she wasn't equipped to address?

She tugged at a persistent weed, freeing its roots from the soil. Tossing it into a bucket with others she had pulled, she glanced at Marc Rayne's cottage. If what he said about the portraits was correct, she might have a significant windfall. She could pay off Eva's debts and have enough remaining to get Luc the proper care he needed. But she still found their presumed value difficult to believe, although she didn't know much about art. Marc had suggested holding an auction at one of the major houses—if the paintings were authentic and as valuable as the professor claimed they were.

It seemed like a dream, a fairy tale about to vanish before it began. Regardless of what was to come, somewhere in the process a mystery had to be solved, although she wasn't sure if she was equipped to do it. Samuel, her husband, had never mentioned the paintings. Not even once. He didn't seem to know their worth, or even if they existed, although he must have seen them at some point. Eva had to know. She had probably put them there. But where had they come from? And why hadn't she tried to sell them to settle her gambling debts?

"I brought you some lemonade," Marc said, suddenly appearing behind her.

She was startled, lost in her thoughts. She turned, shielding her eyes from the sun. "Thank you so much," she said as she stood and took the glass.

"Let's sit a minute," he said, motioning to a set of wrought-iron chairs perched under a chestnut tree. "You've earned a break."

"I just feel like I have so much to do," she said as they walked over and sat down. "It'll take me all summer to get the garden back to how it used to look."

"Eva declined quickly the last year or so," he said. "She didn't bother much with the upkeep."

Zélie was quiet for a moment, reliving days that were best forgotten. "She was mourning her son," she said softly.

"She had no other relatives?" Marc asked. "No one nearby who could have helped her?"

Zélie shook her head. "No, my husband was an only child, just like Luc. Gaston, her husband, died during the war, right before the Allied invasion."

"No siblings?"

"She did have a brother and a sister," Zélie said. "But they're both deceased. I think in the war, also—or just before it."

"Too many lost their lives," he muttered. "And some who survived are shadows of what they once were."

"A generation destroyed, like the war before it."

They were quiet for a moment, sipping their lemonade. "Were you surprised by the paintings?" he asked.

"Absolutely shocked," she admitted. "Not only by their presence but the mystery they've revealed."

He nodded, sharing her thoughts. "How did they get there?"

"Exactly," she said. "I feel like I know nothing about my husband or his family."

He shrugged. "I'm not trying to be sinister, but maybe you don't."

She paused, suspecting he might be right. "It makes me wonder what else is in the attic, especially hidden in all the boxes. How about all of those books? Are they lost treasures, too?"

"We should go through everything. We can separate what we think is valuable and have an appraiser come, if needed."

"I'll definitely need someone for the paintings," she said and sighed. "I feel like everything I find poses more unanswered questions. I'm afraid to look at anything else."

"Maybe you should focus on the paintings," he suggested. "Worry about everything else later."

"Yes, I suppose I should," Zélie said. "Deal with a little at a time."

"I did call the professor, but there wasn't any answer. Maybe she was running errands. I'll keep trying."

"I hope she's willing to meet. I'm sure she has much to teach us."

"She does," he agreed. "She said she would find some research books that show more of Jean-Pierre's works, which should be helpful. I'll call her again when I go inside."

"I am anxious to know," she said. "Because I feel like my husband and mother-in-law were strangers, hiding who they really were, with valuable paintings hidden in their attic and no explanation as to how they got there. Where did they get them? Were they gifts? Are they stolen? They certainly didn't buy them. They were working people, not rich or privileged."

Marc shrugged. "I don't know," he admitted. "But I bet we can find out."

Chapter Twenty-Eight

Montmartre, 1874

"It's time we spoke to Andre Sinclair," Inspector Babin said as they climbed from their carriage at Normandy Mines. It was a narrow limestone building tucked between a café with charming outdoor tables and a bank. "Especially if Henri Lyon believes he has reason to fear him."

"I don't think Lyon fears him at all," Dumont said. "I think he mentioned his name to damage Sinclair's credibility."

"You think?" Babin scoffed. "My dear Lieutenant, we do not merely think. We interrogate, and we investigate. And in the end, we prove who committed the crime."

They stepped into the office and were greeted by a male clerk behind a mahogany desk. "What can I do for you?"

"We are here to see M. Sinclair," Babin informed him. "I am Inspector Babin, and this is my underling, Lieutenant Dumont."

"May I ask what this is about?" the clerk said with a wary expression.

"It's in regard to a recent incident in Montmartre," Babin replied pompously. "And that is all you need to concern yourself with."

The clerk cast him a look of disdain but rose from his desk. "Just a minute."

Babin was indignant. "Who did he think he was talking to? An inspector commands respect. Was he raised in a cave?"

"Obviously, the man does not know who you are," Dumont assured him.

A moment later, the clerk emerged from a hallway. "Gentlemen, please come this way."

He led them down the corridor, framed paintings of coastal scenes on the walls interrupted by closed office doors. He knocked on the last door, waited a few seconds, opened it, and led them inside. "Inspector Babin and Lieutenant Dumont," he announced.

"Please come in," said the man behind the desk, motioning to two plush chairs with armrests. He rose to shake their hands. "I'm Andre Sinclair, president of Normandy Mines."

"M. Sinclair," Babin said, "Inspector Babin, Paris Police. And this is my trainee, Lieutenant Dumont."

"M. Sinclair," Dumont nodded as he shook his hand.

"What can I do for you?" Sinclair asked as the two men were seated.

"We have a few questions to ask you," Dumont began, "in regard—"

"Where we you on Tuesday evening, around seven p.m.?" Babin interrupted with a stern gaze.

Sinclair was stunned, and he looked at them strangely. "I was probably walking home," he said indignantly. "I normally leave here just after six."

"You were walking home, or you were already home?" Babin asked. "Details are very important, M. Sinclair."

"It would have been just after dark," Dumont clarified.

Sinclair shrugged. "I should have been home by then."

"And where is home?" Babin asked.

"I have an apartment a few blocks away."

"Are you married, M. Sinclair?" Dumont probed.

Sinclair looked confused. "No, I'm not married but recently engaged. Although I don't understand why it's any of your concern."

"Do we know your fiancée?" Babin asked. "A Parisian socialite, perhaps?"

Sinclair shifted in his chair. "No, you don't know her. She's not from Paris." He paused, studying their faces. "What is this all about?"

"Lieutenant, you may continue with the questioning," Babin said, ignoring Sinclair. "I will intervene to correct, as needed."

Dumont nodded meekly, paused to collect his thoughts, and then began. "Do you know Henri Lyon?"

"Yes, of course, I do. We're business acquaintances."

"Are you on good terms?" Dumont asked.

Sinclair hesitated. "We're occasional competitors, depending on the asset. But normally, we have little interface. I suppose that's the best description of our relationship."

"Does Henri Lyon have anything to fear from you, M. Sinclair?" Babin asked.

Sinclair laughed. "Not at all," he said. "It's actually the reverse. I have much to fear from Henri Lyon."

Dumont cast a quizzical glance at Babin who nodded for him to continue. "What do you have to fear?"

Sinclair hesitated as if reluctant to continue. "Normandy Mines is not a huge company, at least when compared to Lyon and Son."

"Which still gives you no reason to fear Lyon," Dumont remarked.

"No, it doesn't. But there's more."

"Then you had best explain," Babin scolded. "Because you may find yourself in a difficult situation."

Sinclair's eyes narrowed. "I don't see how," he replied. "I've done nothing wrong."

"Henri Lyon seems to think you may have," Babin retorted.

"Then he's misinformed," Sinclair declared. "Or flinging gossip, another trait he's mastered. I fear Lyon and for good reason."

"Then please, explain," Dumont requested. "We're not making accusations."

"At least, not yet," Babin interjected with a warning glance, wagging a finger.

Dumont paused for effect. "We're only trying to gather information, finding pieces of a puzzle."

Sinclair nodded but didn't seem to understand. "Just after the war, Normandy Mines pursued an aggressive expansion program, investing in mines and real estate both on the continent and in our colonies. To finance that expansion, we borrowed very heavily."

"What type of businesses are you referring to?" Babin asked.

"Natural resources and real estate, commercial buildings primarily. Sometimes we own a percentage of an asset. In other instances, we own the entire enterprise. For example, we have several properties in northern Africa. Algeria specifically."

"Isn't financing assets standard practice in the business world?" Dumont asked.

"It is and always has been," Babin interjected with a condescending glance at his underling.

"But in our case," Sinclair continued, "we were too aggressive, and now we're left with little cash, barely enough to meet overhead and interest payments. At least until the economy recovers from the war."

"Again, I don't find that unusual," Babin said, a man knowledgeable in many things. "The course of doing business, I assume. Every risk taken can't reap rewards."

"That's quite true," Sinclair said. "But in this case, one of my largest loans was purchased by Henri Lyon."

The policemen looked baffled. "Which means what?" Dumont asked.

"Don't you just make payments to Lyon instead of the banks?" Babin asked, fingering his moustache.

"Normally that's the case," Sinclair said. "But not this time."

"And what is so different, M. Sinclair?" Babin asked. "Please tell us because we are trying to unravel a mystery without any clues."

"Yes, of course," Sinclair replied. "The loan is due, but Lyon refuses to extend it. He wants full payment by the end of the month, potentially forcing Normandy Mines into bankruptcy."

"I assume Henri Lyon will then graciously pick up the pieces," Babin concluded.

"At very steep discounts," Sinclair added.

"Can you pay the loan in full?" Dumont asked. "Borrow from another bank?"

"Not without liquidating assets or transferring assets to Lyon," Sinclair explained. "And funding from another bank will take time."

"Time that you do not have because the payment is due," Babin clarified.

"Exactly," Sinclair said. "I'm in a very precarious position."

"Can't you compromise?" Dumont asked.

"I've tried," Sinclair said. "I offered Lyon my percentage of production from a coal mine in exchange for extending the payment for two years. But he wants more."

"What will you do, M. Sinclair?" Babin asked, eyebrows arched.

"Negotiations will continue, but time is limited. The closer to the deadline, the more I will likely have to surrender."

"Ah, and that is why Lyon fears you," Babin observed.

Sinclair's eyes narrowed. "As I said before, Lyon has no reason at all to fear me. I have everything to lose. Lyon can lose nothing."

"It's about revenge, M. Sinclair," Babin said grandly. "And that's why you're a potential suspect in a most serious crime."

Chapter Twenty-Nine

Deauville, 1956

When Anton LaRue arrived back at his cottage, he saw Marc and Zélie sitting under the tree. “Hello,” he said as he approached. “I have information about Golden Cross.”

“Let me get you some lemonade first,” Marc said, as he got out of his chair. “Here, sit. I’ll be right back.”

Anton sat beside Zélie and smiled. “How are you today?”

“I’m doing well,” she replied. “I did some gardening. Marc got information on the paintings from an art professor, and now you have news about the horse.”

“It’s much more than a horse,” he said, smiling. “As you will soon see.”

“Interesting,” Zélie said. She thought of the paintings and why her mother-in-law had kept them a secret. “Was Eva interested in the history of horse racing?”

He paused, thinking. “No, not that I remember. But she did know her race horses.”

“But only current day?”

“Yes, she was obsessed with racing.”

Zélie sighed. “It’s too bad she couldn’t pick winners.”

“I suppose she left you with quite a mess.”

She shrugged. “I don’t know if I would say that. She was kind enough to leave us the house. She just had problems and didn’t know how to handle them. Like most of us.”

“I’m surprised she lost so often. She studied horses. And jockeys, too. She had a very scientific approach.”

"Did she ever win?"

"Oh, yes. She won much more than she lost. At least I thought she did. I suppose you could say she made a living out of it."

Zélie was quiet for a moment. Maybe that explained why income from the cottages was secondary, the occupancy rates not important. Eva earned an income from playing the horses. But it still didn't make any sense. "Maybe she lost before she became a winner, and that's how she incurred all the debt."

Anton hesitated. "Could her debt have come from something else?"

Zélie rolled her eyes. "I don't know what to think."

Marc returned with a glass of lemonade and handed it to Anton.

"Thank you," Anton said, rising so Marc could sit. "I posted a notice in the clubhouse to rent the cottage. Should you get any calls."

"Thank you so much," Zélie said. "That's nice of you."

"It's perfect for someone who frequents the track or works at the stables."

"I asked my son, also," Marc said. "Maybe he knows someone."

"I don't know what I'd do without you two."

"Everything will work out," Marc said. "You'll see."

She smiled. "That's what people always say. People that aren't having the problem."

They laughed and then turned to Anton. "Please, tell us what you learned," Marc said.

"I told you that a portrait of Golden Cross hangs in the clubhouse gallery," Anton said. "It's a hallway, actually, that contains about fifteen portraits."

"How does that painting compare to the one in the attic?" Zélie asked.

"Nowhere near as good," Anton said. "When you look at the portrait you have, it seems like the horse is running right at you. Not so with the painting in the clubhouse."

Marc glanced at Zélie. "An art professor told us that Jean-Pierre, the artist of the works in the attic, was an extremely gifted painter."

"It shows," Anton said. "Wait until you see the painting in the clubhouse."

Zélie was hopeful. "It seems the professor knew what she was talking about then."

"Yes, she did," Anton said. "Golden Cross was also the first great champion in the history of racing at Deauville."

"Really?" Zélie asked, surprised.

Anton nodded. "He commanded a high price at the yearling sale in 1874, and two years later, he won the Grande Poule des Produits."

"Impressive," Marc commented.

"But just the beginning," Anton continued. "Golden Cross won thirty-seven races. And never lost once."

"That explains why a gifted artist would paint his portrait," Zélie said.

"I suspect the owner commissioned the painting," Anton said. "He had to be wealthy to pay the price he did for the horse. It's the equivalent of several hundred thousand francs in today's currency."

Marc whistled softly. “That’s a lot of money. Do you know the owner’s name?”

Anton removed his notebook from his pocket and scanned his notes. “Andre Sinclair.”

Marc shrugged and looked at Zélie. “Does that sound familiar?”

“No,” she said, shaking her head.

“One of the managers at the track, Philippe Armand, is going to research the horse,” Anton said. “Maybe he’ll have some information on the owner, too.”

“That would be great,” Marc said. “We’re trying to put all these pieces together.”

“Why not come to the track with me?” Anton asked. “And we can all talk to M. Armand.”

Chapter Thirty

Montmartre, 1874

The carriage arrived at Jean-Pierre's studio, and the coachman helped Elise to step out. Mme. Michel stood by her stoop, talking to an elderly woman, but she interrupted her conversation and came to greet Elise.

"How are you feeling, Mme. Lyon?" she asked.

"I'm doing much better, thank you," Elise replied.

Mme. Michel looked at her closely, and then lightly touched her face. "Your bruises are healed. I can't even tell they were there."

Elise smiled. "The swelling is gone, and so is the discomfort."

Mme. Michel leaned toward her and whispered, "Inspector Babin had more questions for me."

The studio door opened, and Jean-Pierre stepped out. He nodded at Mme. Michel, then smiled at Elise. "Have the police found the man who attacked you?"

"No, not yet," Elise said.

"I told Mme. Lyon that Inspector Babin asked me more questions," Mme. Michel said. "Such a competent man. He'll find the culprit."

"I received another visit from Lieutenant Dumont," Jean-Pierre said. "He asked questions about those who visit my studio—models and customers."

Mme. Michel lightly touched his arm, again glanced up and down the street, and then leaned closer. "Inspector Babin asked me about those who live on the street," she confided. "I think he trusts me to provide accurate information."

"I can understand why," Jean-Pierre said, his expression serious as Elise hid a smile.

If Mme. Michel knew she was being teased, she didn't show it. "What does your husband think?" she asked Elise.

"I'm not sure," Elise replied. "He has different theories, just as the police do."

"We should begin," Jean-Pierre said, eyeing a cloud. "Before we lose the light."

"I may watch," Mme. Michel said, glancing back to her house. "But I do have to sweep my stoop."

"The windows are always open, Mme. Michel," Jean-Pierre said as he led Elise inside.

Elise sat in the straight-backed chair while Jean-Pierre went behind the canvas and put different shades of paint on a palette. He fussed for a moment, making sure everything was just the way he wanted, and then studied her closely.

"Tilt your chin up, just a bit," he said, paintbrush in hand.

She did as he requested, raising her head a few centimeters.

"Yes, like that. Perfect."

"Should I stay in this position?"

"For now."

Elise was quiet, watching him. "My husband thinks the attack is related to the murder of the young woman."

Jean-Pierre glanced at the window as if he suspected they could be heard. "It was a terrible tragedy."

"I'm told she died in the same place. Just down the street. Only twenty-five years old."

"Her killer has yet to be apprehended," he said. "Which makes those in the neighborhood anxious."

"I can understand why."

He looked at the portrait and then at her, his gaze intense, as the paintbrush teased the canvas. "And what do the police think?"

"Inspector Babin said there are few similarities, so it's not likely related."

"Babin is an arrogant jackass," Jean-Pierre muttered.

She laughed. "He is pompous. Poor Dumont. I feel sorry for him sometimes. But Babin has had a long and illustrious career."

"Does Dumont agree with Babin?" he asked, stopping abruptly to look at the window, frowning at a darkening sky.

She shrugged. "I'm not sure. Whenever he speaks, Babin interrupts."

"Does your husband believe they're related?"

"Yes, he does," Elise said. "He's losing patience with Babin and Dumont."

"Any suspects?"

"They think it could be a business rival of Henri's," she said, glancing at the window. "Andre Sinclair."

"Normandy Mines," Jean-Pierre mumbled.

"Henri holds one of their loans and has requested payment."

"And we're to believe that Andre Sinclair, an upstanding citizen, wants to kill the beautiful Mme. Lyon because her husband has called a loan?" Jean-Pierre asked. "What would he gain by that?"

"Revenge."

Jean-Pierre laughed. "That's absurd."

"Henri agrees but claims it's a possibility."

"Of course he does," Jean-Pierre said, still chuckling. "It puts his competitor at a disadvantage, making it easier for Henri to negotiate. What other theories does the brilliant Inspector Babin have?"

She shrugged. "The random robbery."

"That also doesn't make sense."

"I agree," she said. "But regardless of the motive, they'll find the man eventually."

"And in the meantime?"

"I come to have my portrait painted while my coachman waits outside the door."

He smiled. "I'm pleased our work won't be interrupted." He looked at her for a moment, and then at the light streaming into the window. "Can you turn just a bit to the left?"

Elise did as he requested. His brush moved about the canvas, his palate in his left hand. She watched his eyes as they studied her and then the work before him, never satisfied. It was the mark of a true perfectionist, she suspected, and fascinating to watch.

He painted for almost thirty minutes, continually glancing at the window and the light that came through it. As the skies darkened, threatening rain, he stopped.

"Are we finished for today?" she asked.

"Yes, the clouds are not good," he said as he put down his palette and brush. "Do you want to stay and see if the weather clears?"

She glanced at the window, wondering if Mme. Michel was still there. "Yes, I would like that."

"And what shall we discuss?" he asked, coming closer.

She hesitated, not knowing whether or not to reply but eventually decided to ask, "Tell me about Giselle."

Chapter Thirty-One

Deauville, 1956

Zélie sat in the parlor, enjoying a glass of wine after Luc had gone to bed. She thought about the paintings, unable to explain what they were doing in her attic. They'd never been mentioned by her husband or mother-in-law. How long had they been there? And why were they hidden in a widow's house? Was there a connection between Eva and the artist—some sordid secret that no one knew?

The art professor claimed Jean-Pierre painted portraits to earn a living, but his passion was landscapes. The portrait of the woman fit—it represented his livelihood. If she added the painting of Golden Cross to that category, a portrait even if it was an animal, they could be grouped together. So could the nude painting of the woman with blond hair and possibly the painting of the same dark-haired woman with the young man. The street scene could be classified as a landscape, or cityscape, as could the portrait of the café and the artist's studio. And then the painting of the two policemen in front of the police station fit somewhere in between. Maybe it did make sense—the paintings offered a mix of the artist's creative output.

She finished her wine and went upstairs, made sure Luc was sleeping soundly, and crept to the third floor, leaving the door open should he awaken. The paintings were lined against the wall, and she studied them for a moment, looking for any links. Then she rearranged them, trying to assign some sort of order. She placed the portrait of Golden Cross at one end, the painting of the beautiful woman with dark hair next to it, followed by the portrait of the same woman on the beach with the young man. The dark-haired woman was the only person who appeared twice in the paintings. Next to those, she set the nude of the blonde woman with blue eyes. The two policemen in front of the police station followed, then the street scene, the café, and the artist's studio. Eight paintings, now lined in a row, loosely organized.

Zélie studied each in turn, admiring the beauty, trying to see what made them so vibrant and unique. Was it the use of colors—not yellow, red, blue and green like a million other paintings—but subtle variations, softer at times, harsher when necessary? She studied the portrait of the dark-haired woman, the hint of a smile, the mischievous twinkle housed in her eyes that seemed so inviting. It was almost as if she were about to speak.

And the scenes of the city were dramatic, like the crisp details in the café painting—the newspaper read by a patron, the tarts on his plate, flowers spilling over their window boxes, even a puddle, remnants of a morning rain, that reflected a passing carriage. She moved closer, daring to touch the canvas, and felt the rich textures the brush had left behind, making each scene seem alive and every person about to step from the portrait.

The frames were also beautiful. Hand-carved or molded wood in gilt, cherry, or walnut, they made a statement just as bold as the portraits did, celebrating wealth, style, and grace. She stepped back, viewed them as a group, each painting signed in beautiful curving letters, either JP or Jean-Pierre. In a matter of minutes, she was able to appreciate the artist's genius, his gift, the talent he possessed. And for the first time since Marc told her that the paintings might be valuable, she believed it.

As she continued to study the portraits, she wondered if any of the paintings besides the ones of Golden

Cross and the dark-haired woman were dated. No reference appeared on the paintings themselves or the frames, leaving their birth a mystery. Unless there was a date on the back, where the canvas was tucked into the frame. She delicately took up each portrait and turned it.

On the backs of the first few paintings she found nothing but cobweb remnants. But when she got to the portrait of the two policemen and spun it around, she noticed a folded paper stuck in the bottom right corner. She studied it for a moment, assuming it only filled a gap, keeping the painting tight to the frame. Almost as an afterthought, she touched it lightly and then tried to pull the parchment from the frame.

The paper was wedged securely. She didn't want to tear it, and, even though she thought it had been innocently placed, she was curious. She left the attic, went to check on Luc, and retrieved a letter opener from a desk in the parlor. She returned to the attic and tenderly turned the portrait.

As carefully as she could, she pried the paper from the frame, tediously lifting and tugging. The paper was thick, perhaps a piece of canvas, and folded. Little by little it loosened, and she pulled it free.

She unfolded the paper, which was several centimeters long and not quite as wide. Scrawled across the paper was a neatly printed message: *These eight paintings are the clues needed to solve the crime. CD*

Chapter Thirty-Two

Montmartre, 1874

"Andre, I'm feeling generous," Henri said. "If you give me the yearling, I will extend your loan for two years. The interest can be paid monthly or can be added to the principal at final payment, whichever you prefer."

Sinclair leaned back in the chair, folding his arms across his chest. "Why isn't the coal production I offered an adequate swap for a two-year extension?"

Henri pursed his lips. "Your business sits on a shaky foundation. I incur risk to extend the loan, because you may default on another, starting a cascading effect."

"I know I'm overextended," Sinclair said tersely. "I don't need you to explain it to me. I only asked why the coal output isn't acceptable."

"Because I would assume even more risk," Henri said, mimicking teacher to pupil. "The output is too unpredictable."

Sinclair hesitated. "Then I would prefer to transfer another asset to pay the loan in full."

"You're assuming you have assets I want," Henri said, determined to destroy Sinclair if he had to. "And that we have time to assess them."

"I'm not parting with the yearling," Sinclair insisted, glaring at Henri. "He's worth far more than you claim. Golden Cross will be the greatest champion France has ever known."

"He could be," Henri agreed. "But so can any other horse, pedigree or not. You're letting emotion interfere with logic—a dangerous trait in a businessman."

"It's almost certain, and you know it. Look at the horse's bloodline."

Henri tried to be patient, but he could feel his temper beginning to boil. "We have a few weeks before payment is due. You may feel differently by then."

Sinclair leaned across the desk. "You're asking for the yearling, my most prized possession, but with no incentive for me."

Henri shrugged. He enjoyed watching Sinclair squirm, only now beginning to understand his predicament. "You have no alternative," he said softly. "The loan is due, regardless of what arrangements you may have been making with the bank that previously owned it."

"I'm sure we can agree on assets," Sinclair continued, sounding desperate, his voice beginning to tremble. "Perhaps another mine, in Africa?"

Henri paused, feigning interest. "I may consider full ownership of a specified asset. But I would need time to evaluate it."

Sinclair sat back in the chair. "Why are you being so difficult?" he asked crossly.

Henri thought of Babin and Dumont and their clumsy attempt to link Sinclair to the crime. It was useful ammunition. "Why are you trying to kill my wife?"

Sinclair's eyes widened. "What are you talking about?" he declared. "That's preposterous, and you know it."

"Desperate men do desperate things, so say the police."

"Nice try, Henri," Sinclair said with disgust. "But I already spoke to Babin and Dumont. They think nothing of the kind."

Henri smirked. "The two buffoons," he muttered. "When did they see you?"

"Just the other day."

"They talked to me, too. But they hinted that you are their prime suspect, regardless of what you may think."

Sinclair slowly shook his head. "Absolutely ridiculous."

Henri hid a smile, pleased Sinclair was rattled. The accusation was one more weapon in his arsenal. He doubted Andre Sinclair had anything to do with the attack on his wife. But he would never admit it.

"A totally unfounded accusation," Sinclair scoffed. "Made only to give you an advantage in our negotiations."

"I don't need an advantage," Henri countered. "You took a premier company and destroyed it. I only need to pick up the pieces." He looked at the door, signaling that the meeting had ended. "Think about the yearling. A two-year extension on favorable terms."

Sinclair glared at him. "What's your intention, Henri? Do you want to ruin me?"

Henri paused, letting the tension ease, even though he was enjoying their heated discussion. "I understand how desperate your situation is. But you don't."

Sinclair blinked as if he didn't want to see his options. "I'll transfer ownership of an Algerian mine if you cancel the debt in its entirety."

"I don't want the Algerian mine."

"Then I'll sell it to someone else and pay you off."

"You don't have time."

"Give me an extension."

"You have until the end of the month," Henri said firmly. "Unless I get the yearling."

Sinclair's eyes blazed. His face showed that it took all of his strength to avoid coming across the desk and attacking Henri Lyon. "You know how important Golden Cross is to me."

Henri shrugged. "That sounds like your problem, Andre. Not mine."

Chapter Thirty-Three

Deauville, 1956

The following morning, Zélie watched Luc warily while he ate his breakfast. "Are you all right?"

He picked at his food, ham and cheese with a buttered croissant. "I don't what to go to school."

She sat next to him. "But you have to go to school," she said, brushing his hair from his eyes. "Why don't you want to go?"

"Because nobody likes me," he said sadly. "They make fun of me."

She felt like her heart had been torn from her body. "Oh, Luc, don't listen to them. They're bullies. Ignore them." She reached over and hugged him.

"I try to, but it's hard," he said, fighting not to sob.

"They'll stop, I promise," she said, wondering if she should speak to his teacher. "You'll find friends. It just takes a while."

He sighed and then sipped some apple cider. "I miss grand-mère, too."

"So do I," she said as she wiped a tear from the corner of her eye. She so desperately wanted to help him but wasn't sure what to do.

"And I miss papa," he added softly. "Why did he have to die?"

"Honey, I miss him, too," she said, relieved he was finally revealing his feelings. "But think about how blessed we were to have him as long as we did."

"It's still not fair," he pouted. "Why don't I have a papa? Everybody else does."

"Because God needed him to help the angels," she said, not knowing what else to say.

He didn't reply. He thought for a moment, took a bite of his croissant, and then drank some cider. "Can I stay home?"

She glanced at the clock. "No, Luc, you have to go to school. You know that. Now come on, it's time to go."

"But I don't want to."

"You have to, honey. Everybody does. Today will be better, I'm sure."

He rose reluctantly and walked slowly toward the front door, his head down.

She stopped him, lifted his chin and straightened his shirt collar. She forced a smile, trying to change his mood. "I may have a surprise for you when you get home today."

"What kind of surprise?" he asked without much enthusiasm.

"You'll see," she said. "Now, you have a nice day. And listen to your teacher."

He went out the door, down the walkway, and out the front gate. Across the street, three children his age passed on their way to school. None called to him or waited. A second group followed, laughing amongst themselves, passing Luc as if he didn't exist. She watched, heartbroken, as he went down the street alone.

She went back inside, poured another cup of coffee, and looked out the kitchen window. Anton LaRue was exiting the back door of his cottage. She hurried out the door. "Anton," she called, crossing the lawn toward him.

"Good morning, Zélie, how are you?"

"I'm well," she said.

"And little Luc?"

She grimaced. "He's a little sad today. Missing his papa and grand-mère. And the kids at school are giving him a hard time."

"Aww, the poor child," he said. "Maybe you should talk to the teacher."

"I'm afraid that will make it worse. I thought I would wait a few days."

Anton slowly shook his head. "I wish I could help him somehow."

"Maybe you can," she said, not sure how to ask for a favor, but deciding she had to. "Do you remember offering to show Luc the horses?"

"Yes, of course."

"Is there any way you can do that?"

"Absolutely," he said with a broad smile. "I can do it today, if you like. He'll love it, I promise. Come to the stables after he gets home from school."

"Oh, Anton, thank you so much. He'll be so excited."

Chapter Thirty-Four

Montmartre, 1874

Shortly after Andre Sinclair left Henri Lyon's office, Babin and Dumont arrived. The clerk at the registration desk, a young man with aspirations of someday managing the company, announced their arrival.

"To what do I owe this honor?" Henri asked, tiring of the two detectives.

"We're here to provide an update on our investigation," Babin said.

Henri nodded, not expecting much, but hopeful just the same. "Please, sit down."

"Lieutenant Dumont," Babin said. "I will allow you to present our progress to M. Lyon."

If Dumont was annoyed by Babin's constant patronizing, he didn't show it. "Yes, of course," he said. "Our initial investigation included interviews with you and Mme. Lyon, M. Sinclair, the artist Jean-Pierre, Mme. Michel, who lives adjacent to the studio, the witnesses who assisted Mme. Lyon and helped thwart the attack, and other residents who live in the houses on the top of the hill."

Henri frowned. It was no different from what they said when they visited his home. He suspected they had made little progress, if any. "Your conclusion?"

"Those we interviewed offered no further information," Dumont replied. "Although Mme. Michel spoke highly of Mme. Lyon whom she's met on several occasions."

"However," Babin interjected, "M. Sinclair does appear to have motive. Even though you've not yet taken action that harms him, he suspects you have devious intentions."

Henri snickered. "He harms himself. I am a simple businessman."

"How are negotiations progressing?" Dumont asked.

"They continue," Henri said. "Not that it's any of your business."

Dumont ignored the comment. "Will you be forced to liquidate Normandy Mines?"

Henri shrugged. "Sometimes an innocent issue, like the due date of a loan, starts the collapse of an entire enterprise. Not from my doing, but I've seen it before."

"A good result for you, is it not?" Babin asked, his hands resting on his large belly.

"If I wanted to clean up the mess that Andre Sinclair created, I would. But I don't."

"What are your intentions, M. Lyon?" Babin asked. "Please, enlighten us."

Henri's face firmed. He was tired of meaningless questions. "I'm negotiating the terms of a loan."

"Why is Normandy Mines so close to default?" Dumont asked.

Henri wanted to frame his reply carefully, to skew their impression in his favor. "Normandy Mines is overextended with very little cash. Sinclair knew this loan was coming due but assumed he could convince the bank to extend it."

"Why didn't they?" Dumont asked.

"The bank had so little faith in the future of Normandy Mines that they sold the loan at a steep discount. They lost money because they feared losing even more.

They suspected Sinclair would default—regardless of the terms."

Babin glanced at Dumont. "It seems M. Sinclair will soon be desperate, if he isn't already, and might act irrationally."

"He still has time," Henri said. "Not much, but some."

"Why can't you come to terms?" Babin asked.

"I've presented a generous alternative," Henri said. "But Sinclair found it unacceptable. He's searching for a different solution."

Babin eyed Henri skeptically. "I don't understand why an agreement is so difficult."

"It's a matter of value," Henri explained, his patience ebbing, his tone harsher. "An asset is only worth what someone is willing to pay for it. What I consider valuable, M. Sinclair may not."

"We saw M. Sinclair leaving as we arrived," Dumont said. "He was very aggravated. Are you any closer to resolution?"

Henri paused, carefully wording his reply. "Sinclair places far more worth on his holdings than I do. Especially given the shaky state of his finances."

"Shall we assume that an agreement cannot be reached?" Dumont asked.

"You can assume it's none of your business," Henri snapped.

"But it is our business," Babin declared, leaning across the desk. "We have a desperate man, someone who may do anything to save his business—including an attack on your wife."

Henri tried to stay calm. "I don't know if an agreement can be reached," he admitted. "A likely resolution is the transfer of a minor asset as a fee to extend the payment. Two years seems reasonable to both parties."

Babin eyed him cautiously. "Our questions are relevant, M. Lyon," he said. "Maybe your disagreement with M. Sinclair is only related to business and doesn't extend to other areas of your lives. But I often find that is not the case."

Henri eyed Babin skeptically. Regardless of the reason, business negotiations were none of his concern. Solving crimes was. "Perhaps you would best be served by finding the murderer of that young woman. And then, I believe, you will find the man who attacked my wife."

"A distinct possibility," Dumont admitted, "and an avenue we're exploring."

"Where were you, M. Lyon, on the evening of Tuesday last?" Babin inquired abruptly.

Henri looked at him incredulously. "Certainly you're not suggesting that I am involved?"

"Your whereabouts, please, M. Lyon?" Babin repeated.

"Sebastian, your butler, told us you arrived home only minutes before Mme. Lyon," Dumont clarified.

"And what if I did?" Henri bellowed. "I come and go as I please. I don't answer to the servants."

"Were you here at the office?" Babin asked.

"No, I was at the Le Royal, the gentlemen's club across from the Paris Bourse."

"Ah, that should be easy to verify," Babin said. "You were playing cards?"

Henri rolled his eyes. "I had a cigar and a cognac before going home. I do that often."

"With others who belong to the club?" Dumont asked.

"I don't normally socialize," Henri said tersely. "I sat alone and read the newspaper."

"But others saw you?" Babin asked.

"I assume so," Henri replied. "Not that it matters."

Dumont leaned back in the chair. "It seems you have a credible alibi."

Babin held up a finger, advising caution. "But it may not, Lieutenant," he offered. "We cannot assume M. Lyon has a valid alibi simply because he says so. All must be validated. That's what detectives do."

"I suggest you focus on solving crimes, Inspector," Henri retorted. "Instead of where I spend my afternoons."

Chapter Thirty-Five

Deauville, 1956

Zélie had just finished her second cup of coffee when Marc knocked at the back door. "May I practice piano early today?" he asked. "I'm visiting my son this afternoon."

"Yes, of course," she said. "Let me get you a cup of coffee."

"That would be nice," he said as he came in the kitchen.

"I actually have something interesting to show you," she said as he sat at the kitchen table.

He looked at her curiously. "What might that be?"

"It's a clue," she said, walking into the parlor. "I'll be right back."

Zélie went to a desk in the parlor, tucked in a corner by the window. She opened a drawer and removed the message she found in the portrait. She also grabbed a pad of paper where she had made a list of the paintings and returned to the kitchen.

"I found this note wedged in one of the picture frames," she said as she sat beside him.

Marc took the note and read it. "Interesting," he muttered. "But what crime is being referenced?"

She shrugged. "I don't know. But it seems we have all the clues to solve it."

"Which painting hid the message?"

"The one with the two policemen," she said. "It was tucked in a corner of the frame."

He reread the note, fingering the canvas on which it was written between his finger and thumb. "The note offers a completely different aspect to the paintings."

"We know that they were meant to remain together, based on the note. But we still have no idea why Eva would have them."

"No, we don't," he said, pensive. "Maybe Professor Dufour can offer some insight on our latest mystery. I did manage to reach her last night. She asked if we can visit Friday morning."

"Friday is fine," Zélie said. "Did she discuss a fee?"

"I mentioned it, but she laughed and said it wasn't necessary."

Zélie breathed a sigh of relief. "That makes it easier. We just can't take advantage."

"She didn't seem to think we were," he said. "I got the impression she enjoyed discussing Jean-Pierre. She said she found a reference book that might prove helpful."

Zélie slid the notepad across the table. "I made a list of the paintings and included a brief description with a column for comments. And I added a note about the message."

Marc eyed the list, scanning each entry. "We have some information about Golden Cross, which is one of two paintings actually dated. We can add a note about the owner, too."

"Yes, I had forgotten," she said, thinking for a moment. She then neatly printed Andre Sinclair.

"I suspect the dark-haired woman is the common thread, the link to all the paintings. She's in two portraits."

Zélie nodded. "One painting with her husband, or a lover, perhaps. We need to find out who he is."

"I'm fairly certain it depicts the beach here in Deauville," he added. "See the promenade? Although it could be another small town along the coast."

"Which leaves four portraits in a city, probably Paris, since one is labelled as Montmartre."

Marc studied the list for a moment. "The police station should be easy to find. After we figure out where it is, we can probably identify the policemen."

Zélie leaned across the table, scanning the list with him. "The artist's studio might be Jean-Pierre's."

"Yes, it could be," he agreed. "Most likely, actually."

She scribbled more notes in the comments as they discussed each portrait.

Marc sipped his coffee. "That leaves the café and the street scene."

"Both in Paris, I suspect."

"Yes," he muttered, studying her notes. "Didn't the café have a business next to it?"

"Normandy Mines," she replied, making another note.

"I should be able to find something about that, too."

Zélie looked up from the page and smiled. "It seems we have some research to do before we visit the professor."

"The police precinct, Normandy Mines, and Andre Sinclair, owner of Golden Cross."

"All good leads," she said. "But I have a feeling each question we answer will reveal still more that we do not know."

"You're probably right," he agreed. "I'll make a few phone calls when I get back home. I can start tracking some of this down."

Zélie scanned the notes again and looked at Marc. “I never dreamed this house would come with so many mysteries.”

Chapter Thirty-Six

Montmartre, 1874

"You want to know about Giselle?" Jean-Pierre asked.

Elise nodded, anxious to hear what he had to say.

He went to the window and looked out. "A light rain washes away yesterday's sins."

"Should I ask my coachman to come in?"

"He sits in the carriage, reading the newspaper," Jean-Pierre said as he craned his neck, looking down the street. "And Mme. Michel is nowhere to be found."

"We are alone for the first time," she said, and laughed. "I don't know how to behave without Mme. Michel leaning in the window."

He smiled, closed the window and then the curtains. He grabbed a chair by the wall, moved it in front of Elise, and sat down. "What do you want to know about Giselle?"

"Tell me everything. What was she like, where did she come from?"

He sighed, reminiscing. "In many ways, she was like you," he began. "And in many ways, she was not."

Elise looked at him curiously. "How is that?"

He slid his chair closer until they almost touched. "You're both beautiful," he said, reaching to capture a few renegade strands of her hair and tucking them behind her ear. "She was blond with blue eyes. You have dark hair and eyes."

She smiled. She liked when he touched her, and she was sure he knew that. Very soon, she would have to make a decision. She knew it was coming, a force she couldn't control, an emotion she couldn't contain. And she suspected she would have to make that decision quickly—in minutes. "You probably tell all your models that they're beautiful."

"No, not always," he assured her. "But all people are beautiful in some way. Beauty comes in many forms and on many levels. But you, my dear Elise, define all the beauty that exists."

She laughed. "You're flirting."

"Perhaps," he said, his eyes twinkling. "But you know I speak the truth. I describe what my eyes see. And what my heart feels."

Elise smiled. "I don't see what you do."

"Ah," he said, "but you do. And I suspect you always have."

She pointed to a painting of Giselle. "How did you meet her?"

"She asked if she could model for a modest fee," he said, smiling as he remembered. "She was one of my first models after I came to Paris. That seems like long ago, but it wasn't."

"It feels the same for me," Elise said. "I've been here only a year. Since I married Henri. But Deauville seems like a different life."

"Do you miss the coast?"

"I do. Life is different."

"So are the people."

"They are," Elise agreed. "Was Giselle from Normandy?"

"No, Giselle was from Paris, from Montmartre," he said, studying an unfinished painting.

"What else is different about us?" she asked, prodding. "Other than how we look."

"You are exciting," he continued. "You love life, always searching for adventure. Giselle was reserved, brooding. She never seemed happy."

"Why are so many paintings unfinished?"

He shrugged. "I was never satisfied."

"Are you satisfied with mine?"

"I struggle," he admitted.

"Why is that?" she asked softly.

"I can't capture perfection."

Her gaze met his, and she saw a vulnerability she had never noticed before, a desire not yet quenched. She leaned closer, inches away, her eyes closed. Her lips met his, tentative at first, and then lingering. She pulled away, but only slightly, leaving the impression that she wasn't offended, only surprised.

"You are angry?" he asked.

"No," she said softly. "Not angry."

He kissed her again, briefly. When she didn't resist, he kissed her cheeks and ears and neck, slowly and softly, until his lips again found hers. He pulled her close, holding her tightly, his hands moving, tenderly touching, lightly caressing.

She broke the kiss, breathless. "We shouldn't be doing this."

"No, we shouldn't," he agreed, but his lips again found hers.

She wrapped her arms around him, keeping him close, her hands in his hair, touching his face. She kissed his neck, nibbling on his ear.

"This is going to be complicated," she whispered.

Chapter Thirty-Seven

Deauville, 1956

Luc stayed close to Zélie as Anton led them into Stepping Stone Stables. A long rectangular building with stalls aligned on each side, it sat on private property at the fringe of the Deauville Race Track. Pasture sprawled beyond it with a series of oval tracks surrounded by split-rail fences. The stream for which the stables were named sliced through the far corner.

As they walked farther inside the building, a horse neighed, startling Luc.

"No need to be afraid," Anton assured him. "All the horses are friendly."

Luc hesitated but then followed Anton, Zélie right behind him.

"I'll introduce you to a very friendly horse," Anton said, leading him to a stall near the entrance. "Her name is Matilda."

Anton opened the gate and entered the stall. "You can come in."

"Go ahead," Zélie urged. "You can get closer. She won't hurt you."

Anton removed a brush from a shelf on the wall and pushed a short, two-stair stool next to the horse. "She likes when I brush her."

"Maybe M. LaRue will let you do it, too," Zélie said to Luc.

"It's very easy," Anton said, gently moving the brush over the horse's body. "Would you like to try?"

Luc seemed wary of such a large animal but advanced cautiously.

"Come on, I'll help you," Zélie offered. She took his hand and led him up the short stairs.

Anton gave Luc the brush. "Just lightly move it across her body."

Luc paused, not sure if he should. But after a few seconds, he started softly sliding the brush, slowly at first, and then a bit faster.

"She likes it," Anton said as Matilda snorted, pawing at the ground with her left hoof.

Luc giggled. "I think she does."

Zélie watched, amused by his reaction. "You have a new friend, Luc."

Anton was struck with a thought. "Hey, I know what we can do. Let's take Matilda for a ride."

Luc hesitated. "I don't know how to ride a horse."

"It's easy," Anton assured him. "Come on, I'll show you."

"Go ahead, Luc," Zélie coaxed. "M. LaRue will help. It'll be fun."

Anton saddled the horse, explaining each step of the process to Luc. He then took the reins and led the mare from the stable, Luc beside him. They stopped just outside the building, at a short set of open stairs.

"Come on, Luc," Anton said. "Climb up the stairs, and I'll help you get on the horse."

Luc looked at his mother timidly but slowly proceeded.

Anton lifted him onto the horse's back. "Are you ready?"

Luc nodded. "I think so. But can you go slow?"

"Yes, of course," Anton promised. "We're just going to walk around the track."

Anton led Matilda around a dirt path, worn and rutted from hundreds of hooves that had walked on it. He told Luc about her—how she liked to be brushed and hosed down on a hot day, how she loved to eat apples, and seemed to prefer the sun to the shade. Then he explained the various equipment and the layout of the stables.

Luc turned to Zélie. "Look at me, Maman!"

Zélie smiled. "Yes, look at you. I knew you could do it."

Anton was good with Luc. As Matilda slowly walked around the oval, Luc's expression changed from reluctance to gradual acceptance to a broad smile. He seemed so pleased that he could ride a horse, something he never dreamed he could do.

After about fifteen minutes, Anton led Matilda back toward the stable and helped Luc dismount.

"Was that fun?" Zélie asked, so pleased to see her son happy.

Luc nodded his head, his eyes bright. "It was, Maman. I can't wait to do it again."

"How many other six-year-old boys at your school have ridden a race horse?" Anton asked.

Luc laughed. "I don't think anyone has."

Anton's eyed widened. "Then you must be a very special little boy," he said. "Don't ever forget that."

Chapter Thirty-Eight

Montmartre, 1874

"Mme. Lyon has been in there a long time," Inspector Babin observed as he sat with Dumont in the café at the foot of the hill. He looked at the sky, gray clouds shifting to expose the sun. "In spite of a little rain. It's hard to believe she's been posing for a portrait."

"Which doesn't mean she isn't," Dumont said. "You know how artists are."

"No, I don't, Lieutenant. I deal only in facts. Please, enlighten me."

"They're unpredictable," Dumont said. "She might pose for fifteen minutes one day and, if the light isn't right, the session ends. Or if the light is right, she could pose for hours."

Babin snickered. "Nonsense, I suspect. Sometimes you believe whatever you are told."

"My closest friend is an artist," Dumont explained. "I grew up with him. He showed me much of his work and what it takes to create it."

"But now we have an artist who may be a killer."

Dumont paused, eyeing his superior. "Except no evidence supports that theory."

Babin moved an empty plate, once home to two beignets long since consumed, and parked it next to his coffee cup. "It's a strange coincidence," he observed. "Jean-Pierre had a favorite model named Giselle who ended up dead."

"But Jean-Pierre was never linked to foul play."

"He now has a model named Elise Lyon," Babin said. "And someone tried to kill her."

"Jean-Pierre's neighbor, Mme. Michel, speaks highly of him," Dumont offered. "Apparently she watches many of his sessions."

"At the invitation of Jean-Pierre," Babin scoffed. "It could easily be arranged, my friend, and I suspect it probably was—the appearance of innocence where only guilt exists."

"We never proved that Jean-Pierre is anything but an artist."

"Mme. Lyon was attacked just outside his studio," Babin said. "In the same location where Giselle was murdered."

"But you said it was likely a robbery."

Babin's eyes widened in amazement. "Lieutenant Dumont, I suggested robbery as the most likely motive only as an exercise. I'm teaching you the art of investigation—which is no easy task, I assure you."

Dumont frowned, started to speak but stopped.

"Is there something you want to say, Lieutenant?" Babin asked. "Because there are many policemen who would be honored to receive my tutelage."

"And I am, also, Inspector. I assure you," Dumont said. He glanced up the hill, the carriage still sitting in front of the studio. "But I am confused even though I recognize robbery is still a potential motive. Why do you think Giselle's killer may have assaulted Mme. Lyon?"

"How could I suspect otherwise? There are no coincidences, Lieutenant. Not unless facts prove a coincidence."

"Assuming you're correct, we lack a motive for Jean-Pierre. To me, he seems an artist. Nothing more."

Babin shrugged. "Some killers need no motive. They merely like to kill. I've seen several over the years. It is sometimes impossible to mirror the demented mind of a killer."

Dumont was quiet, considering details known to him. "Some similarities do exist."

"Yes, they do," Babin admitted. "Giselle was strangled, and someone tried to strangle Mme. Lyon—and in the same location. Both are tied to Jean-Pierre. Even a novice detective would connect those dots and find his way to the artist's studio. But that alone makes me think otherwise. The case would be too easy to solve."

"We do have at least two other suspects," Dumont said.

"The husband and M. Sinclair. But I keep asking myself why either would do it."

Dumont shrugged. "Sinclair for revenge, and I suspect Lyon has a temper he cannot control. We see hints it exists, but he hides it. Maybe he tires of his wife and prefers a mistress."

"An unlikely motive for a likely suspect," Babin said, correcting him. "Many men have mistresses. They think it is their right. But I know of none who commit murder. But M. Lyon's temper may be another matter."

Dumont sipped his coffee and sat back in the chair. "I suspect Lyon, and you suspect Jean-Pierre."

"Sometimes you don't listen, Lieutenant," Babin scolded. "I simply presented an observation of Lyon and Jean-Pierre as well as M. Sinclair. All three are strong suspects."

"Our investigation will reveal which is guilty."

"But wait, my good Lieutenant," Babin said. "There could be another suspect, based on what a witness saw."

Dumont looked at him strangely. "None of the witnesses I talked to had further information."

"But one that I interviewed did."

Dumont's face firmed. "Do you intend to share that information? I am your assistant."

"That depends on where you were on the night Mme. Lyon was assaulted."

Dumont chuckled. "You're joking, I assume."

"Policemen never assume, Lieutenant. I told you that many times. Where were you?"

Dumont's eyes lit with anger. "I was in my apartment, Inspector."

"Did anyone see you?"

"No, I was alone."

"Not a good alibi."

"Why would I need an alibi?" Dumont asked incredulously.

"Because a witness claims he saw Mme. Lyon's attacker. And he wore a policeman's uniform."

Dumont rose from the table, lips taut. "I have an appointment, Inspector. Let me know how long Mme. Lyon remains in the studio. Although I suspect it has no bearing on the case. It seems you have already solved it."

Chapter Thirty-Nine

Deauville, 1956

The following morning, Zélie watched closely as Marc finished his piano scales, using both his left and right hand. "You're doing well."

"I'm enjoying it," Marc said. "I feel like I'm using a different part of my brain. It's challenging, but also fun. Especially when I get it right."

"You are using different parts of your brain. Reading music requires eye-hand coordination, and your foot must press the pedal at the right moment while your fingers move in the proper sequence."

"Yes, I suppose you're right," he said, learning to appreciate what was required to play even the simplest of songs.

"It keeps the mind sharp," she added.

"It's such a different world from police work. I think that's some of the attraction."

"Next week we'll focus on chords, then we'll gradually work through relationships."

Marc grabbed a book from the stack on top of the piano, and turned to a chart on the last page. "I was looking at this the other day. Is that what you mean by relationships?"

Zélie glanced at the page. "Yes, it's known as the circle of fifths, or fourths, depending on how you address it, and shows minor keys, too. After that, we'll learn different modes—Dorian and Mixolydian are a few."

He started laughing. "That seems advanced for my next lesson."

She smiled and lightly touched his arm. "No, not for your next lesson, but we'll get there soon. Our next focus is major chord construction—the first, third, and fifth note of the scale."

"I realize learning theory is important, but my first goal is playing an Edith Piaf song."

"It won't be long," she promised as she stood, signaling the lesson had ended. "A few more weeks."

"That's something to look forward to. Sometimes the routine gets boring."

"It can be monotonous.," she agreed. "Luc has the same problem. I have to push him to practice. But once you get past the jingles in the lesson book and start to play songs you know and like, it's much more fun."

He walked toward the back door, his first few steps stiff, his leg cramped from sitting. "Can I move my practice time, maybe after lunch?"

"Yes, of course," Zélie said. "I'm usually here all day, come whenever you want. Although I have added two students. They come on Tuesday, at two and three."

"Good for you," Marc said. "Three students already, counting me. Everything's falling into place."

"I sure hope so," she said, a cloud crossing her face. "If I could only find a tenant for the vacant cottage."

"Someone will rent it, you'll see," he said. "Just give it some time."

Zélie smiled, but it wasn't as bright as it normally was. "I still have the portraits, too," she said. "Wherever they may lead."

He paused, his hand on the doorknob. "Can I look at one of them before I go?"

"Yes, of course," Zélie said. "Have you thought of another clue?"

He shrugged. “No, not really. I’m just trying to make sense of the note.”

“It’s quite a mystery,” she said as they walked down the hallway and into the foyer. “Are you trying to determine what crime was committed?”

“Not just yet,” he said, leaning on the railing for support as he climbed the stairs. “But if it’s a violent crime, like murder, the victim may be in one of the portraits.”

Zélie shivered. “That’s a creepy thought,” she said. “But it’s likely true,”

“I also wondered if the policemen featured are those who conducted the investigation.”

“They probably are,” she said as they reached the attic. “Why else would they be in one of the portraits?”

Marc was tiring, slowly climbing the attic steps. “We may be making it harder than it is,” he suggested, pausing halfway to rest.

Zélie considered what he said. It made sense. If the portraits were the clues, they should contain the answers to any questions they might have. “Maybe we should study the paintings more closely.”

“That’s what I was thinking,” he said as he reached the attic. They paused in front of the portraits, looking at them with a different perspective.

“It seems an odd assortment,” Zélie muttered. “It’s hard to see a connection.”

Marc was quiet for a moment, pensive. “But they must be connected somehow. The horse is the most confusing. I don’t know where it fits.”

“Unless it only represents the owner, Andre Sinclair.”

“I suppose that could be,” he said, kneeling in front of the portrait with the policemen.

"What are you looking at?"

"This painting is so detailed, the eye drawn to the life-like depiction of the policemen, especially the older man with the handlebar moustache. But it's the building I wanted to look at."

"We know it's a police station," she said, pointing to brass letters imbedded in the limestone atop the entrance.

"I'm focused on this little plaque beside the door," he mumbled.

"What does it say?"

"Eighteenth arrondissement."

Zélie hesitated, recalling the districts of Paris. "Montmartre?"

Marc stood, taking one last glance at the portrait. "Yes, Montmartre. I think that must be where the crime occurred."

Chapter Forty

Montmartre, 1874

Elise stepped from Jean-Pierre's studio, remnants of rain melting in the returning sun's rays. Her coachman stood by the carriage and opened the door.

Jean-Pierre was behind her, and he waved to Mme. Michel who stood on the pavement with a small boy.

"The window was closed," Mme. Michel complained as she came closer. "I couldn't watch you paint."

"Oh, I'm sorry," Jean-Pierre said. "It wasn't intentional, I assure you. I closed the window for the rain."

She looked at him curiously. "The rain stopped a while ago. It was only a brief shower."

"You can watch the next one," Jean-Pierre promised.

"Mme. Lyon is my favorite," Mme. Michel said. "A beautiful model."

Elise smiled. "Thank you so much, Mme. Michel. That's very kind."

Jean-Pierre steered Elise toward her carriage.

"Did you ever complete Giselle's portrait?" Elise asked, continuing their discussion.

Jean-Pierre looked at her awkwardly and didn't reply.

"She doesn't know," Mme. Michel said, listening in as always.

Jean-Pierre's expression was suddenly somber. "No, I never finished it."

Elise tilted her head. "Why not?"

"He couldn't," Mme. Michel interjected, moving beside her, holding the toddler's hand.

"But you have seven or eight unfinished portraits and sketches," Elise said. "Surely you completed one of them. Was the light wrong? Or maybe the model didn't want to pose?"

"There is no model," Mme. Michel said softly.

"Ask her to return," Elise said with a quizzical look.

"Not possible, I'm afraid," Jean-Pierre said, glancing at Mme. Michel.

"But why?" Elise asked. "You must like painting her. Or you wouldn't have started so many portraits."

"Giselle is dead," Jean-Pierre said abruptly.

Elise raised her hand to her mouth. "I'm so sorry," she exclaimed. "I didn't know. What happened?"

"She's the woman who was murdered last month," Mme. Michel said, pointing down the hill. "Just over there, where the tree limb hangs above the street."

"Jean-Pierre, I'm so sorry," Elise said, glancing at Mme. Michel. "How was I to know?"

"You couldn't," he said. "No one ever told you."

"Please forgive me. I didn't mean to pry."

Jean-Pierre shrugged. "There's nothing to forgive. A tragedy that can't be undone."

Mme. Michel lightly touched Elise's arm. "It was so tragic. I haven't recovered, and neither have the neighbors, including Jean-Pierre. But nothing can be done. At least not now."

Elise hugged Jean-Pierre as any friend would. "I'm so sorry."

"Yes, we all are," he said.

She held him a moment more. "I must go. The servants will wonder where I am."

"Of course, I understand."

"Goodbye," Elise said, smiling. The look in her eyes said more than words ever could. She turned to his neighbor. "Goodbye, Mme. Michel."

The coachman checked his pocket watch and helped Elise into the carriage. As he closed the door and climbed on his perch, she realized she was being watched more closely than she thought. As the coach pulled away, she looked at the paintings displayed in the studio window—seascapes and scenes of Paris, different worlds that invited an observer to walk within them.

The carriage rattled down the hill, the driver gently guiding the horses along the incline and onto the boulevard. They came near the corner café where a handful of people sat outside, eating and drinking and reading the newspaper, the horses hooves clicking on the cobblestone. Carriages and wagons loaded with produce passed, and people strolled along the pavement, a woman carrying a hat box, a man with two long loaves of freshly baked bread.

They went toward the eighth arrondissement where Henri Lyon's luxurious townhouse was located. Elise looked from the window, watching the sights of Paris, familiar with the route they normally took. After a few minutes, the driver turned onto a street they had never before taken. For a minute she wondered why, curious why their route had changed—not that it mattered. She studied the scenery, some buildings in disrepair with peeling paint and patched roofs, others well-maintained, bright and cheery and looking as if they didn't belong.

The carriage rounded a corner and entered a slender alley lined with outbuildings and stables, cluttered with worn wagons, a leaning carriage that was missing a wheel. A seedy gentleman watched them pass, his clothes baggy and threadbare. Elise was overcome with curiosity, wondering why their route would take them somewhere so ill-suited for travel. She banged on the panel behind the driver and slid open a tiny door.

"Where are we going?" she asked.

"It's a shorter route," the coachman explained. "I thought I'd save time since we're late."

"Yes, of course," she said. "Thank you, I appreciate that."

"We don't want to arouse suspicion."

She closed the door and sat back on the seat. If the coachman was suspicious that she'd overstayed her appointment, the other servants would be, too—especially if he told them. And then Henri would find out. Now she was concerned.

"Woah!" the coachman shrieked, pulling up on the reins, the coach quickly coming to a stop. "Move along!"

"What happened?" Elise asked.

"The road is blocked, Madame," he said. "But it should be cleared in a minute."

A few seconds later she heard a scuffle, and then a shout.

"What's going on?" she asked, leaning to look out the window.

The door behind her flung open. A man leaped in, grabbing her from behind. He covered her mouth and nose with cloth, a sweet smell invading her nostrils before she was overwhelmed and drifted into darkness.

Chapter Forty-One

Deauville, 1956

Philippe Armand was an interesting man, older and a bit rough, but very polite. He sat in a cramped office behind a desk cluttered with papers, a half-empty pack of cigarettes, and a brass figurine of a horse. Anton LaRue and Zélie sat in front of him while he described a long career at the Deauville race track, including the many celebrities he had met.

"You do such a marvelous job with the grounds," Zélie remarked, looking out a window that showed a stretch of grass behind one of the tracks, not a single weed within it. "If only my garden were that perfect."

Armand chuckled. "I enjoy it," he said. "Most people retire at my age. But I have no desire to do so. Why would I? I love what I'm doing."

Zélie smiled, impressed with the man's optimism. "I wish I had your outlook on life."

"But you can, Mme. Girard," he exclaimed. "You can."

She smiled as the others laughed. She had been optimistic when she'd inherited the house in Deauville—before she knew about the debt that came with it. But she would get through it.

"Can you tell us all you learned about Golden Cross?" Anton asked, coming to the purpose of their visit.

"Yes, of course," Armand said, his tone more serious, realizing the discussion had strayed. "I went through all the records we have here at the track."

Zélie leaned forward. "I can't wait to hear about it."

Armand shuffled through some papers. "I listed all of Golden Cross's victories—I told Anton that he won thirty-seven straight races. Horses today don't run that many races. Some are retired after less than a dozen." He paused, glancing at a written report, which he gave Zélie. "I added some details on his pedigree, which is impressive. Although some of the bloodline information is limited."

"The first true champion of Deauville," Anton remarked.

Zélie leafed through the report. It was several pages, describing the horse's lineage, each race, the location and jockey. She gave it to Anton.

"It's very thorough," Anton muttered as he scanned the pages. "Thank you for your effort."

"Do you have information on the owner?" Zélie asked.

"Very little," Armand replied, handing another paper to Zélie. "Golden Cross was purchased for a record price, as you can see, by a Parisian businessman who had a summer cottage in Deauville."

Zélie read the paper. Andre Sinclair's address was on a nearby road with wide expanses of property, beautiful mansions, and well-kept lawns. Cottage didn't quite describe the properties, even though it was a common reference. He must have been very successful.

"He owned a corporation called Normandy Mines," Armand continued. "It no longer exists, not with the mergers and acquisitions that occur in the business world. I suppose you could trace what company it became, if you truly wanted to."

Zélie hid her excitement. The portrait of the café showed an adjacent building labeled Normandy Mines.

Two clues pointed to Andre Sinclair: the portrait of the café and the painting of Golden Cross.

"M. Sinclair must have been quite pleased with his initial investment," Anton said. "Especially given the many victories Golden Cross achieved."

"Yes, even in that day, winning purses were considerable," Armand agreed. "But there is one problem as I mentioned when we first discussed Golden Cross."

Anton paused, reflecting on their original conversation. "The transfer of ownership?"

"Yes, exactly," Armand said as he leaned across the desk and pointed to the bottom of the paper Zélie held. "Andre Sinclair transferred ownership of Golden Cross, for an undisclosed sum, before the horse had run his first race."

Anton looked at him curiously. "To whom?"

"Henri Lyon," Zélie said, reading from the report.

Chapter Forty-Two

Montmartre, 1874

"Are you all right, Madame?"

Elise's eyelids fluttered open as someone lightly shook her arm. She didn't know how long she had been unconscious or even where she was. But after a few seconds her mind began to clear, and she remembered the attack.

An elderly woman leaned into the carriage. "Is something wrong, Madame?"

Elise gasped, her hands touching her throat. "Yes, I was attacked," she murmured. "Someone tried to choke me."

"Choke you!" the woman exclaimed. "Are you hurt?"

Elise blinked, trying to regain her senses. "No, I don't think so," she mumbled. "But I'm not sure."

"Stay here, and I'll get a policeman," the woman said, her face disappearing.

Elise managed to sit up, still dizzy from the effects of whatever drug she had been given. She dreamed she had been choked, but she wasn't sure if she actually had been. She touched her neck. It wasn't bruised; she felt no pain. As she moved her fingers over her face, she found nothing sore, no abrasions or swelling. She twisted her torso. It didn't feel like she had been punched or pummeled. But she had been attacked. She was sure of that. And she wondered what, or who, had scared her assailant away. She took a deep breath and sat upright, stretching to restore stiff muscles, and stepped slowly from the carriage.

A wagon blocked their way, parked askew in the alley. It was loaded with furniture, used or discarded, and a man held the tether on the horse that pulled it, guiding him forward. Elise's coachman was slumped on the driver's seat, and she climbed up and gently shook him.

"What happened?" he mumbled.

"I think someone drugged you," she said. "And then they attacked me."

He bolted upright, his eyes wide but glassy. "Are you all right, Madame?" he asked, leaning toward her. "Are you hurt?"

"No," she replied, still dazed. "Not hurt. Only frightened."

"Did you see who it was?"

"No, I didn't. Someone scared him away. But I'm not sure who."

The elderly woman returned with a policeman. "She's the woman who was attacked," she said, pointing at Elise.

"Are you all right, Madame?" the policeman asked.

"Yes, I think so," Elise replied, climbing down from the driver's seat. "Just shaken. My coachman was injured, also."

"Your name, please," the policeman requested as he withdrew a notebook from his pocket.

"Elise Lyon, and my coachman, Pierre Beaufort."

The policeman wrote in his notebook and then looked at the witness.

"Mme. Louise La Branche," the woman said. "And I live just across the way."

The policeman looked to where she pointed and scribbled in his notes. "Now, tell me what happened," he said, looking at Elise.

"I'm not sure," Elise replied, her voice trembling. "It was all so fast." She turned to the woman. "Did you see the man who attacked me?"

"No, Madame, I didn't see anything," the woman replied. "I'm sorry, but I only know what you told me."

The policeman took more notes and then looked up at the coachman. "Tell me what you saw, sir."

The coachman climbed from the driver's seat and stood beside Elise. "We were coming through this cramped alley when that wagon blocked our way," he said. "When I stopped the carriage, I think someone drugged me or knocked me out."

"You didn't see him?" the policeman asked.

The coachman rubbed his eyes for a moment and shook his head. "No, sir. I didn't see anyone."

"Then he climbed in the back and grabbed me," Elise said.

"And you're sure you're not hurt, Madame?" the policeman asked.

"No, I'm not hurt," she said. "But I think he tried to kill me. I just can't remember clearly."

"Did the assailant strike you, Madame?" the policeman asked. He looked closely at her face. "I don't see any bruises."

Elise tried to remember. "I don't think so," she said slowly. "But I know I was drugged. I remember a cloth over my face and then hands clutching my throat."

"And you never saw who it was?" the officer asked.

"No, he fled when this brave woman approached."

"I didn't see him, either," the woman claimed. "I stopped at the carriage because the door was open, and I saw the lady laying on the seat with her leg sticking out. I thought she might be ill."

Elise started sobbing but wiped away tears that trailed down her cheeks. “This is the second time someone has tried to kill me. I was almost strangled a week ago.”

“And the woman murdered just last month,” the elderly woman said. “Wasn’t she strangled, too?”

“She was,” the policemen said sternly. He looked up from his notebook. “Who is investigating the first attack?”

“Inspector Babin and Lieutenant Dumont.”

“I will summon them at once,” the policeman promised. “And we’ll find the perpetrator of this horrible crime.”

Chapter Forty-Three

Deauville, 1956

"M. Armand had some interesting information," Zélie said as she and Anton walked back to her black Citroën. She paused by the rear fender and ran her finger along the edge of a dent, rust forming on the edges. One more problem she had to address.

Anton paused beside her, then climbed in the passenger seat. "The mystery keeps evolving," he said as Zélie got behind the wheel. "The more we find out, the less we know."

"We are making progress, though," she said. "It just doesn't seem like it sometimes."

"It's so hard to determine what's relevant and what isn't."

"Like the yearling," Zélie continued. "We know it's linked to the crime because of the portrait. But why did Andre Sinclair pay a record price for the horse and then sell him before he ever raced?"

Anton shrugged. "Maybe he earned a good profit or needed money or had some other reason that we'll never know."

Zélie wondered what motivated someone to sell a horse—a future champion—and why she might do it. "I should have asked if Sinclair had other race horses."

"I didn't think of that, either," Anton admitted. "Maybe he had a horse he thought had a brighter future."

"But really didn't," Zélie said as she exited the Deauville track and drove back to her house. "We need to tell Marc when we get home. He's obsessed with figuring all of this out."

"And he will," Anton assured her. "Sooner or later."

"I hope it's sooner," Zélie said with a light laugh. She braked, eyeing a cat that sat on the curb, unable to decide whether he wanted to race across the street or not. "I wonder why Eva never mentioned the portraits. Why not tell you, at least about Golden Cross?"

"I've been thinking about that," Anton said. "I suspect there are two explanations. Maybe she didn't know their value and paid little attention to them."

Zélie waited for Anton to continue, but he didn't. "What's the second reason?" she finally asked.

He turned to face her. His expression hinted that he had something to say she might not like. "She knew exactly what the paintings were worth and who Golden Cross was."

"But kept it a secret."

Anton nodded. "It seems more likely. We just don't know why."

Zélie was quiet, negotiating the residential streets in a quiet town. After a moment, she realized Anton was probably right. "It is hard to believe she didn't know what they were."

"They were scattered all over the attic," he said as if trying to defend Eva. "Maybe her husband put them up there, and she never bothered with them."

"Maybe," Zélie muttered. "But not likely."

"She didn't talk much about the house," Anton said, reflecting. "And she never mentioned her past. I didn't know anything about her family."

Zélie thought for a moment as she approached her home. "My husband once told me that she had been married before his father."

Anton seemed surprised. "What happened to her first husband?"

"He was killed in the war, in 1918," she said. "But I know nothing about him."

"Interesting," Anton mused. "Maybe he put the paintings up there. He could have known the artist or had some other connection that we don't know about."

"Yes, I suppose," Zélie said, feeling overwhelmed.

She parked the car in front of the house. As they got out and started up the driveway, Marc came across the yard toward them.

"We have a lot to tell you," Zélie called.

"Really?" Marc asked. "More questions or answers?"

"Both," she said. "We talked to M. Armand at the race track."

He met them in the driveway. "I can't wait to hear about it."

Zélie handed him all the papers. "M. Armand wrote everything up for me. Maybe you can look through it and see if there's anything worthwhile."

Marc scanned through the papers and then looked up, shifting his gaze between the two. "This creates more riddles than it solves."

"It does," Zélie agreed. "But we made some progress."

"We don't know why Sinclair sold Golden Cross," Anton said. "Although it doesn't seem related to the crime."

"Except for the portrait," Marc said. "It has to be a clue of some sort."

"Maybe the painting represents Sinclair," Anton suggested.

Marc kept looking through the papers. "Who is Henri Lyon?"

Anton shrugged. "We have no idea. Just another name to add to our list."

"Normandy Mines, too," Zélie said. "We now know that Sinclair is linked to both Golden Cross and Normandy Mines. We don't know why their connection is important."

Marc sighed. "More mysteries. We'll solve them. It'll take time."

"I'm beginning to wonder about my own family," Zélie said. "We know Eva never mentioned the paintings, and there can only be two reasons why."

"She had no idea they were valuable," Anton said, "or she knew exactly how valuable they were."

Marc gave Zélie an apologetic look. "I'm starting to suspect the latter."

"Interesting, isn't it?" Zélie asked, not offended. "I'm going to look through some of her papers and see what I can find out."

"That's a good place to start," Marc said. "Maybe we can check the rest of the stuff in the attic, too."

"Come for dinner tonight," she offered. "I'll make something simple."

"I have a better idea," Marc said, smiling. "You two go out for dinner. I'll cook up something for Luc."

"That would be nice," Anton said, smiling shyly.

Zélie was surprised by his suggestion—and Anton's response. "I wouldn't want to impose," she said reluctantly

"You're not imposing at all," Anton said. "I'll stop by at six."

Chapter Forty-Four

Montmartre, 1874

A policeman waited impatiently, pacing the pavement outside Elise Lyon's townhouse. He was glancing at his pocket watch, which he had already done several times, when Babin and Dumont arrived.

"Let's hope the officer has captured everything," Babin said as they climbed from the carriage. "Although most would not."

"Inspector," the harried policeman said as he approached. "Another attempt has been made on the life of Elise Lyon."

"As we've been told," Babin said, assessing the man with a practiced eye. "Is Mme. Lyon unharmed?"

"Yes, sir, just distressed," the policeman replied. "It seems she was drugged, but the attack was thwarted by a witness, an elderly woman named Louise La Branche. I have all the details recorded."

Babin took the notebook from the policeman, leafed through the pages, and handed it to Dumont. "You've done your job well," Babin said. "Now let us go inside and see Mme. Lyon."

As the policeman tapped on the door and waited for a reply, Babin leaned toward Dumont. "Please study M. Lyon closely," he whispered. "His response will tell us much about what we need to know. I will conduct the questioning."

Sebastian answered the door and led them into the parlor where a pale Elise Lyon sat sipping tea, a small bottle of cognac on the table beside the saucer. Her coachman stood by the fireplace.

Babin entered first, glancing at those in the room. "Where is M. Lyon?"

"A coachman has been sent for him," Elise assured him. "He should arrive any moment."

Babin turned to Dumont, sharing a secretive glance. He sat across from Elise, eyeing the bottle of cognac.

"To soothe my nerves," she said.

"Yes, of course," Babin replied as Dumont sat beside him. The policeman stood by the coachman, notebook in hand. "Whatever is needed."

Dumont watched Elise warily, compassion crossing his face. "Were you hurt, Mme. Lyon?" he asked. "You look quite shaken."

"No, not hurt," she said, smiling weakly. "I must have been drugged. I'm still groggy."

Babin arched his eyebrows. "Are you certain you were not harmed in any way, Madame?"

Elise shook her head. "No, I'm not injured. But I don't remember much. The attack was not as physical as the last. It ended before it began."

"And how was the attack foiled?" Babin asked.

"It was interrupted by an elderly woman," Elise said. "The attacker must have fled when she approached."

The policeman held up his notebook. "Mme. La Branche as we've already discussed. She did not see the attack, only Mme. Lyon in distress."

Babin turned to the coachman. "Give me your recollection of what occurred, good sir."

"Yes, of course, Inspector," said M. Beaufort, the coachman. "We were returning from Mme. Lyon's portrait session when the attack occurred. I took a different route, a bit shorter, that went down a narrow alley."

"Who told you about the shorter route?" Babin asked.

"M. Lyon," Beaufort replied.

Babin eyed Dumont warily. "Can you please repeat that?"

Beaufort looked at him strangely. "I took a route that was recommended by M. Lyon."

"Thank you," Babin replied, scribbling in his own notebook. "What happened in this alley?"

"A wagon loaded with furniture pulled out of a narrow carriage house," he explained. "The driver halted, left the wagon blocking the alley, and went back inside."

"Did you think his actions suspicious?" Dumont asked.

"Not really," Beaufort replied. "I thought he'd merely forgotten something."

"And what occurred next?" Babin asked.

"I leaned forward in the coach, trying to peek into the carriage house, and that's all I remember until Mme. Lyon roused me. I was either drugged or knocked unconscious."

"You have no injury?" Babin asked.

"No, sir."

"Then you were drugged," Babin concluded. "You never saw the attacker?"

"No."

"That is all you can remember?" Babin asked.

"Yes, it is, Inspector," Beaufort replied.

"You are free to go," Babin said.

The coachman walked to the exit, looking guilty for failing to protect his mistress.

"What do you recollect, Mme. Lyon?" Babin asked.

"I felt the carriage stop abruptly," she recalled. "So quickly that I shifted in the seat. There was a ruckus in the driver's area, but I didn't know what it was."

"Were you tempted to look out?" Dumont asked.

"Yes, I did look from the coach window. But I couldn't see anything."

"And then?" Babin asked.

"The carriage door opened, I was yanked backward, and a wet cloth was held over my mouth. As I started to faint, I felt hands wrap around my throat."

"Did you struggle?" Dumont asked.

"I weakened quickly," Elise said. "But I do remember screaming and kicking open the other carriage door."

Babin was scribbling in his notebook, eyeing Mme. Lyon. "When did the witness arrive, the elderly woman?"

"She appeared just as I regained consciousness and asked if I was all right. The attacker was already gone."

"You never saw him, Mme. Lyon?" Dumont asked.

"No, I did not."

Babin turned to the policeman. "Does the statement from Mme. La Branche match what Mme. Lyon has just described?"

"Yes, sir, it does," he said.

Their discussion was interrupted when the front door opened and slammed closed. Seconds later, Henri Lyon burst into the parlor.

"What's going on here?" he demanded.

"Ah, M. Lyon," Babin said, glancing at Dumont. "Where have you been for the last two hours?"

Chapter Forty-Five

Deauville, 1956

Marc Rayne borrowed the documents that Philippe Armand had given to Zélie and sat at his kitchen table reviewing them. First, he read them straight through, then put the information on Golden Cross off to the side. Although he knew the horse was somehow related to whatever crime had been committed, he didn't think his lineage or stellar success had much to do with anything—at least not yet.

He took a notepad and described the two portraits, linking the words together with a line—Golden Cross and the café painting that included Normandy Mines in the adjacent building. He then wrote on the side of the paper: Andre Sinclair and Henri Lyon.

Next, he grouped two more paintings together: the portrait of the dark-haired woman, wealthy if he judged by her clothing, and the painting of the same woman and a young man, picnicking on a beach. He connected the descriptions with a line and then wrote a large question mark.

He listed the police station next, writing Montmartre beside it, and then added: Who are these policemen? He described the street scene, which was labeled Montmartre and drew a line connecting the two, related by location, if nothing else. He listed the artist's studio and wrote Jean-Pierre, followed by a question mark. And last, he described the blond model. After he had listed all the paintings, he wrote another question in large letters at the bottom of the page: Who is CD, and what is the crime he referenced?

On a separate page, he made a list of other unanswered questions: Where did the paintings come from; how long were they in the attic; who put the paintings in the attic; how did Zélie's mother-in-law get them; did she know how valuable they were? After glancing at the two pages of notes, he realized he had much to learn, many avenues to explore. But he knew more today than he had yesterday.

When he was done with his mental exercise, he went to the house to get Luc. Zélie opened the door, dressed in a casual blue dress and heels, her hair done up nicely in a chignon.

"You look great," he said as she opened the door.

"Thank you so much," she said as she let him in. "I don't get out much."

"Anton will be very impressed, I'm sure."

She laughed. "I'm not trying to impress anyone. It's just a casual dinner." She had no interest in a relationship, and she had to make sure Anton understood that. They were too painful, especially when death stole love. She would rather be alone.

Marc smiled. "It's whatever you want it to be."

She turned away. "Luc," she called. "M. Rayne is here."

Luc came running into the kitchen. "Hi, M. Rayne."

"Luc, how are you," Marc said, mussing the boy's hair. "Are you ready for a fun dinner? Maybe we can play *les dames* afterwards."

Luc's eyes widened. "That'll be so much fun."

Marc chuckled. "It will be fun. What do you want for dinner?"

"Macarons!"

"Luc," Zélie said sternly. "You be a good boy for M. Rayne."

"I will," Luc promised. "But I like macarons."

"How about macarons for dessert," Marc suggested. "We'll have ratatouille for dinner."

"Luc, that sounds good," Zélie said. "Maybe I'll skip the restaurant and have dinner with M. Rayne, too."

Marc smiled. "You have a nice time tonight," he said. "You deserve a night out. Relax a little."

Chapter Forty-Six

Montmartre, 1874

Andre Sinclair watched from his coach as the police carriage came to a halt in front of Henri Lyon's townhouse. He opened the slotted door and addressed his driver. "Wait here for a moment. I'll let you know when to continue."

His carriage had stopped by a large plane tree, stout branches swinging over the road, as Sinclair leaned back and observed. A policeman entered the Lyon residence, followed by Babin and Dumont. They were an interesting pair—the pompous instructor and overshadowed underling. Sinclair knew he had nothing to fear from Dumont. But Babin was easy to underestimate, and he had been studying the inspector closely, gathering whatever information he could. Sinclair suspected that, although Babin seemed pompous and dismissive, as if only his opinion mattered, there was likely very little he didn't notice.

Babin's primary objective was to promote Nicolas Babin in every way possible—or so it seemed by the newspaper headlines. Sinclair was afraid of him but only because he was a difficult man to assess. Babin was a highly skilled investigator, which no one would question. But Sinclair suspected that he always acted in the interest of Babin, sometimes subtly, sometimes with motives that were much more obvious. If necessary, he would create the crime to fit the man but only if the situation demanded. For in the mind of Babin, only he determined right from wrong, not the law, the circumstances, or the Supreme Being. He had little regard for anyone or anything, including whoever he might hurt or treat unfairly in the course of his investigations. Babin was dangerous.

Fifteen minutes later, Henri Lyon arrived, glancing at the police carriages as he rushed into the house. Sinclair wondered where he had been—he looked slightly disheveled as if he had been somewhere he shouldn't have been. Sinclair knew that, like Nicolas Babin, Henri Lyon was also a dangerous man. He had built an entire empire by destroying other men. Sinclair suspected he enjoyed that above all else—the slow devastation of any financial foe. Their demise was his prize. Finance, and all that revolved around it, was secondary.

Everyone had faults, shortcomings, vices, and secrets that they hoped were never revealed. Sinclair had only begun to unearth those of Henri Lyon, covertly observing him and dissecting every second of his life, searching for a weakness he hoped to exploit.

Andre Sinclair would do to Henri Lyon what Henri Lyon did to everyone else.

Chapter Forty-Seven

Deauville, 1956

A few minutes after Marc had left with Luc, Zélie answered a knock at the front door, dressed in her casual blue dress with heels. She found Anton at the entrance, holding fresh-cut tulips and daffodils.

"Anton, you didn't have to do that," she exclaimed, wondering if he had the wrong impression. "That is so nice."

He was dressed in a green shirt and a dark sports coat. He smiled shyly. "I know you like flowers because I see you in the garden all the time."

"Come in, and I'll put these in some water. Thank you so much."

Zélie went in the kitchen and poured water in an Art Deco vase—twirling light green glassware—added the flowers, and put it in the center of the table. "They're beautiful."

"I'm glad you like them," he said, smiling, as they turned to go. "Where would you like to eat?"

She paused, thinking of different restaurants in town. She didn't want to give the impression that they were on a date, just a casual outing between friends. "How about some place informal," she suggested. "A café along the water?"

He arched his eyebrows. "Are you sure?" he asked. "We can go wherever you like."

She considered the expense, knowing he couldn't afford it. "How about the café," she said. "We can get a table outside. And we split the bill."

"There's no need for that," he assured her.

"No, I insist," she said, making sure he understood it was dinner between friends.

He hesitated but then shrugged. "Whatever you wish."

They left the house and walked to the curb, climbing into his battered green Renault, which looked to be about ten years old. Zélie had always liked his car even though it was dated. She paused as he opened her door.

"Thank you," she said as she got in, impressed by how polite he was.

They drove a dozen blocks to the restaurant through residential streets that yielded to shops and passed a casino perched along the waterfront. Minutes later they were seated at a table facing the ocean, a wide stretch of sand between them and the white waves that washed up on the shore. Most of the tables were occupied, the hotels in town starting to fill with tourists as the weather got warmer. They scanned the menu, ordered wine, and selected entrées.

"Are you originally from Deauville?" he asked, making conversation to ease the awkwardness.

"No, from Amiens," Zélie said. "I have a large family—three sisters and two brothers. I had a fabulous childhood." She paused and then smiled. "Although being an adult hasn't been what I had hoped."

He chuckled and shrugged. "Life takes turns we never expect," he said. "But that is a large family. Are they all still in Amiens?"

She paused for a moment, reflecting on her family and how the war had torn it apart. She didn't like to think about it. "My parents are," she replied. "In a quaint cottage outside the city. We didn't have much growing up."

"How about your siblings?" he asked, his gaze fixed on hers, interested in learning about her life.

Zélie looked out at the waves as the whitecaps spilled onto shore, reflecting on years that hadn't been kind. "They're scattered now," she said. "I lost one brother in the war. I try not to think about it."

Anton nodded, sadness crossing his face. "I'm so sorry," he said. "It's sad, I know. I too lost a brother. I don't think you ever recover."

Zélie thought of her husband, gone too soon, her brother, her mother-in-law. Life was hard. It hurt sometimes. "We all grieve," she said. "And we always will."

Anton paused for a moment, reflecting. "I grew up in Deauville," he said, as if searching for a happier topic. "My father still lives in that same house, a small farm out past the race track. My mother passed when I was young, in an automobile accident, but I have a sister that lives just down the coast. I see her often."

Zélie thought of her sisters. They had been so close. For a moment she wondered what had happened. "Your father and sister must be so proud of you," she said. "Such a successful jockey."

He smiled but weakly, doubt written on his face. "I'm actually not very successful," he admitted. "I recently won a race, a new stallion named Silver Shadow. But prior to that, it had been years since I'd won anything. My career as a jockey isn't beginning. It's close to ending."

Zélie watched him for a moment, a man whose dream was beginning to die. "But you said you just won a race on Silver Shadow."

He shrugged. "Yes, I did. But that's one race. He's a marvelous horse though. The best I've ever ridden." He laughed lightly. "Maybe he'll be the next Golden Cross."

"Maybe he will," Zélie said, urging him to be more confident. "Especially if he won his first race."

"He's such a strong horse," he continued. "I think he'll surprise everyone."

"Then your career is only beginning," she said, correcting him.

Anton beamed, swelling with pride. "Yes, maybe you're right," he said, unable to hide his enthusiasm. "His next race will be tough—he's running against some very strong competitors. But the next few races will tell. If Silver Shadow remains undefeated, then there's no stopping him. I honestly believe the entire country will soon know his name."

She smiled in admiration of a man chasing his dreams. "They'll soon know yours as well."

He laughed. "I'm not so sure about that. But it would be nice."

Zélie wanted to support him. "I'll be at your next race, cheering you on. I promise."

He gazed in her eyes, maybe seeing something he hadn't before noticed. "That would be nice," he said softly. "I've never had anyone cheer me on before."

"You do now," she declared. "How about your father? You had mentioned he was involved with horses. Was he a jockey?"

"No, he trains horses. My grandfather did, too."

Zélie felt for him, trying so hard to be successful but finding nothing but failure. At least until now. "How did you come to rent Eva's cottage?"

"I wanted to stay close to the stables," he said and shrugged. "I can't afford much right now."

Zélie smiled. "I'm sure that will change now that you're about to become a champion jockey."

He laughed. "Yes, perhaps it will."

"What will you do when you're rich and famous?" she asked, trying to make him see in himself what she was able to see. "What does Anton want, other than to become the greatest jockey in the world?"

He again smiled shyly. "I hope to marry and start a family. Of course, my wife will help with the decision on where we live, but I would like to stay in Deauville. Family should come first."

She watched him closely as he described the life he wanted to live, so close to what she'd once dreamed—before God took it all away. "I'm sure you'll make someone very happy."

Chapter Forty-Eight

Montmartre, 1874

Henri Lyon paused in the parlor entrance, glaring at the inspectors and the policeman standing meekly behind them. He hurried to Elise, sitting on the sofa with a cup of tea in a saucer on the table.

"Are you hurt?" he asked as he sat beside her, warily looking at those in the room.

"No, darling, I'm fine," she assured him. "Only distraught."

He tenderly moved her hair away from her face. "You're pale," he said, his eyebrows knitted. "Tell me what happened."

"Mme. Lyon was assaulted once more," Babin said, answering for her. He cast a knowing glance to Dumont.

"But the attempt was thwarted by a passerby," Dumont added.

Henri eyed the inspectors, his face flushed, his anger rising. "How did this happen?"

"An interesting question," Babin posed. "Apparently her coachman was directed to take a different route. The assailant waited, ready to leap upon his prey."

Henri rose and stood in front of Babin, a stance meant to intimidate. "You're an incompetent fool," he bellowed. "What difference does it make what road she took? You're tasked with finding the culprit, yet you fail time after time. And here we sit once more, pontificating on what must be done. Why can't you just solve the crime!"

"Please, M. Lyon," Dumont urged, stepping between them. "Calm yourself. We are trying to solve the crime, I assure you. But it takes time."

Henri sighed, moved away from Babin and sat beside Elise, lightly caressing her hand. "I'll hire private security to protect you," he promised. "You no longer have to fear for your safety."

"Henri, there's no need," Elise said softly. "The inspectors will find the man."

"Mme. Lyon was not seriously hurt," Babin said, his eyes fixed on Henri. "Should you be interested in the extent of her injuries."

Henri ignored him and spoke to Elise. "Are you sure you're all right?"

She nodded meekly. "Yes, it wasn't as bad as the first time."

Henri turned to Babin. "What are you doing to protect her?"

"We continue to make progress investigating the crime, M. Lyon," Dumont said.

"Progress?" Henri asked, his eyes wide. "You're sitting in my parlor, offending me, while my wife suffers from the second attack on her life in as many weeks!"

"It's more difficult than it seems," Babin postured.

"I don't see how," Henri declared, his voice louder. "A young woman has already been murdered. Obviously, the lunatic who perpetrated that crime has chosen my wife as his next victim."

"The investigation continues into the murder of the young woman," Dumont said. "And although they appear related in some aspects, in all likelihood they are not."

"What if they are?" Henri asked. "What if the murderer is after Elise?"

"Let's address the facts, M. Lyon, shall we?" Babin proposed. "The second attack on Mme. Lyon makes motive a primary consideration in contrast to the apparent random attack on the woman who was killed last month."

"We have yet to rule out someone seeking revenge, perhaps related to your business dealings," Dumont added.

"Which you claim implicates Andre Sinclair," Henri said. "I do find that difficult to believe. He's a businessman, a bad one, I grant you. But he's not a killer."

"Perhaps," Babin said, fingering his moustache. "Or perhaps not."

"You say that, Inspector, as if it's the most profound statement man has ever made," Henri uttered with disgust. "It only proves to me that you have no idea what you're talking about."

"Tell me, M. Lyon," Babin continued, ignoring him. "Where have you been for the last two hours?"

Henri's face grew taut, his eyes lit with rage. "I left the office and went for a walk."

"A walk?" Babin asked. "I assume you were alone?"

"Did anyone see you?" Dumont asked. "Perhaps a friend or acquaintance who passed you on the street."

Henri shook his head with disgust. "It shouldn't matter if anyone saw me or not."

"Gentleman," Elise said, intervening. "Aren't we being ridiculous, accusing a loving husband of attacking his wife?"

"You would be surprised, Madame," Babin said smugly. "If you only knew, from a statistical perspective, the number of murders committed by spouses."

"What would my motive be?" Henri asked. "I have none."

"Still a missing piece to the puzzle," Babin said, his gaze trained on Henri. "Which doesn't mean it won't be found."

Henri pointed his finger at Babin, eyes blazing. "I suggest devoting your time to the unsolved murder. You may find the man who attacked my wife."

"Perhaps," Babin said, his hands resting on his large belly. "Or perhaps not."

Chapter Forty-Nine

Deauville, 1956

The morning after she had dinner with Anton, Zélie sat with Luc for breakfast, the vase with her flowers proudly displayed in the center of the table. She sipped her coffee while Luc described his dinner with Marc.

"I was so surprised when M. Rayne gave me a new bicycle!" Luc exclaimed. "Did you see how shiny it is?"

Zélie smiled. "Yes, I did. I hope you thanked M. Rayne."

"I did," he said. "He let me ride it around the block, too."

"I bet that was fun," Zélie said. She didn't know Marc had refurbished a bicycle for Luc, but she wasn't surprised. He was a good man. And he was good to Luc.

"After I had macarons, M. Rayne let me have ice cream, too," Luc continued.

"Really?" Zélie asked, eyes wide. "You must have had so much fun."

"I did," he said. "Can I have dinner at M. Rayne's house again?"

"Yes, of course," she said. "As long as it's all right with M. Rayne. But now you have to finish your breakfast so you can go to school."

Luc returned to his buttered croissant, took a bite, and washed it down with apple cider. Zélie waited patiently while he finished, keeping an eye on the clock. As soon as he was done, she urged him on his way.

"Come on, Luc, let's go," she said, leading him into the foyer. She paused at the door. "I was talking to M.

LaRue yesterday, and he wants to know if you would like to ride Matilda again."

"I sure do," Luc said, bubbling with excitement.

She grinned, pleased he was happy. If she could only keep him that way. "Maybe after school, we'll see."

"I can't wait," he said, flinging the door open with a burst of energy.

She laughed. "Have a good day at school," she said as he scampered down the walkway. "I'll talk to M. LaRue."

Luc was in such a good mood that Zélie wondered if his visits to Marc's for dinner and Anton's for horseback riding should be more frequent. Maybe if she kept him busy doing things he enjoyed, he would forget about his nightmares and problems at school.

After Luc was on his way, Zélie decided to go through some of her mother-in-law's papers. There was a desk in the parlor, stylish and petite with the swirling curves of the Art Deco design, that she had avoided going through. But now it was time. There might be something that needed her attention. Or she could find clues to the many mysteries she was trying to solve.

She sat at the desk and opened the middle drawer, removing all that was in it and setting everything on top of the desk: a stapler and box of staples, several pens and pencils, a box of paper clips, a small magnifying glass, and a stack of bills. She looked everything over, and then put it back in the drawer except for the bills. She leafed through them, finding a year's worth of statements from the phone and electric companies, mortgage information, receipts for taxes paid to the city of Deauville, and a copy of a handwritten receipt for the sale of her mother-in-law's automobile, made out just as she started to become ill. Zélie studied it with a sickening feeling. It seemed Eva had known she was terminal and had started to get her affairs in order.

She searched the remaining drawers but found nothing of interest. Some holiday cards, old Nazi currency, now worthless, receipts and warranties for household items, including the kitchen appliances, and proposals for home improvements and house repairs. Also tucked in the drawers were boxes of different sized mailing envelopes, rental agreements for the cottages, various pads of paper, and an address book. She put everything away except the address book. She leafed through it quickly, recognized no names except her own and her family members, but left it on the top of the desk. It might prove valuable at some point.

Zélie rose from the desk and paused, pensive. It seemed her mother-in-law had used the desk for managing daily activities: paying bills, dealing with tenants, maintaining the property. Important papers must be kept elsewhere, especially those she was looking for—birth and death certificates, school records, information on distant relatives—anything that might tell her about Eva's life.

She went in the kitchen, poured a cup of coffee, and sat at the table, pondering her next move. She suspected what she wanted was in the attic, hidden away in the piles of boxes and crates that contained everything from books to Christmas decorations. It would be a chore to go through them, and she wasn't looking forward to it.

She had just finished her coffee and was about to go up in the attic, when Marc came to the door.

Chapter Fifty

Montmartre, 1874

Elise lay wrapped in Jean-Pierre's arms on the cot in the studio storage room, a thin sheet draped over their naked bodies. "I don't ever want to leave," she whispered, nuzzling her face against him.

"But you must," he said, lightly kissing her head.

A light rap sounded on the studio door. Jean-Pierre leaned up on one elbow, listened for a moment, and started to get out of bed.

Elise grabbed his arm. "Ignore them."

"I can't," he said, pulling on his pants. "What if it's your coachman?"

She sighed and rolled over. "I suppose I should get dressed, too."

"Jean-Pierre," a voice called as the knocking persisted.

"Who is that?" Elise asked, the voice familiar.

"Jean-Pierre, open the door," the visitor demanded. "It's Babin. I know you're in there."

"And we know Mme. Lyon is with you," Dumont called.

Elise leaped from bed and grabbed her clothes. "What are we going to do?" she hissed.

"Hurry," Jean-Pierre whispered. "Get dressed and act like you're posing."

He put on his shirt, tucked the tail into his trousers, and slid on his shoes while she fumbled with the buttons on her dress. "Just a minute," he called, "I want to finish what I'm doing."

"We're not waiting much longer," Babin said. "I'll break the door if I have to."

"All right, be patient," Jean-Pierre called. "I'll just be a second."

Elise finished dressing and slipped on her shoes. Jean-Pierre helped her buckle them, and she hurried to the chair and sat, as if posing.

"I'm coming," Jean-Pierre said loudly, walking to the door. He paused before opening it, ensuring Elise was ready.

She nodded. "It's all right," she whispered.

Jean-Pierre opened the door, looking annoyed. "What is the meaning of this, Inspector?"

Babin brushed by him and hurried in, followed by Dumont. "I ask the questions, Jean-Pierre," he said. "Do not forget that." He stopped beside Elise, gazing around the room.

"Hello, Inspector," she said. "Lieutenant Dumont."

"Mme. Lyon," Dumont said. "How is the portrait coming?"

"Very well," she said. "Although it's hard to sit still for such long periods of time."

Dumont chuckled. "I don't have the patience. I wouldn't make a very good model."

Babin faced Elise. "Do you feel safe here, Mme. Lyon?"

She looked at him strangely. "Yes, of course, Inspector. Why wouldn't I?"

Babin started to pace the floor. "You survived two attacks, failed robberies or attempts on your life. Both occurred when you left this studio."

"Jean-Pierre had nothing to do with them," she said. "And my coachman is much better prepared should an additional attempt be made."

"How do you know Jean-Pierre had nothing to do with the attacks?" Babin asked, pausing dramatically. "Especially if I don't?"

Her eyes widened. "Because he couldn't possibly have done it."

Dumont intervened; his tone was much softer than Babin's. "Anyone you associate with is a suspect," he explained. "At least until we prove otherwise. Isn't that right Jean-Pierre?"

Jean-Pierre watched the inspectors, a twinkle in his eye. "Whatever you say, Lieutenant."

"It's typical in an investigation," Dumont continued, "to include everyone as a suspect, and then eliminate them through evidence and interrogation."

Babin continued pacing the floor, walking from the front of the studio to the back. "Ah," he said, pointing at one of the unfinished portraits. "Poor Giselle. Do you know what happened to Giselle, Mme. Lyon?"

"Yes, I do," she replied. "She is the woman who was murdered last month."

"She was strangled," Babin said. "Doesn't that seem strange to you?"

"It does," she replied. "The madman who killed her could be after me. My husband is sure of it."

Babin stopped pacing in front of Jean-Pierre and eyed him sternly. "The madman could be closer than you think."

Jean-Pierre laughed. "Don't be ridiculous, Inspector."

"Where were you on Tuesday afternoon after Mme. Lyon left your studio?" Babin asked.

"I was here," he replied. "Painting."

"Who can verify that?" Babin asked.

Jean-Pierre shrugged. "No one," he said. "Or perhaps Mme. Michel. She's often nearby."

"So you said before," Babin said. "She's often nearby. Whenever you find it convenient, it seems."

Dumont addressed Elise. "Jean-Pierre couldn't prove his whereabouts during the prior murder."

"Which doesn't mean he killed anyone," Elise said crossly.

Babin chuckled. "So quick to defend, Mme. Lyon. Although I'm not surprised. But you may not know the man as well as you think."

She glanced at Jean-Pierre but quickly looked away, afraid her gaze might say too much. "He's my friend," she said. "I don't think he's capable of wrongdoing."

Babin walked behind the easel and looked at the portrait, studying the brush strokes, the progress made compared to the time expended. "How is the portrait coming along?"

"It's almost finished," Jean-Pierre said.

"A little more gets done each session?" Babin asked.

"Yes, it's a tedious process."

Babin turned to Elise. "Your coachman said you have been here for about an hour."

"Yes, Inspector, I have."

Babin looked at Jean-Pierre. "Is your progress today typical of any other session?"

Jean-Pierre nodded.

"Interesting," Babin muttered, studying the portrait. "Absolutely fascinating."

"What's the matter, Inspector?" Dumont asked.

"An hour's worth of progress, a typical session, yet no brush is wet with paint."

Chapter Fifty-One

Deauville, 1956

Anton LaRue sat astride Silver Shadow, trotting around an oval course. He rode daily, exercised several horses, and trained a few more. Adjacent to the Deauville track, Stepping Stone Stables was one of a series of horse farms that stretched across the Normandy terrain, the sprawling pastures divided by white rail fences and groves of trees.

He had enjoyed his dinner with Zélie Girard, and he suspected she had, also. It had been good for her to get out, to forget she mourned a husband, missed a mother-in-law, worried about a troubled son. An hour into their dinner he had noticed what a beautiful smile she had, because she didn't often display it, how bright her eyes were when they twinkled, and what a warm and funny person she was—when she allowed it. Although dinner had been casual, two friends enjoying an evening, it left him hoping they could do it again. He was attracted to her and suspected she felt the same about him, if only she could accept it. But he sensed she wasn't ready, and he wondered if she ever would be.

Silver Shadow was the thoroughbred many hoped would propel Stepping Stone Stables to the forefront of French racing circles. With good height and nearly perfect conformation, a bright chestnut coat and two stockings, he had a natural ability that only the greatest racehorses possess. Anton LaRue's dreams of becoming the most celebrated jockey in France rested on Silver Shadow. He realized that, and so did many others. He was the horse Anton favored and spent most of his time with and, even at such an early stage in the horse's career. With only a single win and no losses, many believed he would soon be considered one of the greatest—like Golden Cross.

Anton slowed Silver Shadow to a walk and wandered to the end of the straightaway. As they rounded the turn, Anton coaxed him into a trot, a canter, and then a full gallop, amazed at the power he possessed. He was born to run, preferred nothing else, and Anton knew that, one day soon, the world would know both Silver Shadow and Anton LaRue. He raced the horse halfway around the track, eased him back to a trot, and then to a walk—a process he would repeat. As he exercised Silver Shadow, he thought of Zélie Girard, little Luc, and Eva, the gambling mother-in-law who loved race horses. And for a moment he felt pangs of guilt.

Eva had a secret. And Anton knew it must be told.

Chapter Fifty-Two

Montmartre, 1874

Babin and Dumont left the studio and climbed into the police carriage. "It doesn't seem that much painting is getting done," Babin scoffed.

"We don't know that for sure," Dumont said. "Jean-Pierre said he was doing charcoal sketches."

Babin chuckled. "Yes, he did, didn't he? And we both must be very stupid to believe it."

"We didn't prove otherwise."

"We didn't have to," Babin said. "You'll learn to be more observant, Dumont, as time passes, and you're exposed to similar situations. Observation and logic are the building blocks of a good inspector. Someday you will acquire these skills. I have high hopes for you."

"But I saw exactly what you saw," Dumont protested.

"Yes, you did," Babin agreed. "But you didn't process it as I did. You can't yet assess the subtle clues so obvious to the seasoned investigator. But I will teach you."

"Maybe you can start by explaining what we just witnessed."

"Gladly," Babin said pompously. "First, the most obvious clue is the time it took before the door was opened."

"But Jean-Pierre said he didn't want to stop painting and lose the light."

"Yes, yes, I know," an amused Babin replied. "And you know all about light because your best friend is an artist."

Dumont looked at him, surprised. "I didn't think you were listening when I told you that story."

Babin chuckled. "I am always listening, my dear Dumont. Whereas you hear but don't listen. As we have already discussed."

"You don't believe him?" Dumont asked. "He claimed he wanted to finish sketching before he lost the light. It seems a plausible explanation."

"Yes, that is what he claimed, and, for the novice investigator, it would certainly suffice. But both Jean-Pierre and Mme. Lyon appeared flushed and disheveled, much different from what one would expect from a sedentary activity like posing and painting."

Dumont bit his lip, appearing annoyed with himself. "I didn't see that."

"No, but you did," Babin insisted. "You just didn't process it."

"I'm not sure I understand."

"Did you not notice that Mme. Lyon's hair was mussed—just a bit? But she wouldn't pose for a portrait unless it was perfect."

Dumont shrugged. "I'm not sure that's significant."

"Perhaps it is, or perhaps it is not," Babin said. "But did you also see that Jean-Pierre's shirt was only partially tucked into his trousers?"

"It could have pulled free while he painted," Dumont offered.

Babin shrugged. "Yes, it could have, I suppose. But lastly, and this was most obvious to me, was a charcoal sketch was supposedly in progress, but Jean-Pierre's hands were clean—no smudge could be seen. And even though a sketch of Mme. Lyon did exist, it rested on the floor beside an unfinished portrait of Giselle, victim of a brutal killer."

"I hadn't noticed that," Dumont admitted.

"Because you are learning, that is why," Babin said. "It's no fault of your own. Your skills will develop in time. But our observations today pose an interesting question."

"What is that?"

"If we know that Mme. Lyon visits the artist Jean-Pierre but is not posing for portraits, does Henri Lyon also know?"

Dumont's eyes widened. "A motive to kill Mme. Lyon."

"Exactly," Babin said. "Not only do the attacks mimic the murder recently committed as if to show that the culprit is one and the same, they all occurred as Mme. Lyon left Jean-Pierre's studio."

"As did the attack on Giselle," Dumont said. "Which could point to Jean-Pierre."

"Possible but not probable," Babin said. "Although Jean-Pierre is still considered a suspect in both the killing and the assaults on Mme. Lyon. But maybe someone wants us to think Jean-Pierre is the culprit. Someone who is very clever." He chuckled and fingered the curving sweep of his moustache. "Someone who underestimates Inspector Nicolas Babin."

"M. Lyon did identify a different carriage route for Mme. Lyon's coachman," Dumont said. "And that is where the second attack occurred."

"Ah, my dear Lieutenant, you are starting to piece things together," Babin said. "Very good of you. It is all a puzzle, is it not? We just have to place every piece where it belongs."

Dumont smiled meekly. "Do you think we have two strong suspects?"

"What about Andre Sinclair?" Babin asked. "Have we forgotten him, at risk of losing his business to Henri Lyon? Does revenge not count as motive for murder?"

"Yes, I suppose it does," Dumont admitted.

"We know very little about M. Sinclair, but we will soon learn more."

"Three strong suspects," Dumont said, weighing the evidence against each.

"Four," Babin said sternly, correcting him.

"Four?" Dumont asked.

"You forget that a witness claimed the assailant wore a police uniform."

Chapter Fifty-Three

Deauville, 1956

"How was dinner last night?" Marc asked as Zélie let him in the kitchen door.

"It was nice," she said. "I needed a night out."

"Good, I'm glad you enjoyed it."

"Thank you so much for Luc's bicycle," she said. "That was very nice of you. It must have been a lot of work to repair it."

Marc shrugged. "No, not really. I tinker with them all the time. But I wanted to build something special for Luc."

"We both appreciate it," she said. "And thanks for looking after him while I went out."

"Anytime," he replied. "Luc and I had fun, too."

Zélie smiled. "So I heard. Macarons and ice cream?"

Marc laughed. "He was having such a good time. I didn't want to spoil it."

"He couldn't stop talking about it. I hope he wasn't too much trouble."

"No, not at all."

Zélie set two cups of coffee on the table and sat down. She pointed to the worn address book. "I found that in Eva's desk. Nothing else worthwhile."

Marc picked it up and leafed through it. "Maybe as we learn more about the paintings, we'll stumble upon a name or address that's listed in here."

"I scanned it quickly," she said. "I saw some family members but didn't know anyone else."

"Probably Eva's friends."

“I was going to look in the attic next.”

Marc sipped his coffee. “I’d be glad to help if you like.”

Zélie gave it some thought. It would certainly go a lot faster. “If you don’t mind,” she said. “I don’t even know what to look for.”

“Let’s take our coffee up and get everything organized.”

They went upstairs and entered the attic, pausing in front of the paintings. Zélie studied them for a moment and then stepped closer. “We still have the mystery to solve. What are they doing here?”

Marc glanced at the boxes, crates, and furniture, haphazardly crammed into two rooms. “Maybe the answer lies up here somewhere.”

Zélie sighed. “I don’t even know where to start.”

Marc looked over the items. “I think if we organize this a bit, you’ll have much more room, and it won’t seem like such a daunting task.”

“I’m open to anything.”

He looked at each room and all that was stored there —stacked boxes, crates, and furniture shoved against the walls. “Let’s move all the furniture into one room and all the boxes and crates into the other.”

Zélie shrugged. “Sounds good to me.”

They spent an hour moving everything: a chaise lounge, a half dozen tables, a wardrobe with clothes from the ‘20s that they eased against a wall, baskets, bins of holiday decorations, bookshelves, chairs of different designs that spanned a half-century, a marble pedestal with a life-like bust of Napoleon—it seemed like inventory from an antique shop. They separated everything, furniture in the larger room, boxes and crates in the second room, against the wall.

"This should work nicely," Marc said, eyeing their progress. "As we explore a box, we'll move it to the other side of the room."

They got started, working their way through several dozen boxes and crates.

"Old records," Marc said, sliding a box across the floor.

Zélie studied the contents of an opened box. "All cookbooks. I'll have to look through these later."

"More books."

"Old photographs," Zélie said. "A task for a rainy day."

"More photographs."

"Here's a box of lace," Zélie said. "Doilies, mostly. They're beautiful."

"Children's games. I'll put this by the door. Maybe Luc will like them."

"A box of jigsaw puzzles."

"More for a rainy day."

Zélie took the wooden top from a crate and studied what was inside. "Marc, come here a minute."

"What is it?"

"Coins," she said, turning to face him. "But valuable coins. Silver and gold, some a hundred years old."

He glanced in the crate and opened the one next to it. "More of the same," he muttered.

She went to a third crate, removed the top, and looked inside. "Look what I just found."

Marc moved closer. "It's a lockbox, the crate built around it, with both a combination and a key lock." He leaned over, tapped on it, and studied it more closely. “It’s German military, marked as Gestapo.”

Chapter Fifty-Four

Montmartre, 1874

"Inspector Babin and Lieutenant Dumont came to my portrait session today," Elise told Henri at dinner, steak au poivre, the sauce made with cognac and served with roasted potatoes and green beans. She didn't trust Babin and didn't want him telling Henri something he didn't need to know.

He looked up from his meal, his eyebrows knitted. "Why did they pester you there?" he asked. "Or did they have information on your assailant?"

"No, they knew nothing more, and they never said why they came. It seemed they only wanted to disrupt the session."

Henri put a forkful of steak into his mouth and chewed thoughtfully. "Do they suspect the artist?"

She hesitated, phrasing her replies carefully. "I don't know who they suspect, if anyone. But they were blunt and accusatory. Not Dumont so much as Babin."

He pursed his lips, a tiny vein on his forehead flexing. "They act like we're the criminals," he muttered. "Accusatory in what way?"

"They questioned why it took so long to answer the door."

He cast a confused glance. "Why did it?"

"Jean-Pierre ignored them," she said, framing the conversation for her benefit. "He thought it was his neighbor, who can be annoying. But then they called out and demanded that the door be opened."

"And he still delayed?" Henri asked, his eyes narrowing.

"Briefly," she replied, pretending she didn't notice the suspicion in his expression. "But he only wanted to finish what he was doing."

"But why provoke them?" he asked, giving her his complete attention. "Not that Babin and Dumont deserve any courtesies."

"I thought it rude at first, too," she said, providing the explanation she had rehearsed. "But Jean-Pierre said he didn't invite them, and they had no appointment. I was the one—or you, actually—who was paying for his time. He made them wait until he was ready."

Henri laughed. "Good for Jean-Pierre. Those two need to be humbled. Especially Babin."

Elise smiled. "They were angry that Jean-Pierre made them wait."

Henri chuckled but then eyed her warily as if struck with a revelation. "What was he doing that couldn't be interrupted?"

She shrugged, trying to act casual. But she knew his suspicions were mounting. "Something to do with the light. He wanted to finish while the sunlight streamed in the window at a certain angle."

He sighed, studied her a moment more, and returned to his dinner. "I don't pretend to understand any of it," he said. "It's taking weeks to paint a portrait I thought would be done in a day."

"I know as little as you. But I realize there's much more involved."

"Yes, I suppose," he said. He paused, sipping his wine. "What did Babin want?"

"I don't know," she replied, relieved he no longer seemed suspicious. "He asked some questions, was somewhat rude, referred to Giselle, the victim murdered earlier in the year."

"Why discuss her?"

"She was one of Jean-Pierre's models."

Henri's eyes opened wide. "But you said he wasn't a suspect. Does Babin think Jean-Pierre is the killer?"

"No, of course not," she said, hastily dismissing his concerns. "His innocence has already been proved. But I did get the impression that Babin doesn't like him."

"Babin doesn't like anyone," Henri mumbled, satisfied with her explanation.

"But he's a very good investigator," Elise said. "Most say he is the best."

"If he's so good, why hasn't he found whoever attacked you?"

"He must be close. Although he didn't say that. I learn more from Dumont."

"He seems a good man," Henri admitted. "He has the patience of someone who's never been wronged. Especially the way Babin badgers and bullies him."

"Babin is trying to teach him," she said.

"I would rather not learn, if it were me," Henri muttered. "But I am concerned about this artist. Although he came highly recommended. He does portraits for many socialites—even the wives of government cabinet ministers."

"Yes, I see them when I go for my sessions, in various stages of completion."

Henri laid his fork on the plate. "What if he were involved in this woman's killing?"

"He couldn't be," she assured him. "Or he would have been arrested. It must be someone else."

"I'll tell you who it is," Henri said, his eyes lit with anger. "It's some lunatic who still roams the streets. Babin won't admit it because it proves he can't solve the crime. But he better find this maniac quickly. Or the whole city will turn on him. And I will lead the charge."

Chapter Fifty-Five

Deauville, 1956

When Luc got home from school, Zélie brought him to Stepping Stone Stables so he could ride Matilda as Anton had offered. When they got out of the car, she saw Anton by the fence, watching three horses feed on thick clumps of grass.

"Luc," Anton called when he saw them. "I've been waiting for you. Matilda is ready for a ride."

Zélie waved, watching as a broad smile crossed Luc's face.

"Can I go, Maman?" he asked, unable to contain his excitement.

She smiled. "Yes, go ahead. Just be careful."

Luc raced through the gate and hurried over to Anton as Zélie leaned on the fence to watch.

"Come on, Luc," Anton said, winking at Zélie. "Let's get Matilda saddled up."

They disappeared into the stables. Zélie was so grateful for the tiny improvements Luc seemed to be making. He was a little better every day, less depressed, looking more to the future than the past, although he wouldn't discuss school even when prompted. She suspected he still had issues with classmates. But she hoped, in time, they would disappear. For now, he needed an escape, and the stable seemed to provide it.

While she waited for them to saddle Matilda, she considered what she had found in the attic. The crates of coins, once she and Marc evaluated them, were probably worth a lot of money. Some were highly collectible, well over a hundred years old, and most were in very good condition. They initially thought the coins had come from a collector. But someone who loved what they collected wouldn't have dumped the coins into a wooden box without sorting or cataloguing them. Unless they had a very good reason to do so.

The paintings still remained a mystery, although she knew they would learn more when they visited the professor. Why were they stored in her mother-in-law's attic, and why had they never been mentioned by the lawyer, Eva, or her husband? But they'd never mentioned the coins either.

The last box she and Marc had found was the most mysterious. She didn't know what to think about it. For some reason, she suspected it offered answers to every question they had ever asked.

"Maman, look!" Luc exclaimed, sitting astride Matilda. Anton held the reins, walking the horse into the yard.

"Yes, I see," Zélie said. "You're a brave little boy to ride such a big horse."

Luc beamed and turned to Anton who was providing instruction. She watched them, her son in need of an escape to help him cope—something new that he could cling to, an interest to embrace. And Anton, a jockey fighting to rise above all others, taking the time to help a little boy. She hoped Silver Shadow propelled Anton to greatness, first in Deauville, then France, and eventually throughout the world.

As Anton led Luc around the pasture, he started teaching him how to use both his knees and the reins to give the horse directions. After a few minutes of instruction, Anton handed the reins to Luc and stepped away, letting him guide the horse in a grand circle.

"Look at me, Maman!" Luc called as he came close to the fence where Zélie was standing.

"What a big boy you are!" she said. "I'm so proud of you."

"He's doing good," Anton said as he passed.

Zélie watched the jockey for a moment, so patient with her son, so willing to help. He was a good man, kind and compassionate. She so hoped that all his dreams would come true.

After almost an hour, Anton led Matilda and Luc to the stable. Ten minutes later they emerged, and Luc scampered through the gate as Anton came over to where she waited.

"You did so good," Zélie said to Luc as she gave him a quick hug.

"He's a natural," Anton said. "Matilda likes him."

"It was fun, Maman!" Luc exclaimed. "Can I do it again?"

Zélie laughed. "That's up to M. LaRue."

"Yes, of course you can," Anton said. "Whenever your maman says."

"Thank you so much," Zélie said as they turned to go.

"You're welcome," Anton said. "I enjoy it, too."

Zélie took Luc by the hand and started back to the car.

"Zélie," Anton called. "I meant to ask you something."

She turned, smiling. "What is it?"

Anton hesitated. "How well did you know Eva?"

She shrugged, not expecting the question. "I knew her for eight years. But I know little about her life before that."

Anton studied her for a moment.

"Why, what is it?" she asked. She could sense he had something to say but wasn't sure if he should say it.

Anton sighed, looking guilty. "I think it's time I shared some of her secrets."

"Secrets?" she asked, wondering what he could possibly mean and why he hadn't shared them before.

Anton glanced at Luc. "Not now," he said. "It's a long story. But it needs to be told. I've given it a lot of thought, and I think it might explain the paintings."

Chapter Fifty-Six

Montmartre, 1874

Henri Lyon pushed the contract across the desk toward Andre Sinclair.

"You seem surprised, Andre," Henri said, hiding a smirk. "Although I don't know why."

"More irritated than surprised," Sinclair snarled. "I don't understand why this is so difficult. I'm not interested in trading the yearling."

"But none of what you've offered is acceptable. Your company is in trouble, and now I hold a risky asset."

Sinclair rolled his eyes. "I've given you options: proceeds from a direct sale or a swap for specified asset—real estate, percentage of production, direct ownership. I can satisfy the loan, or we can extend payment for two years. Yet nothing is acceptable but the yearling?"

Henri eyed his competitor carefully. He forced a passive expression, not wanting Sinclair to know how much he enjoyed destroying him. "It's a good contract," he said, ignoring the question. "In exchange for the yearling, I extend the due date of the loan for three years, with nothing due until final payment."

Sinclair's face was flush. It seemed he recognized defeat was inevitable. His only option was to try for better terms. "But interest still accumulates."

Henri shrugged. "No different from any other bank. But you have no payments at all for three years—your problem is pushed into the future. All in exchange for a horse that may or may not be a champion. I assume all the risk. You assume none. You should be grateful."

Sinclair frowned. "How about this?" he asked. "Give me a two-year extension with no interest and then four payments spread over the third year."

Henri pretended to consider the offer. Sinclair had already given up the yearling—even though he didn't seem to realize it. He could afford to be generous. "Four equal payments, due quarterly, to retire the entire debt?"

"Yes."

"How do you propose to raise the money?"

"I'll find a way."

"I do need to know," Henri said, offering one more obstacle to further frustrate his adversary. "Especially if I'm assuming more risk on what is already a shaky investment."

Sinclair closed his eyes. But when he opened them, he still sat in Henri Lyon's office, struggling to save his business. "I'll sell production or assets to someone else."

Henri inched the contract closer. "I might consider another property to retire the debt. But you still need the extension I'm offering."

Andre Sinclair studied his nemesis closely. He sensed a trap, a financial solution he might live to regret. He was caged, caught in a corner. He knew it and so did Henri Lyon. "What would you consider?

"Your gold mine in Madagascar."

"Impossible," Sinclair said, aghast. "That mine is one of my most precious assets."

"Yes, I know."

"And it's worth far more than the debt you're calling."

Henri laughed. He found the discussion enjoyable. "I know that, also."

"I cannot agree to your terms."

"Andre, it doesn't matter what you want or what you think you can agree to. You have no choice. I know that. And I suspect that you do, also."

Sinclair was confused. "I don't understand."

"You can't pay the loan," Henri said, his voice getting louder. "It's that simple. If I chose to, I can force default, seek relief in the courts, and take over Normandy Mines. The sooner you realize that, the better off you'll be."

"I intend to change that," Sinclair insisted.

Henri chuckled, knowing his reaction would further frustrate Sinclair. "I don't see how. You're closer to bankruptcy than you realize. I'm offering a tremendous opportunity. You have three years to improve your balance sheet—regardless of how you choose to do it. It's very generous."

"I can't surrender my prize gold mine, or I will go bankrupt."

Henri sat back in his chair, studying his adversary. He gained the most pleasure from taking what his opponents valued most—regardless of worth. "I want the yearling," he insisted. "That's the only deal I'll accept."

"You can't do that."

Henri hesitated. He knew Sinclair was trapped. He could do nothing and still win. "I can do whatever I want because you're helpless to stop me. This is the best offer you will ever get."

Andre Sinclair sighed and reached for the contract. He read through it, taking his time, and signed it.

Chapter Fifty-Seven

Deauville, 1956

"Zélie Girard, this is Professor Marie Dufour," Marc announced, making introductions.

"Please, sit down," the professor said. "Call me Marie."

They sat on the same terrace where Marc had originally met Professor Dufour around the oval table that offered such a commanding view of the sprawling ocean beyond.

"This is lovely," Zélie said, breathing in the salty scent of the sea, her gaze drifting to waves walking on shore and then quickly running away. "What a fabulous view."

"It's a pleasant place to spend retirement," Marie said, smiling. "I loved it the first time I saw it."

Zélie turned to her host. "I can understand why. It's beautiful."

"Thank you for allowing us to visit," Marc said. "We really appreciate it."

"I've been looking forward to it," Marie assured him. "What a fascinating story. So, it seems you've inherited quite a cache of paintings."

Zélie chuckled. "Apparently, yes. But quite unexpectedly."

"Since Marc's last visit, I've done some research on Jean-Pierre," Marie said, pointing to an art history book laying on the table. "Although this is a limited resource, we'll at least have photographs of some of his paintings for reference."

"Thank you so much for helping us," Zélie said.

Marie smiled. “I’ve been enjoying it.”

Marc withdrew some papers from a leather satchel. “I have a list of the paintings along with descriptions and some comments.”

“The paintings also came with a mystery,” Zélie said. “I found a note inserted in one of the frames. It claimed that the eight paintings provide the clues needed to solve a crime.”

Marie’s eyes widened. “Oh, my,” she said. “I don’t think I can help solve the crime. But hopefully I can provide some insight into the paintings.”

“Anything you can offer will help us tremendously,” Zélie said.

Marc scanned the notes that he and Zélie had made. “I described two of the paintings when I last saw you,” he began. “The portrait of the dark-haired woman, identity unknown, who appears to be quite wealthy, and the race horse who was known as Golden Cross.”

“I’m afraid I can’t help with those,” Marie said. “Jean-Pierre painted many portraits, so we would have to narrow that down a bit. Maybe if I saw the portrait, it would be easier. But I found no listing of any horses among his work. At least with this resource.”

“We learned that the horse was one of the first champions at Deauville,” Zélie said. “Owned first by a man named Andre Sinclair and then by Henri Lyon.”

The professor thought for a moment and then thumbed through her reference book. “Neither of those names are referenced.”

“How about a nude portrait of another woman, blond, blue eyes, early twenties?” Marc asked.

Marie looked through her book. "There are limited examples of Jean-Pierre's work—at least in this book. I don't think I can help with that one, either."

"A painting of an artist's studio," Zélie said, hopefully.

"Jean-Pierre did do a painting of his Montmartre studio," Marie said. "Even though he spent much of his time on the Normandy coast. Let me find it to show you." She leafed through the pages of her book. "Yes, here it is."

Marc and Zélie leaned across the table. "That's it," Marc exclaimed. "Perfect. Now we know what one of the paintings is—Jean-Pierre's Montmartre studio."

Zélie looked at the image closely. "There's also a painting of a street scene that's labeled as Montmartre, a rising road enclosed by stone walls. Maybe it's near his studio."

The professor turned pages, scanning references for Jean-Pierre. "I'm sorry, no listing."

Marc looked at their notes, systematically addressing each item. "There's a painting of the same dark-haired woman with an attractive man on what appears to be the beach at Deauville."

Marie turned more pages. "It's not listed among his works—at least not in this book. But not many portraits are. I may be able to identify it if I see it."

"A café, in Paris," Marc said, continuing down their list. "Normandy Mines is the building beside it."

"Normandy Mines is also the company managed by the man who owned the race horse—Andre Sinclair," Zélie added.

"I'm sorry," Marie said. "It's not listed here." She paused and looked at them curiously. "Are you sure all of these have Jean-Pierre's signature?"

Marc nodded. “Yes, although a couple have only the initials JP.”

“But in the same handwriting,” Zélie clarified.

Marie thought for a moment, reading a note in her reference book. “Do you have any more?”

“The last is a painting of the Montmartre police station with two men standing in front of it,” Marc said. “One is an older man, stout, with an unusual handlebar moustache.”

“I found the note about the clues to the crime in that painting,” Zélie said.

“I am familiar with that one,” Marie muttered, turning pages. “Yes, here it is. Inspector Babin is the name of both the man and the portrait. Is this it?”

“Yes,” Zélie exclaimed, looking at the book. “Finally! A clue we may be able to follow.”

“Is the second policeman identified?” Marc asked.

Marie shook her head. “No, I’m afraid not. A note in the book claims that Babin was a famous detective, known for his manicured moustache.”

Marc glanced at Zélie and shrugged. “Why do you think the others aren’t listed?”

“They may be elsewhere, just not in this book, which is more of a history of European artists,” Marie explained. “Several Jean-Pierre paintings are listed by name with no corresponding photograph, but I wasn’t able to reference them by your description. Some of his work, especially portraits, were held by private collectors, taken by the Germans during the wars. More specific reference books do exist. I only have to find them.”

“Is there another explanation for why they’re so difficult to find?” Marc asked.

Michelle hesitated for a moment. "Yes, there is," she said, almost apologetically. "The paintings may not be authentic."

Zélie frowned. "I hadn't considered forgeries."

"Neither had I," Marc said. "If true, that casts a completely different spin on everything."

"But the paintings may have been commissioned by a private client and never offered for sale or exposed to the public," Marie said. "Especially the portraits. Let me check additional references before we make any assumptions. It should only take a few days. The library at Rouen has an excellent selection on French artists."

"How much would these portraits be worth?" Marc asked, glancing at Zélie. "Assuming they are original works of Jean-Pierre."

Marie thought for a moment. "First, I would have to see the paintings, to ensure they're authentic. I would also have to locate a corresponding reference."

"And if you prove all eight are works were done by Jean-Pierre?" Zélie asked, her heart beginning to race.

Marie paused dramatically, her gaze shifting between them. "Probably close to a million francs."

Chapter Fifty-Eight

Montmartre, 1874

Inspector Babin sat in Andre Sinclair's office, Lieutenant Dumont beside him, and eyed Sinclair warily. He found the man evasive, replying to questions without giving answers.

"I was still at my office," Sinclair said, his gaze shifting around the room.

"The attack on Mme. Lyon occurred at four p.m.," Babin said. "Just to clarify."

"And I rarely leave until five or six," Sinclair said. "I told you that the last time you questioned me."

"But your clerk told us otherwise," Babin said, caressing the curve of his moustache with his fingers.

Sinclair shrugged. "I must have gone for a walk or ran an errand," he said. "Because I don't leave the office until later."

"Except on this particular day," Babin countered. "Which also happens to be when Mme. Lyon was assaulted."

"Could you have had an outside appointment?" Dumont asked.

"I may have," Sinclair said, considering his calendar.

"It was only two days ago, M. Sinclair," Babin scoffed. "It shouldn't be hard to recollect."

"I did meet with a client," Sinclair said slowly. "I remember now."

Babin wasn't convinced. "Nothing is listed in the appointment book that your clerk showed us. And he knew of no other appointments."

Sinclair sat back in his chair, his arms folded across his chest. "Not all of my appointments are listed, Inspector. Some are personal."

"It's not a crime to have a private appointment," Dumont assured him, trying to ease the tension.

"But assaulting a woman is a crime," Babin declared.

Sinclair banged his fist on the table. "I did not attack Mme. Lyon!"

Babin shrugged. "But you cannot provide an alibi," he said calmly. "Or for some reason that is incomprehensible to two investigators, you refuse to do so."

Sinclair sighed, hesitating. "If it's truly needed, I'll provide an alibi for both occasions. But not until absolutely necessary."

Babin's eyes narrowed. "And why is that?" he asked. "What are you trying to hide?"

"I won't impact the lives of other people," Sinclair said.

"An affair, perhaps?" Babin probed.

Sinclair's face firmed. "I have no reason to kill Mme. Lyon."

"Except her husband is destroying your business," Babin said. "Most would think that is a very good reason."

"Are you seeking revenge, M. Sinclair?" Dumont asked. "It is a viable motive."

Sinclair rolled his eyes. "Hardly," he replied. "If I wanted revenge, and I was that devious, I would not attack Mme. Lyon, who is a woman I barely know. I would take my revenge out on her husband."

Babin studied Sinclair closely, resting his hands on his big belly. "Since M. Lyon is taking something precious from you," he surmised, "maybe you are taking something precious from him—like Elise Lyon."

Sinclair shook his head in disgust. He leaned on the desk and arched his fingers, impersonating the great detective. "Perhaps, or perhaps not."

Babin frowned and looked at Dumont. "Lieutenant, this is a good lesson for you, an excellent example of the human psyche. We have an uncooperative suspect. He could very well be innocent, merely caught in a spider's web meant for another fly. Or he could be guilty, clumsily attempting to murder his competitor's wife. And what is much worse, he may have already killed an innocent woman, intending to make Mme. Lyon his second victim."

Sinclair's eyes flashed angrily. "Or you could be an inspector with a marvelous reputation who can't begin to solve a crime—even if you committed it yourself."

Chapter Fifty-Nine

Deauville, 1956

Zélie took one last look at Luc, eyes closed with his head on the pillow, and turned out the light and went downstairs. He seemed better every day, less afraid, more confident.

"He's asleep," she said as she entered the parlor. Anton and Marc were sitting by the radio, enjoying a glass of wine.

"I think he's improving," Marc observed. "He seems happier."

"He is," Zélie said. "You two have a lot to do with it."

Anton seemed surprised. "We're just spending some time with him."

She poured a glass of wine and sat down. "I think that's all he needs. You may not realize it, but you're helping fill the void his father left. I appreciate it. I really do."

"We're glad to help," Marc said, glancing at Anton, who nodded in agreement.

It was quiet for a moment, and Marc and Zélie then turned and looked at Anton.

"I suppose it's time to tell you about Eva," Anton said.

"We have been waiting," Marc said.

Anton smiled. "I didn't want to speak in front of Luc. But now I'm ready."

Zélie pointed to the bottle of wine on the table. "Should anyone need refills during the story."

Anton paused, collecting his thoughts. "The war is a vivid memory for all of us," he began. "Some endured the Nazi occupation, doing what they had to, merely to survive. Others actively opposed the enemy. Deauville was inundated with Germans, especially as the war progressed. Men and boys were forced to build the German's defenses—pillboxes, roads and supply depots. Germans occupied all the grand hotels, the casinos, even the three little cottages that sit beside this house."

Zélie listened intently. "My husband spoke very little of the war, my mother-in-law not at all."

"Their memories were probably too painful," Marc said.

"Throughout the war," Anton continued, "a group in Deauville belonged to a Resistance network that helped downed Allied airmen escape to England. The village was the last stop in their route before they were smuggled onto fishing boats in the harbor."

Marc's eyes widened. "Even with such a heavy German presence?"

"Yes, it's surprising," Anton replied. "But if you think about it, the Germans would never suspect a Resistance operation in the midst of one of their strongholds."

"Who belonged to this network?" Zélie asked.

"My father," Anton replied, "who rarely speaks about it, Eva and her husband Gaston, and an older couple named Marie and Louie Chard, who were the ringleaders."

"My husband told me his father was killed in the war," Zélie said.

"He was," Anton replied. "The Germans stumbled upon a Resistance safe house in the countryside, not far from here. Gaston, your father-in-law, was killed. Two others escaped, and some airmen were captured."

Zélie was quiet, now knowing the root to some of her husband's behaviors—extreme patriotism, a career in the military—perhaps a subconscious attempt to help the father he couldn't save as a teenage boy.

"After the raid on the safe house, the entire network unraveled," Anton continued, "betrayed by someone within."

"Who was the traitor?" Marc asked.

Anton hesitated, then shrugged. "No one knows. Or no one will say."

"What happened to the other members?" Zélie asked.

"Eva was held by the Gestapo but later released, the Chards were caught and executed—apparently some incriminating evidence was found on their property—and all their personal belongings were confiscated. Several others were also executed: a fisherman, a farmer, a man who worked at the railroad station in Rouen. My father was imprisoned for weeks—tortured almost to death."

"Did he escape?" Marc asked.

"The Allied invasion saved him," Anton replied.

"Was the traitor ever identified?" Marc asked.

Anton shrugged. "If my father knew who it was, he never said."

Zélie shifted in her seat. "Only Eva and your father survived?"

Anton nodded. "I'm sure others may have, but I can't say for sure. Identities were protected for just such an occurrence—a betrayal. I'll ask my father for more information. Maybe he'll tell me now that time has passed.

But some say Eva and my father were heroes—only because they survived."

Zélie shared a furtive glance with Marc. "I suspect there may be another explanation."

Anton cocked his head. "I don't understand."

"Your father avoided the Gestapo's wrath because of the Allied invasion," Marc said. "But we don't really know how Eva did it."

Chapter Sixty

Montmartre, 1874

"We have to be cautious," Elise said as she sat, not moving, her head tilted slightly to the right. "We could spoil everything."

At first Jean-Pierre didn't reply. He was focused, the brush dancing across the canvas. After a few moments, he stood, looking past the portrait to her. "You're so close I can almost taste your lips, see the strands of hair that escape the pin, and revel in the scent of your perfume. But I cannot hold you."

"It's too dangerous, yes," she insisted, even though she suspected he was toying with her. "It's hard for me, too."

"Am I to ignore your beauty, deny the attraction that pulls us together and pushes all others away, and pretend you're nothing but an object to paint, like a flower in a vase or a cobblestone street? My heart races when your carriage arrives and hangs heavy when it leaves."

She grinned. "You're teasing."

He shrugged, smiling. "In some ways. But a man cannot deny his most basic needs, what his heart feels or his soul requires."

"We're being watched constantly," she warned. "Both of us."

"Who watches now?" he asked. "We're alone in my studio."

"We thought we were alone during the last session, too. But Babin barged in, demanding to know what we were doing."

"You're a model, and I'm an artist," he said. "You pose, and I paint."

"There's much more. We both know that."

"But we are alone. Even the delightful Mme. Michel, who knows every secret this quiet lane has ever whispered, is nowhere to be found. Why waste what precious moments we have?"

"Mme. Michel may only be buying bread or pastries. She can tap on the window at any time."

"Or she may not," he said, grinning. "And we will have wasted an entire hour only painting and posing."

"We only appear to be alone," she stressed. "But we're not. More eyes watch than Mme. Michel's. You know that, and so do I."

"Both the door and the window are closed."

"The coachman watches with detailed instructions from both the police and my husband. I'm sure he sees all."

Jean-Pierre twisted his head to glance out the window. "The coachman reads the newspaper and naps. As long as you leave in an hour or so, nothing else concerns him."

"Babin and Dumont may be watching, just like the last time."

"The street was empty when you came, and now only your carriage sits upon it."

"Just as it was when I last came. They can be anywhere—at the café on the corner or around the bend in the road. And Mme. Michel is somewhere near, I assure you. Whether the window is open or closed, she knows all. Don't underestimate her."

"But if no one can see, does it matter if I paint you or touch you?"

She smiled. "Yes, it does. If we've learned anything, it's to be careful for a little while longer. Look how close we were to getting caught."

"You're assuming Babin is a great detective," he said, his attention drifting back to the canvas. "He is not."

"We would be foolish to underestimate him. He is said to be the most gifted detective Paris has ever known."

Jean-Pierre chuckled, put down his brush, and walked toward her. "I have yet to see a hint of brilliance."

"You should be wary. He suspects you."

"I'm sure he does. And I suspect him. But only of being a fool."

She frowned. "Both attacks came when I left you. Only minutes later."

"Babin can claim I'm a suspect but to no avail," Jean-Pierre said, kissing her lightly on the forehead, the cheek, and then the lips. "I am innocent. You know that, and so does he."

Chapter Sixty-One

Deauville, 1956

Zélie sat at the kitchen table with her second cup of coffee. Sometimes she felt overwhelmed. So much had happened in so short a time: moving to Deauville, trying to get Luc adjusted to all the changes in his life, finding the paintings and crates of coins—and all the mysteries surrounding them—and now learning that Eva had been a member of the Resistance, a hero who had helped save downed Allied airmen. She thought briefly of Deauville, only a dozen years before, inundated with German soldiers. It added one more mystery just as others unraveled, all somehow leading to the attic.

She now knew the paintings were valuable even though Professor Dufour needed to examine them to ensure they were authentic. But if they were, she could sell them at auction and reap enough money to pay off all of Eva's debts and give Luc a life he'd never dreamed of. But first she wanted to know where the paintings had come from. They had never once been mentioned by her mother-in-law or her husband. They could, of course, have had no idea what they were. The paintings could have been in the attic for seventy years. The coins, however, had been placed there more recently, given some of the dates. But anything of such monumental value comes with riddles that must be solved. And she had stumbled upon more than her share.

Zélie was fortunate to have found such devoted friends and tenants as Anton and Marc. It was sweet how protective they were. Any doubts she had about being a landlord or managing the property had disappeared. The estate agent still advertised for summer lets, income that she desperately needed, while Anton and Marc asked family and friends for prospective tenants. Her parents and siblings had all made arrangements to visit, and she could comfortably accommodate them in the spare room and even Luc's bedroom if too many came at the same time. She had posted an advertisement to give piano lessons and had added her third student, not counting Marc. Deauville had been good for her. She just had some finances to sort and mysteries to solve.

She buttered a croissant and chewed it thoughtfully as she sipped her coffee. Two boxes of coins that had significant value. Eight paintings that provided clues to a crime. The dark-haired woman appeared in two paintings. Zélie suspected she played a central role in the mystery. Andre Sinclair, the original owner of Golden Cross and owner of Normandy Mines, was referenced in two paintings also, but the artist had not actually depicted him. He, too, must be a central figure. The police station was most likely where the crime had been investigated, the artist's studio where Jean-Pierre worked. The paintings that remained were of an isolated street and a nude woman with blond hair and blue eyes. Sometimes Zélie felt like she was close to finding the thread that tied them together and only lacked the critical clue.

As she looked out the window, she saw Anton leave his cottage, likely destined for the stables. She agreed with his assessment—horses were good for Luc. It gave him a sense of accomplishment, distracted him from the dark days he had just endured, and seemed to make him happier. She could only hope it lasted.

Zélie smiled. Anton was an attractive man, kind and compassionate, ambitious and hard-working. He would make someone a good husband. She also had no doubt he would rise in the world of horse-racing, soon to be a jockey all would know and respect. Their dinner had been nice—she had enjoyed their getting to know each other. She would love to see him again, but she didn't know if it would ever amount to anything. She wasn't ready.

And she didn't know if she ever would be.

Chapter Sixty-Two

Montmartre, 1874

A man sat in the office of Andre Sinclair, his clothes shabby, his face not clean shaven. A hat was perched on his head, pulled low, keeping his face in shadows. "He has many secrets," the man revealed. "I can assure you of that."

"What did you learn?" Sinclair anxiously asked Fabien lecture, the man he had hired to spy on Henri Lyon.

"He usually leaves the office around three p.m.," lecture said.

"I thought he once mentioned working into early evening?"

"He does sometimes, but not too often."

Sinclair sat back in his chair, knowing there was more to come. "Where does he go?"

"He belongs to a gentleman's club, The Royal. It's not far from his office, by the Paris Bourse."

"Does he gamble?" Sinclair asked, hoping for a weakness to exploit.

"He plays cards, but not too often. He smokes a cigar, reads the newspaper, and has a glass of cognac or sherry. But he doesn't stay long. From there he goes to this location." He handed Sinclair a slip of paper with an address written on it.

Sinclair tried to picture the street. "Rue Brongniart. I'm not familiar with it."

"It's near his office," lecture said. "He rents a small apartment, just one bedroom. But it's on a quiet street, no one notices when he comes or goes. The neighbors seem to mind their own business."

"He has a mistress?"

"More than one, it would seem."

"Really?" Sinclair asked. "How does no one know that?"

LeClere shrugged. "Maybe no one cares. A lot of men have mistresses. Lyon actually has three."

Sinclair's eyes widened. "Unbelievable," he said. "His wife is beautiful. Have you ever seen her?"

"I have, M. Sinclair, and I agree with you."

Sinclair was still digesting the information. "Do these women compare to Mme. Lyon?"

"No, they're not as attractive."

"Then why the mistresses?" Sinclair asked. "Are they intelligent, prone to sophisticated conversation that might elude Mme. Lyon, or do they possess some other skill that captivates M. Lyon?"

LeClere grinned. "I suspect they have talents Mme. Lyon may not possess. Don't most mistresses?"

"Interesting," Sinclair said, thinking of how to use it for his benefit. "Have you identified them?"

"I have, sir," LeClere said. "The first is Mlle. Sophie Delacroix. She is young, barely a woman, and lives with her parents."

"Is she a prostitute?"

LeClere shrugged. "Possibly."

"The next?"

"Angelique St. Pierre. She's closer to M. Lyon's age, the daughter of a friend to Lyon's mother and married to a railroad official."

"A longtime affair?"

"I suspect so," LeClere said. "He sees each woman at least once a week."

"And who is the third?"

"She's the most interesting—Mme. Jeanette Richelieu."

Sinclair sat up in the chair. "Is she—"

"Yes, sir, one and the same."

Sinclair chuckled, having snared the bear in the jaws of a trap. "Henri Lyon, owner of an investment conglomerate, is having an affair with Mme. Richelieu, wife of the government official who oversees financial corporations."

"Yes, sir, it's true."

"What a wonderful time I will have with that."

LeClere chuckled. "Tell me when the time is right, and I'll inform the newspapers."

Sinclair smiled. He would enjoy destroying Henri Lyon, his revenge for losing the yearling. "One more request."

"What is it?"

"Can you get into Lyon's apartment?"

"Sure, it's no problem at all. What for?"

"I want you to hang a portrait on his wall," Sinclair said. "But only when the time is right."

"What is it?"

"It's a nude painting of a blond model."

Chapter Sixty-Three

Deauville, 1956

Marc arrived just after ten to play the piano. "I asked a locksmith to come by around eleven. We can see what he thinks about the third crate."

"I suppose the sooner we know, the better," Zélie said, wary of what the crate contained, especially with its Gestapo marking.

"My thoughts, too," Marc replied. "I'm going to practice a bit before he gets here."

Zélie went upstairs and tended to some laundry, still listening with the critical ear of the teacher. Marc was doing well. He enjoyed playing, had a desire to improve, and practiced daily. She had just finished folding clean clothes and was putting them away when the music stopped.

"Zélie," Marc called.

"I'm upstairs," she said. "I'll be down in a minute,"

She gathered some laundry, made another pass through the bedrooms to make sure Luc didn't have more dirty clothes, and went downstairs, carrying the wash basket. She put it in the kitchen and came into the parlor.

"How does it sound?" Marc asked.

She smiled. "Absolutely wonderful. You're doing great."

"I can't wait to play for my son," he said eagerly. "He'll be shocked."

"Invite him over," she suggested.

"Soon," he replied. "I have to get a little better first. When can I play Edith Piaf?"

She laughed. "It won't be long. Not at the rate you're going."

He closed the lesson book and set it on top of the piano. "If you're not too busy, I thought I would look at those coins again. I can do some research and find out what they're worth."

"Sure," she said. "Come on, I'll go with you."

They went up to the attic, now neatly arranged.

"At some point you should inventory all of this," Marc said, glancing around. "You can sell what you don't want."

She scanned the cramped rooms. "It's hard to believe it all fits."

"Some of these items are valuable—paintings, coins, antiques. I'm still surprised your husband or Eva never mentioned anything."

"No, they never did," she mused, wondering the same. "I think I was only up here once or twice. I didn't really pay much attention to what was here."

"Maybe no one else did, either."

"Maybe not," she agreed. "But don't you wonder where it came from?"

He shrugged. "Accumulated over the last hundred years, I would guess. Maybe no one realized how much some of this stuff is worth."

"But eight paintings that provide clues to a crime?" she asked. "How did they stay as a set over the last seventy years?"

"They were probably part of a private collection."

Zélie hesitated, hoping he could see what she did. "That's exactly what I was thinking."

He looked at her strangely. "Which then begs the question: What are they doing here?"

She nodded. “Especially when neither my husband nor Eva ever mentioned them.”

Marc paused, pensive. “It’s as if they were a secret.”

“I’m convinced there’s a good reason why the paintings were never sold. The same for the coins.”

He was starting to understand. “Because they couldn’t be sold.”

“No,” she said, shaking her head. “They belong to someone else.”

Chapter Sixty-Four

Montmartre, 1874

"We may lay a trap for the culprit," Inspector Babin said to Dumont. "But I would suggest, as you become more familiar with police work, that you use this technique sparingly."

"Why is that?" Dumont asked. "Especially if it's effective."

"Because in this instance it would place Mme. Lyon in danger,"

Dumont looked at Babin warily. "Then it doesn't seem worth the risk."

"Ah, my dear Lieutenant, sometimes a risk is worth taking. As you will learn once you've been exposed to more cases."

Dumont paused, pensive. "I did have a thought," he said slowly as if reluctant to reveal it. "The attacks on Mme. Lyon may have been staged, intended to illicit a grisly result."

Babin's eyes widened. "Lieutenant Dumont, your mind is starting to work like a true detective. Very good, my friend. What is the basis for your suspicion?"

"Both attacks failed and were poorly planned. Especially the attack in her carriage, which was carried out in broad daylight."

Babin nodded, considering the suggestion. "Not premeditated but maybe in response to provocation."

Dumont studied the great inspector. "Doesn't any assault require some planning?" he asked. "The perpetrator must know the location of the victim."

"Let me paint a picture for you," Babin said and then laughed. "I'm referring to the artist, of course and whatever it is he is doing with Mme. Lyon. We surely know he isn't painting."

"Do you still rank him highly as a suspect?"

Babin hesitated, eyeing his assistant. "Perhaps," he said. "But not for a crime of passion, where emotion tramples logic. The criminal reacts to a stimulus. He has no time to plan."

"Who is capable of such an irrational act?"

"A crime of passion defines the actions of Henri Lyon," Babin explained. "He is a man who struggles to control his temper. Have you not noticed how enraged his eyes become when challenged, or how the tiny vein in his forehead throbs when he's angry? I believe the slightest provocation could trigger his temper. He is unable to control himself."

Dumont considered his theory. "Wouldn't evidence of such behavior already exist?"

"Not necessarily, my dear Dumont. The provocation has to be sudden and severe, causing the uncontrollable reaction. If M. Lyon discovered what we already know—that his wife and Jean-Pierre are likely lovers—I don't think his rage could be contained."

Dumont was quiet. "Both attempts on Mme. Lyon's life were made after she left modeling sessions."

"Modeling sessions?" Babin started to laugh. "I would hardly call them that, but we can if you choose to."

"Are you ruling out other suspects?"

"No, of course not," Babin said. "But Henri Lyon is at the top of my list."

"Along with Andre Sinclair and Jean-Pierre?"

"Let us examine each, in turn," Babin suggested. "We have a potential madman, linking Giselle to Mme. Lyon. But I tend to think this the least likely scenario."

"I rank it higher," Dumont countered, "given the similarities between attacks."

"But a madman doesn't know his victims. He kills indiscriminately, whenever he has the opportunity. If but one attempt had been made on Mme. Lyon's life, I would say yes, a madman could be the killer. But when the second attempt occurred, I thought otherwise."

Dumont nodded, understanding the logic. "Is Andre Sinclair still a suspect?"

"I believe so," Babin said. "Because he might also fit the definition, reacting to provocation. M. Lyon is taking a terrible toll on Normandy Mines, at least according to Andre Sinclair. Perhaps the assaults coincide with failed negotiations."

Dumont pursed his lips. "It doesn't seem enough of a catalyst. Sinclair lives in a world of financial risk. Failed negotiations, even those as serious as he describes, wouldn't warrant that severe of a reaction."

"Yes, my friend, that is true," Babin agreed. "Although he could still be the culprit, I contend that Henri Lyon is more likely."

"And Jean-Pierre?"

Babin shrugged. "Possible, but unlikely. Who makes love to a woman and then tries to kill her?"

"A madman would."

"Perhaps, or perhaps not."

Dumont looked at his superior strangely as if wondering whether the man made any sense. "Four suspects: a madman, Lyon, Jean-Pierre, and Sinclair."

"I count five."

"Who is the fifth?"

"Did you forget the witness who claimed the attacker wore a policeman's uniform?"

"I remember," Dumont said. "I assumed it was a mistake."

"Good detectives never assume," Babin lectured. "They prove."

"A fifth suspect, potentially a policeman."

"Correct, a policeman," Babin said, eyeing his partner sternly. "Maybe even you, Lieutenant Dumont."

Chapter Sixty-Five

Deauville, 1956

Zélie left Marc in the attic and went downstairs. She put dirty laundry into the washer and made more coffee. As she waited for it to perk, she considered the source of the paintings and coins. If they belonged to someone else, who could it be? And why had Eva been storing them? Maybe the third crate held the answers.

Fifteen minutes later, she went back to the attic with cups of coffee. Marc had removed the lids from the two wooden crates, and coins were scattered on the floor beside him, roughly arranged in groups. The third crate remained undisturbed, waiting for the locksmith.

"Have you found anything good?" she asked as she handed him a cup of coffee and sat on the floor beside him.

"This first box has a wide variety of coins, although it's not very well organized."

"What does a wide variety mean?"

Marc paused, looking at the coins on the floor. "It seems that the overall theme is historical. The oldest coins are from ancient Greece."

Zélie's eyes widened. "From two thousand years ago?"

He nodded. "Roman coins follow. I need a reference book to verify everything, but I think that there's a coin for every emperor of the Roman Empire. Not that unusual, actually. Many Roman coins survive."

"Are you serious?" she asked, wondering why a collection would focus on such an ancient period in history.

"Absolutely," he said, grabbing another handful of coins from the box. "But there's more. The historical theme continues with coins minted throughout the Middle Ages, mainly from England and France."

Zélie hesitated, trying to absorb it all. Then she realized what he was implying. "It took a lot of effort to create this collection," she said. "Research, auctions, antique shops."

He nodded. "The coins present a timeline. For example, I found a coin for every king or queen in the Tudor dynasty."

"It's a collection that was painstakingly assembled —someone who loved what they were doing."

"Exactly," he said. "And they likely spent a lifetime doing it. Or it may have been passed down through generations."

She was quiet, wondering where it came from. "What do you think their value is?"

Marc shrugged. "It's hard to say. We need an expert to assess them. But I think they're probably priceless."

Now she was even more suspicious. "What about the second box?"

"Silver and gold coins, dated over the last seventy or eighty years, from Australia, Canada, and South Africa. All highly collectable, though more for their gold and silver content than anything else."

"It's almost like someone was hiding their wealth," she said. "There are no receipts, bank statements—no trail of where it all came from or what it might be worth."

He looked at her with a solemn expression. "That's what it seems like."

Zélie studied the boxes, more mysterious than ever, and maybe more valuable than the paintings. Never mentioned by anyone. Secrets protecting a fortune.

"The coins are like the paintings," Marc said. "They're surrounded by questions."

She pointed to the third crate. "Maybe the answer lies in there."

Almost on cue, the doorbell rang. "We may know in a few minutes," Marc said.

Zélie went down to answer the door and returned a few minutes later with an older man wearing work clothes —matching green slacks and shirt—and carrying a pouch with tools in it.

"M. Lambert," she said. "This is Marc Rayne."

Marc nodded and pointed to the third crate, the face of the exposed lockbox showing. "Do you think you can do anything with this?"

The locksmith knelt beside it, a wary look on his face. "The crate was built around it. The lockbox wasn't put into an existing crate."

"Does that matter?" Zélie asked.

"It could," Lambert replied. He spent the next few minutes fingering the combination lock and studying the key cylinder.

"Any suggestions?" Marc asked.

Lambert shrugged. "You don't have many options. These Nazi lockboxes can be tricky."

"Can't you drill out the locks?" Marc asked.

"I can," Lambert replied. "But sometimes they're rigged. If the locks are tampered with, a chemical is released to destroy the contents." He paused, his expression stern. "Sometimes it's worse than that."

Zélie was alarmed. "Are we in danger?"

"I don't think so," Lambert said. "But I'm very reluctant to tamper with the locks."

"Can we just cut the side of the lockbox with a saw and gain access that way?" Marc asked.

Lambert hesitated. "That might work. But it won't be easy."

"What do you suggest?" Zélie asked.

Lambert stood and glanced at the collection of crates and boxes. "Make every attempt to find the key and combination. They might be here somewhere."

"What if we can't find it?" Zélie asked.

"Then and only then should you make any effort to breach the lockbox," Lambert said sternly. "It's just too dangerous."

Chapter Sixty-Six

Montmartre, 1874

Elise Lyon sat in the parlor with Henri, enjoying a glass of wine after dinner. It was a rare moment spent together—he normally retired to his study—and she wondered if he had a motive, something he wanted to share or a question he might want to ask.

"I've received no updates from Babin," she said, assuming he might be dwelling on the assaults.

Henri sipped his wine and slowly shook his head. "He may have an excellent reputation, but he hasn't demonstrated how he earned it."

"Do you think he should have made an arrest?"

"I expect anything resembling progress, but I haven't seen it."

She hesitated, not sure whether to continue or change the subject. "He seems to be taking some action," she said. "I think someone is watching me."

His eyes widened. "Why do you say that? Have you seen them?"

"No," she admitted. "It's just a feeling. I thought it might be Babin or policemen he assigned to thwart another attack."

"Someone stalked the woman who was murdered, too," he warned. "He then waited on a dark, deserted lane until she wandered along. Just as someone did with you."

She shivered, his words so eerily spoken. "I'm not concerned," she assured him. "The coachman has been very diligent in protecting me. He waits outside the studio door during my sessions and does the same wherever I go, even the orphanage."

"Someone could still be watching you," he said. "Although I doubt it's Babin. The thought wouldn't occur to him."

"I'm sure the inspector is making progress. He just can't share it with us. He's probably identified a suspect and waits to make a move."

"I don't think so," Henri muttered. "Babin and Dumont are spinning in circles, accomplishing nothing."

"Babin has never had an unsolved crime," she said delicately.

"He hasn't found the murderer, nor has he found the culprit who attacked you," Henri said. "I suspect he assigns his unsolved crimes to underlings just to keep his reputation intact."

"Like Lieutenant Dumont."

"Yes. I suppose," he mumbled, lighting a cigar. He puffed on it, ensuring the flame caught, and spewed cherry smoke in Elise's direction.

She sipped her wine, watching him closely. "You seem distracted this evening."

He shrugged. "It's a business matter," he said. "I reached an agreement with Andre Sinclair today."

"I'm surprised. You seemed far apart only days ago."

Henri chuckled. "He came to his senses and realized he was in a precarious position."

She hesitated. Henri had a passion for destruction, and she feared he might have employed it. "I hope the agreement benefits both parties."

"I gave him generous terms—better than he'd find elsewhere."

She realized he hadn't answered her question. "Advantageous to each of you?"

He shrugged. "He got what he wanted, and I took what he wanted most."

She wasn't sure what he meant. "You sound like you're waging war. He's not a rival. You hold a loan, nothing more."

He chuckled. "I enjoy the chase, the hunt. The look in an adversary's eyes when he realizes he's cornered, caught in a cage of his own making, and I'm circling for the kill."

"Henri, you sound like a savage!"

He laughed, apparently proud of himself. "It's how you succeed in business," he claimed. "Most of all, I like taking what my opponent values most."

She was leery of his boasted success. "And what does M. Sinclair value most?"

"The yearling."

Her eyes widened. "Golden Cross?"

"Yes," Henri confirmed. "It's his most prized possession, so I structured the agreement around the horse. But I gave him everything he wanted."

"I'm surprised he would part with it. Those in Deauville claim he loves that horse above all else."

"Who wouldn't?" Henri asked. "The horse is a guaranteed champion. You've seen his bloodline."

She nodded. "Yes, I have," she said, thinking it was still unusual. "He had nothing else to give?"

"He had nothing I would take."

She frowned, watching as he blew cherry smoke about the room.

"You don't approve?" he asked, observing her reaction.

She shrugged. "It seems a lot for M. Sinclair to lose."

"Not really," he said. "His business is failing. I helped prop it up. He has enough problems anyway."

She knitted her eyebrows. "What problems?"

"Babin still insists he's a prime suspect."

"I don't understand why," she said, shaking her head. "He seems a quiet man who keeps to himself."

Henri snickered. "Most murderers are."

"Why does Andre Sinclair want to kill me?"

Henri shrugged. "Revenge for losing the yearling, I suppose. Just another of Babin's absurd theories."

She thought for a moment, eyeing her husband cautiously. "It would be very simple to prove."

"How is that?" he asked, looking at her curiously.

"Don't take the yearling, and see if there's another attempt on my life."

Chapter Sixty-Seven

Deauville, 1956

Deauville had a small but well-equipped library, fitting for a town of its size. It occupied a stucco building, white with brown trim, on a corner a few blocks from the beach. Marc Rayne decided to visit, hoping he could learn more about the growing mysteries in Zélie's attic. The details about the WWII spy network should be the easiest to research, having occurred only twelve years before. But he knew much of what had happened was shrouded in secrecy and might not be known for years—after all involved had been dead and buried.

The library wasn't far from his cottage, but it was too many blocks to walk for a man with a crippled leg. Marc got into his red Renault and drove over, finding the building clean, stacked with well-organized shelves and several staff members willing to assist.

"I'm wondering if you can help me?" he asked a young woman behind the counter. "I'm looking for records of Deauville newspapers from early 1944, before the invasion."

The woman rose from her desk. "I'll show you where they are," she said, leading him to the back of the library. "We have originals for later papers, and we just converted some of our older records to microfilm."

"Thank you so much," he said as he followed her into a room filled with wide filing cabinets, a table in the center. "Do you have anything as far back as 1874?"

She paused, thinking for a moment. "Yes, a few," she said, pointing to a micro viewer. "We keep aperture slides in those small drawers, which you insert into this viewer. But we don't have a large assortment. For detailed research you would have to go to the library in Rouen."

"Thank you," he said with a smile. "That's something I should consider, I suppose." Rouen was only eighty kilometers away. He could do that in a day if he left early enough.

She pointed to a cabinet against the back wall. "All the papers from the war are kept here, stored in plastic sleeves. Please handle them carefully and return everything to its original location. If you have any problems with the viewer or the aperture cards, come and get me, and I'll be happy to assist."

"I will," he promised. "Thank you so much for your help."

The clerk left, and Marc started going through drawers that contained copies of a local Deauville paper, neatly arranged in chronological order. It was exactly what he was hoping for. As he scanned the first few papers, he wondered if journalists had any control over what they wrote. Probably not. The Nazis would have censored everything. But even if they had been, the capture and execution of local spies would have been boldly printed, to discourage others from doing the same.

He started in January, 1944 and leafed through the papers quickly. An event as monumental as outing a local spy ring would most likely appear on the first page, so he searched no further, flipping through each daily paper. He found what he was looking for on May 8, 1944. He took the folder out of the cabinet and sat at the table.

He removed the paper from its plastic sheath, the headline screaming: 'Local man killed as spy network uncovered.' He took a notebook from his pocket and started writing. Gaston Girard, Zélie's father-in-law, was identified as the man killed during a raid on a Resistance safe house. Several Allied airmen were captured, but other Resistance members escaped.

Marc continued reading, but the article had no more information beyond what Anton had already told him. He returned the paper to the cabinet and continued searching. He next found what he wanted on May 18, 1944.

The headline read: 'Several arrested in connection with Resistance spy ring.' The article described the arrests of the Chards, Louis and Marie, and claimed the wealthy citizens of Deauville were the ringleaders. Victor LaRue, Anton's father, had also been captured along with several others from neighboring towns. The article claimed they had been betrayed, though the name of the informant was not provided.

Marc jotted down all the information, the names of those apprehended, and the detailed information provided on the Chards, the couple identified as the group's leaders who were apparently citizens of some note. He returned the paper to the cabinet and started looking through the remainder. The next paper that caught his attention was dated May 25, 1944 and described the execution of the Chards by firing squad and confiscation of their personal belongings. A Gestapo colonel named Hans Fischer, his current and former address provided, was quoted in the article, warning citizens that further arrests were expected.

Normandy was invaded by Allied forces on June 6th. Marc leafed through the papers through the end of June. The town had been under siege, so many days were missing; he found no further information. But what he had found was disturbing enough.

Hans Fischer, the Gestapo colonel quoted in the article, had been quartered in one of the cottages now owned by Zélie Girard.

Chapter Sixty-Eight

Montmartre, 1874

The black carriage had no police markings, was unremarkable in design and construction, and was similar to many others that rattled down the cobblestone streets of Paris. It was quietly parked on a winding lane that stretched from the top of the Montmartre hill, just past a bookshop. The crooked road wound around a corner to the artist's studio, the last house in the row, and then ramped down between stone walls to the boulevard below.

The driver wore plain clothes, and, after tending to the horses, he left the carriage and walked to the corner, leaning on a lamp post with a newspaper spread between opened arms. In the passengers' compartment, Inspector Babin and Lieutenant Dumont patiently waited. From their vantage point atop the hill, they could see the back wheels of the carriage parked in front of the artist's studio and knew Mme. Lyon was inside.

Occasionally, her bored coachman appeared, stepping down from the carriage to pace the pavement. A few moments later he was no longer in view, likely returning to the coach to nap or scan the newspaper. Residents wandered the street, children playing, women talking or visiting the handful of shops that occupied the lower floors of the mismatched buildings that made the block. None had any interest in the carriages parked along the lane, scattered among a few others.

"Detective work can be tedious," Babin said after they had waited forty minutes, looking at nothing more than the back of Mme. Lyon's carriage. "Probably not what you expected when you came to Paris."

"I know investigations can be boring," Dumont replied. "I've been a policeman for a decade, although I sometimes wonder where the time has gone."

"I suspect, no matter how tedious our investigation becomes, it is far more exciting than the tiny town from which you came, conducting the minor police work that the community required. Was a serious crime ever committed that warranted a detailed investigation?"

Dumont pursed his lips. "Nothing compares to Paris or the criminals it contains. The villages in the city's shadows sleepily exist, some never knowing how evil people can be."

"I'm sorry to say that Paris does hide the master criminal," Babin continued, "those who have honed their skills through years of illegal activity. They pose a challenge to even the most gifted investigator. But I have dedicated my life to solving the crimes they commit, making the city a safer place for its citizens."

"The residents admire you for it, I'm sure," Dumont said, glancing out the carriage window at two young boys playing ball.

"Yes, perhaps," Babin muttered, craning his neck to see more of Mme. Lyon's carriage. "We've observed three sessions between Mme. Lyon and Jean-Pierre. Let us presume, for argument's sake, that she is posing, and he is painting. Have you identified the established pattern, Lieutenant?"

Dumont rolled his eyes. "I have, Inspector," he replied. "The sessions rotate through the day, morning, afternoon, and early evening."

"Why do you think that is?"

"To capture variations of natural light as the sun travels across the sky."

Babin shrugged. "Yes, I suppose that could be true," he admitted. "But I suspect that lack of routine suggests a more nefarious purpose."

Dumont didn't seem convinced. "What might that be?"

"Could it be that the random schedule prevents M. Lyon from observing the sessions, should he choose to?" Babin asked. "Maybe he's never quite sure, on any given day, when his wife might be at the studio, and the demands of his business prevent his attendance."

"I'm not sure I agree," Dumont said. "M. Lyon likely knows exactly when the sessions are. He probably has no interest in them."

"Ah, Lieutenant Dumont, exactly what a novice would suggest. But that poses a very interesting question."

Dumont sighed, tired of the verbal jousting. "Why isn't M. Lyon interested in his wife's portrait?"

"Exactly," Babin said. "What man wouldn't take an avid interest in his wife's activities, especially after two attempts have been made on her life? Wouldn't most men hover over their spouse, worried for her welfare, ensuring they knew where she was at any time of day and that she faced no danger? Wouldn't the loving husband be concerned?"

"Yes, of course," Dumont said. "But we don't know that M. Lyon isn't concerned. The coachman stands guard over Mme. Lyon, at least when she's in the studio."

"The question I have, the same for any experienced investigator, is what is M. Lyon doing while Mme. Lyon is posing?"

Dumont's eyes widened. "Maybe we should be watching him, instead of Mme. Lyon?"

"You are learning," Babin said. "I'm very impressed with you, Lieutenant Dumont. Because that's precisely what we are about to do. Tomorrow we will watch M. Lyon. We may be surprised by what we see."

Chapter Sixty-Nine

Deauville, 1956

The stands at the Deauville racetrack were packed with a frenzied crowd, all cheering for their favorite horse. Zélie and Luc sat in the highest row on the left, the only seats available. Anton was racing Silver Shadow in the fifth race, and they waited anxiously, watching the races that came before it.

Luc stared, wide-eyed, at everything around him. “Maman, maybe I’ll race horses one day.”

“You might,” Zélie said. “But it’s very hard work. M. LaRue is at the stables all day.” She smiled as she watched him, so mesmerized by the crowds, the excitement, the respect the jockeys earned, and the speed of the horses.

Luc turned to face her. “But I like to ride horses.”

“Yes, I know you do,” Zélie said. Horses had been good for him—and so had Marc and Anton. Two weeks had passed since his last nightmare, and he was slowly adapting, both to his new home and the loss of his papa and grand-mère.

An announcer called each race over the loud speaker as a dozen horses galloped around the track. Zélie wondered why she never knew Eva was such an enthusiast—especially given the excitement true fans felt. But Samuel, her husband, must have known. Maybe he thought it wasn’t important. Or maybe he thought it was, and that’s why he never mentioned it.

When the fifth race came, Anton LaRue was in the eighth gate of twelve horses. Zélie watched intently, her heart racing, her fists tightly clenched. She leaned close to Luc. "M. LaRue is up," she said. "He's in the eighth slot."

Luc started cheering and stood to get a better view. Those in the crowd were loud, screaming for their favorite horse. Zélie leaned forward as the start command was issued, and the horses rocketed from the gate.

"Go, M. LaRue!" Luc yelled. "Go!"

Zélie's body tensed, her gaze riveted to the track, as the horses rounded the first curve. She yelled, as did everyone else, urging Silver Shadow forward, coaxing Anton to victory. Rounding the first turn, he was third, wedged against the rail.

The horses raced for the second turn, their positions barely changing, the jockeys fighting for an advantage. Anton led Silver Shadow away from the rail, finding a narrow gap in the pack, pushing him toward the front. Zélie watched the horse's stride, his muscled legs and torso, the magical rhythm of his movement, amazed at the animal's strength. As the pack rounded the next curve, Silver Shadow edged into second place, challenging the leader.

"Go, Anton, go!" she cheered, leaping to her feet, unable to control herself.

She kept screaming encouragement, Luc beside her also yelling, as Silver Shadow slowly gained. The horses came down the backstretch, Silver Shadow pushing the leader, another horse half a length behind. As they entered the third curve, the three horses were so close together no one could tell who was winning. When they came out of the curve, headed for the final turn, a fourth horse was quickly gaining.

Zélie was overwhelmed, her hands clammy, her heart racing, her voice hoarse. She was beginning to understand what Eva found so addicting, the thrill of having your horse fight for the lead. And it was even better when your favorite jockey rode him. She smiled, suspecting she liked Anton much more than she was willing to admit or that she had even realized.

The three lead horses rounded the final curve, the fourth a half-length behind. Anton lifted his slender frame in the saddle close to Silver Shadow's neck as if whispering in his ear. With each meter they ran, the horses fought harder. A black horse, number nine, who had led the entire race, appeared to falter slightly, and was overtaken by a chestnut horse, number two. But he was quickly challenged by Silver Shadow who rapidly began to pull ahead. Anton had saved the horse's strength for the end when it was needed most.

As the horses sprinted down the homestretch, Silver Shadow sprang forward, responding like the champion he was destined to become. With long, powerful strides no other horse could match, he thrust ahead, faster and more powerful than those who quickly fell behind. By the time they reached the finish line, Silver Shadow won by more than six lengths, his closest competitors bunched together in a battle for second. It was a stunning performance, an awe-inspiring display of power few, if any, horses could match. Those in the frenzied crowd knew it; they sensed they had just seen a champion, and their frantic cries displayed it.

As the race ended, all who saw it realized Silver Shadow was a horse who came once in a generation, destined to be a champion. And so was Anton LaRue.

Chapter Seventy

Montmartre, 1874

Jean-Pierre stood at the studio window, watching Mme. Michel stroll down the cobblestone lane. She walked away from the hill, passing four or five houses, and stopped abruptly. After peeking around the edge of a building, she turned and nodded to Jean-Pierre.

"The fool," Jean-Pierre muttered. "Babin still waits around the corner."

"We need to be wary," Elise cautioned. "He could barge in at any time."

"Mme. Michel will warn us," he said. "She can be helpful at times. Especially when asked to involve herself in someone else's business."

Elise smiled. "She can also be a nuisance."

He shrugged. "She means well. Although not a single secret has been kept for more than a minute or two."

"It will all be different someday," Elise promised, referring to far more than Mme. Michel.

He came close, glanced back at the window to make sure no one watched, and kissed her lightly on the lips. "We wasted the afternoon painting."

She smiled. "Yes, we did. But too many people, like Mme. Michel and Inspector Babin, might see something they shouldn't."

"He's convinced he's a brilliant detective," Jean-Pierre said. "Forgive him because he doesn't realize what a buffoon he is. Did he think no one would find his carriage, only fifty meters away?"

"I don't understand why he watches me. Shouldn't he search for the culprit?"

"He doesn't know what to do," he said, returning to the canvas. "He thinks he's protecting you. I'm sure he'll follow you home again." He shook his head, lips curled with disdain. "As if no one realizes they're the police because no markings appear on their carriage."

"It wouldn't bother me if I truly thought he was protecting me. But I think he has an ulterior motive."

Jean-Pierre chuckled. "He would rather catch us doing something we shouldn't be doing."

"Which he already did," she reminded him. She paused, pensive. "I wonder if Babin suspects Henri."

Jean-Pierre shrugged, moving the brush against the canvas, delicately forming the fine lines that, when combined, create a work of art. "How can he not?"

"Just because Babin suspects we're lovers doesn't mean that Henri does."

"But he soon will," Jean-Pierre said. "Especially if I don't finish your portrait. One or two more sessions, at most."

"I wish we could just leave," she said. "Run away and never come back."

He smiled, still painting. "You would leave Paris?"

"Yes."

"And go back to Deauville, the little village by the sea?"

"I wouldn't hesitate. Or I'd live here and spend summers on the coast."

"You could do that now. Henri has a cottage there. A small mansion, actually."

"Henri and I met in Deauville," she muttered, slowly shaking her head. "It seems like ages ago."

He paused, watching her for a moment. "Regrets are anchors that keep us from swimming away," he said.

"Tomorrow never comes because we keep reliving yesterday."

She hesitated. She knew he was right. "I saved my father from debtor's prison. And I would do it again if I had to. But I've spent a year of my life confined to a cage."

"Surrounded by luxuries," he added, teasing.

She smiled. "I would rather be poor."

"We should stop for the day," he said abruptly. "We don't want our routine to change. It would make them even more suspicious."

"I'll be glad when there is no routine."

"Soon, I'm sure," Jean-Pierre said. "But as long as Babin is watching, we can take no chances."

Chapter Seventy-One

Deauville, 1956

While Zélie and Luc enjoyed their day at the racetrack watching Anton's victory, Marc continued his investigation at the Deauville library. He found no additional information regarding the Resistance movement in the newspaper files and not a single mention of Eva Girard. It seemed strange that every other person Anton referenced was identified in various reports. Maybe Eva had escaped detection, and the Gestapo had assumed only her husband was involved. Even though Anton said she had been questioned, he could have been mistaken.

He next went to the small drawers that held the long, narrow aperture cards, which he slid into a viewer. He flipped from one image to another in either direction using small knobs. It proved to be tedious. The files weren't well labelled, usually marked with only the year, not a complete date. He sorted through what was in the drawer and eventually found several cards labeled 1874, a date referenced on two of the paintings in Zélie's attic.

It was time consuming to scan the cards, which used a few local newspapers as sources, with an occasional article from Paris. His task was made more complicated because he wasn't sure what he was looking for. But he knew everything was linked to Montmartre, so he focused on articles about Paris, especially those related to crimes.

He was halfway through the stack when he found a report about a murder, a young woman believed to be a prostitute, who had modeled for an unnamed artist. The article described the murder scene—a narrow street in Montmartre that climbed from one boulevard to the next, hemmed in by stone walls. Marc read the description several times and then jotted it down in his notebook. It was eerily similar to the painting in Zélie's attic. He continued scanning the story, pushing slides through the viewer, and came to the woman's description: slender, early twenties, blond hair, blue eyes. A sketch at the end closely resembled the nude painting in Zélie's attic. The woman's name: Giselle Picard.

Marc was excited, his heart racing, as the clues gradually emerged. The article went on to describe the murder and the impending investigation—those who might be involved and efforts made by the police to find the killer. Marc had successfully identified two more paintings: the murder scene in Montmartre and the murder victim. He continued combing through slides, finding an update posted the following day, which stated that the killer remained at large, and, even though a multitude of people had been questioned, including the artist Giselle modeled for, there were no suspects. The case was overseen by the famed Inspector Nicolas Babin, known for his investigative flair and a unique handlebar moustache. He was assisted by Lieutenant Claude Dumont.

Marc stared at the viewer, unable to believe what he read. Not only had both policeman in the Montmartre Prefecture painting now been identified, one of them may have left the note claiming the paintings were clues to solving a crime. He had signed the initials CD: Claude Dumont.

He anxiously scanned the remaining slides for 1874 but found only scattered information—several newspapers for a single day, then nothing for an entire week. He finished the slides labeled 1874 and began to check those from 1875, still looking for details: Had the crime been solved? Who was the killer? Who was the artist? What had happened to the policemen? But he found nothing more. Several pages of his notebook were filled with details from two tragedies, the murder of a woman in 1874, and the ruin of a Resistance spy network that met a horrific end only twelve years before. He would have to go to the library at Rouen if he wanted to learn more, and he intended to do so.

He couldn't wait to tell Zélie.

Chapter Seventy-Two

Montmartre, 1874

Inspector Babin sat behind his desk in a cluttered office at police district headquarters. Lieutenant Dumont was perched on a chair against the wall, a painting of the Pont Neuf bridge hanging above him, a coat rack beside him with the inspector's baggy police jacket draped upon it. A clerk tapped on the door and led Andre Sinclair into the office.

"Please, sit down, M. Sinclair," Babin offered, motioning to a chair in front of the desk. "What have you come to tell us?"

"I have some interesting information for you," Sinclair offered.

"And what might that be?" Babin asked, glancing at his pocket watch.

"It's about Lyon."

Babin shared a glance with Dumont, but his gaze returned to Sinclair. "And you think it's something we don't already know?"

"I'm sure it's something you don't already know."

"Then please enlighten us," Babin said. "Lieutenant Dumont and I are always willing to listen. We are trying to solve a serious crime, more than one, it seems."

Sinclair eyed the two men before him as if he wondered whether or not to trust them. "Lyon has a small apartment, nondescript. The entrance is in an alley off the main boulevard."

"How did you learn of this?" Dumont asked, withdrawing a notebook from his pocket.

"I have sources," Sinclair said tersely.

"And why are you spying on Henri Lyon?" Babin asked.

"Because he is trying to destroy me," Sinclair replied. "I have no other choice."

Babin sat stoically, having dealt with many men throughout his career. He paused, studied Sinclair a moment more, and turned to Dumont. "Lieutenant, I will conduct this interview. We'll see if M. Sinclair has valid information to share. Listen closely. The discussion will offer valuable insight into how a proper interrogation should be conducted."

"Yes, of course," Dumont said, blushing faintly. "I'll take notes, as needed."

Babin eyed Sinclair curiously, trying to gauge his sincerity. "All right, M. Sinclair, so you have proven M. Lyon has a small apartment not far from his office. Is that correct?"

"Yes."

"And next you will tell me that he often spends a couple hours there in the afternoon."

Sinclair showed surprise. "Yes, he does."

"Now you are going to tell me he has a mistress."

Sinclair didn't reply. After a moment, he merely nodded.

"Do you think Henri Lyon is the only wealthy man in Paris who has a secret apartment?"

Sinclair hesitated. It wasn't the reception he had expected. "No, I suppose not."

"Do you think he's the only man in Paris who has a mistress?"

Sinclair shifted in his seat. "No."

Babin clasped his hands over his huge belly. "Then you have only told me something that I already knew or that I could deduce from evidence already in my possession."

"He has more than one mistress," Sinclair countered.

"Ah, so M. Lyon has more than one mistress," Babin said. "Do you think he is the only man in Paris with more than one mistress?"

"No, I don't."

"Then perhaps your information is not as valuable as you think."

"The information is valuable because of who the mistresses are," Sinclair clarified.

Babin arched an eyebrow. "I'm listening, M. Sinclair. Who are his mistresses?"

"There are three, actually."

"Please, enlighten us," Babin continued, glancing at Dumont, who jotted down notes.

"A young woman, possibly a prostitute, Mlle. Sophie Delacroix," Sinclair said. "Mme. Angelique St. Pierre, a married woman with whom Lyon has carried on a lifelong affair and Mme. Jeanette Richelieu."

Babin paused, waiting for Dumont to capture the information. "Mme. Jeanette Richelieu, wife of the finance minister?"

Sinclair nodded. "One and the same."

"M. Lyon is having an affair with the wife of the man who oversees financial companies in Paris?" Babin asked.

"Yes," Sinclair said.

"Scandalous," Babin said. "Absolutely scandalous."

Sinclair grinned. "I thought that might interest you."

"Actually, M. Sinclair, it's of no interest at all," Babin said. "Scandal and gossip rarely fuel the crimes that I am forced to investigate."

Sinclair smiled slyly, not deterred. "Maybe the identity of a prostitute that M. Lyon used to frequent would interest you."

Babin shrugged. "Perhaps, or perhaps not. Tell us, and we'll make that determination."

"Her name was Giselle Picard."

Chapter Seventy-Three

Deauville, 1956

Zélie was in the kitchen washing dishes when she saw Marc crossing the lawn, limping badly but moving as quickly as he could. She marveled at how crucial a few seconds in life can sometimes be—all it took for an assailant to take aim, fire, and change his life forever.

"Good afternoon," she said as she opened the door,

"Hello, Zélie."

"You look flustered," she said, eyeing him strangely.

He grinned. "Not flustered, excited. I've just come from the library. They had records of old newspapers."

Zélie gave him her complete attention. "About Eva or the portraits?"

"Both," he said. "Let's go look at the paintings. I want to be sure."

As they started for the attic, Zélie wondered what he could have learned. Marc was a calm man, not prone to excitement. But he certainly seemed excited now.

"I'm starting to tie everything together," he said, winded as he maneuvered the steps.

They entered the attic and paused in front of the paintings, still leaning against the wall in the sequence they had originally placed them.

Marc eyed the paintings carefully and then began. "I believe, from sketches in the 1874 newspapers, that the blond woman is Giselle Picard who was murdered in Montmartre." He moved her portrait to the far end.

Zélie looked at him curiously. "How can you be so certain?"

"Her sketch was in the newspaper along with a description," he said as he moved the painting of the street scene next to Giselle.

Zélie was excited but waited patiently, knowing he had more to reveal.

"This street painting perfectly depicts the Montmartre murder scene," he continued. "The stone walls and dark street, tree limbs reaching over the walls."

Zélie arched her eyebrows. "We now have two of the clues," she said. "Giselle Picard was murdered on this lonely street in Montmartre."

"There's more," Marc said, still looking at the portraits. He moved the painting of the police station beside Giselle and the street scene. "These are the policeman who investigated the murder. A famous detective named Nicolas Babin, which we already knew from Professor Dufour, and this man is his assistant, Lieutenant Claude Dumont."

Zélie's eyes widened. "Claude Dumont! The initials on the note."

"Exactly," he said, beaming. "These three paintings are definitely linked together. The victim was a model for a local artist."

She hesitated. "Was Jean-Pierre the killer?"

Marc shrugged. "If he was, Professor Dufour would have known. She's coming tomorrow to authenticate the paintings. We can ask her."

"Assuming he was caught," Zélie added.

"And if so, was he convicted?" Marc clarified.

"We know from Professor Dufour that the artist's studio is Jean Pierre's," she said, moving the portrait near the three linked with the crime but leaving a space.

Marc pointed at the remaining four, grouped in pairs. "Two portraits of the dark-haired woman and two associated with Andre Sinclair—Normandy Mines and Golden Cross."

"What did you learn about Eva?"

"Nothing specifically," he said, referring to his notebook. "But Gaston, your father-in-law, was killed when the country safe house was raided on May 8th, 1944. Those in the network, including Anton LaRue's father, were arrested on May 18th. And the Chards, who were apparently wealthy and had a large home out past the racetrack, had all their belongings confiscated. They were executed on May 25th. The Allied invasion was June 6th, which is the only explanation for Anton's father being released."

Zélie paused, thinking. "Maybe Eva wasn't involved in the network."

"Maybe not," Marc said. "But the Gestapo colonel who exposed the network lived in one of the cottages—Hans Fischer, originally from Munich."

Zélie had an uneasy feeling in the pit of her stomach. "You're certain?"

"I am," he said. "At least according to the newspapers."

She was quiet for a moment, wondering what to do next. "I went through everything in the attic, looking for the key to the lockbox, but I didn't find anything. Do you think we should search the cottages?"

Marc nodded. "Fischer may have left a clue behind."

Zélie sighed. "I suppose we need to find out."

Chapter Seventy-Four

Montmartre, 1874

"Where were you?" Elise asked as Henri entered the dining room. She had already finished her first two courses and had started on the main entree, chicken confit. He had been habitually late over the past few weeks, often leaving her to dine alone. It made her suspicious. Or maybe he had always been late, and she only recently noticed, alerted by her own behavior.

"Business," he muttered, not really offering a reply. He sat at the end of the table and motioned to Sebastian who stood by the buffet.

"What business?" she asked.

His eyes widened, hinting she may have overstepped. "Business," he repeated louder. "That's all you need to know." He sat back in the chair as Sebastian put a bowl of onion soup before him.

She eyed him coldly for a moment but didn't reply. She returned to her meal but ate slowly, waiting for him as he spooned his soup. When he finished, he again nodded to Sebastian. The servant cleared the empty bowl and served the second course, a plate covered with various cheese wedges.

"No more attacks?" he asked, studying the cheese before placing a piece in his mouth.

"No," she said tersely.

"Have you seen Babin or Dumont?"

She sampled a forkful of chicken before replying. "Sometimes when I leave my session, I notice them at the base of the hill, near the boulevard."

"Good," he said. "They should be protecting you."

"If that's what they're doing."

He looked at her curiously. "What else would they be doing?"

She shrugged. "They never told me they were watching me, but I see them whenever I go to the studio."

He was quiet, focused on dinner. After a few mouthfuls, he sipped his wine. "I told them to protect you. If they don't, and I'm forced to hire private security, I'll ensure the whole city knows how incompetent they are."

"They must have listened because I see them everywhere."

"They should be everywhere. They're paid civil servants. Something Babin often forgets."

She sipped her wine, her thoughts drifting. "Have you finalized the agreement with Andre Sinclair? Is that the business that delayed you?"

"Yes, I did," he said, partially replying. "I took the yearling."

"And extended his loan?"

He nodded. "But Normandy Mines still has issues. I only postponed the inevitable. Although I at least gave him time to recover."

Elise frowned. She wished they could have negotiated different terms. All of Deauville knew how much the yearling meant to Sinclair—it was his most prized possession. Henri could be hostile when he wanted. He enjoyed it. "Do you think Normandy Mines will fail?"

He shrugged. "That's up to Sinclair."

"What about you?"

"If I wanted it to fail, it would have already happened. But I don't."

"He seems like such a good man," she said. "Can't you work with him?"

"He is a good man," he agreed. "But he's a bad businessman. I helped him tremendously, but he doesn't even realize it. Someone will notice that Normandy Mines is in trouble, and they'll take advantage of it."

She was quiet, returning to her dinner. She finished her chicken and sat back while Sebastian cleared her plate. "I'll wait for M. Lyon," she said, referring to the next course.

"When will your portrait be finished?" Henri asked as Sebastian removed his empty plate and replaced it with the main course.

"Another session, maybe two. It's almost done."

"It's taking a long time," he said. "I need to understand why."

She eyed him curiously. "How long does it normally take?" she asked. "I've never had my portrait done before."

He shrugged. "I know nothing about it."

"Then how do you know it's taking a long time?"

"I don't," he replied. "But I do know that you go to the studio two or three times a week. It seems like you should be done."

"I don't think the process is any different for me than anyone else," she said, trying not to argue. She didn't want to make him any more suspicious than he already was. She had to make sure he didn't find out that she didn't spend all of her sessions posing.

"When is your next session?"

"Friday at six p.m."

He took a bite of roasted potatoes and chewed it thoughtfully. "Why in the evening?"

"It has to do with the light. I explained it to you before."

"Interesting," he muttered, although he wasn't very interested at all.

"Artists are fascinated by light."

"What goes on in these sessions?" he asked. "Do you just sit there while he paints?"

"Yes, for the most part," she said. "We stop sometimes, so I can move around. It's hard to pose for a long period of time."

"What happens when he isn't painting?"

"Nothing, really," she said. "We talk for a few minutes, or he goes in another room and cleans his brushes. Sometimes neighbors watch the session and chat through the opened window."

"Friday at six p.m. is the next session?"

"Yes, why?"

"I want to observe it," he said, a hint of suspicion crawling across his face. "Just to see how painting a portrait is done."

Chapter Seventy-Five

Deauville, 1956

Zélie and Marc went out the back door and started across the lawn. "I searched my cottage already," Marc said. "But I didn't find anything."

"I'm not even sure what we're looking for," Zélie said.

He shrugged. "Anything that can be connected to the Gestapo colonel or might lead to the lockbox. A key or note, even a hidden safe."

"It's been twelve years since he's been here though," Zélie said as she unlocked the door of the vacant cottage. "Many people have rented the cottage, especially for holiday lets, and Eva did some upgrades and purchased new furniture—I saw the receipts. If he did leave clues, they're probably gone."

They stepped inside, finding a furnished parlor with a small kitchen behind it, two bedrooms to the right with a bath between them. Zélie eyed the rooms carefully as a prospective tenant might. She had to admit the paint was a bit dated, the furniture worn. Maybe she could gradually start to refurbish it—as soon as she got her finances in order.

Marc watched as she studied the rooms. "No rentals?"

Zélie shook her head. "No, not yet. I'm starting to get desperate."

"It'll rent," he assured her. "Just be patient." He scanned the cottage, assessing where something could be hidden. "Why don't you look in the kitchen?"

She wasn't sure what to do. "Should I just go through the cabinets?"

He nodded. "Look for any hidden compartments, check the baseboards to see if they're loose—anything that doesn't seem right. I'll go through the bedrooms, and we'll do the parlor last."

Fifteen minutes later, Marc emerged from the bedrooms. "Nothing here."

"Nothing in the kitchen," Zélie said. "I'll check the bath."

Marc started in the parlor. He checked for loose floorboards, baseboards that may have been removed and reattached, and then moved pictures on the wall, looking for secret compartments or safes behind them. But he found nothing. He was looking underneath the furniture when Zélie came out of the bathroom.

"I didn't find anything," she said.

Marc stood, struggling with his stiff leg. "No, me either," he said, disappointed. "I don't think there's anything here."

They left the cottage and were locking the door when Anton came up to the walk. Luc was with him, having seen his mother when he arrived home from school.

"What are you doing?" Anton asked. "Making sure the cottage is ready to rent?"

Zélie approached Luc while Marc took Anton aside and explained all they had recently learned. "How was your day at school?" she asked her son.

"It was good," Luc said. "I have a new friend."

Her eyes widened. "You do?"

"Yes, his name is Paul, and he lives two blocks away. We walked home together. And we're going to walk to school together tomorrow."

"Oh, Luc, that's wonderful!" Zélie said, relieved he was starting to adapt.

"Can he come over and play?"

"Yes, of course," Zélie said. "He can come whenever you want. Have him over for dinner if you like."

Anton and Marc finished their discussion and came over to them. "Marc and I are going to search my cottage," Anton said, casting a guarded glance at Luc. "Then I have some information to share. I talked to my father, and he had an unbelievable story to tell."

Zélie suspected she knew what he was going to say. But she hoped she was wrong. "Come over after dinner tonight. We can compare notes once Luc is asleep."

Chapter Seventy-Six

Montmartre, 1874

"It seems Lyon challenges legitimacy in both his business and personal life," Dumont remarked after Sinclair had left.

Babin was quiet, his elbows on his desk, his fingertips joined in an arch. "Does either concern us?"

Dumont looked at him curiously as if he didn't understand. "I think it's quite clear."

"Enlighten me, Lieutenant Dumont. Because we've developed different impressions from the same words that were spoken. Please, present your case for debate."

Dumont paused, framing his thoughts. "A young woman named Giselle Picard was murdered a little over a month ago," he stated. "The cause of death was strangulation."

"That is fact," Babin said, teacher to pupil.

"Two attempts to strangle Mme. Lyon have been made."

"That is a postulation."

"I don't understand," a perplexed Dumont said.

"Let's begin with the first attack on Mme. Lyon, which occurred in the same location as Giselle's murder," Babin said. "Almost as if the perpetrator wanted us to connect the two. But no one witnessed this attack. However, someone claims to have seen a man, possibly wearing a policeman's uniform, flee the scene."

"Mme. Lyon's face was bruised."

"That is fact," Babin said. "Mme. Lyon did have bruises on her face."

"I contend that we can assume they were made by the attacker."

"Assume?" Babin asked. "Policemen do not assume, Lieutenant, you should know that by now. They uncover the facts and systematically apply what evidence they find to frame a case for innocence or guilt. That is what policemen do."

Dumont frowned. "All right, I agree," he said. "But we know for a fact that Giselle was strangled to death."

"Agreed."

"We believe two attempts have been made to strangle Mme. Lyon, at least as it was reported by the victim herself."

"Agreed."

"And now we know that Henri Lyon was a frequent customer of Giselle's," Dumont said.

"No, we don't know that at all," Babin disagreed. "All we know is that Sinclair claims Lyon was a frequent customer of Giselle's."

"If proved as fact," Dumont continued, "then Lyon could have killed Giselle and made two attempts to strangle Mme. Lyon."

Babin nodded slightly. "Continue, Lieutenant. You have my attention."

"We discussed Lyon's temper, the throbbing vein on his forehead that betrays it. We also suggested that Giselle's killer could be a madman. Henri Lyon could very well fit that description, especially if Giselle's murder was a crime of passion."

"Pure conjecture," Babin scoffed and then wagged his finger at Dumont. "But it still warrants further investigation. If detectives did not develop theories, how would they know what to investigate? You surprise me sometimes, Lieutenant Dumont. I think you very well could have a future in police work."

Dumont paused, not sure if he had been complimented or insulted. "Do you doubt Sinclair's story?"

"What is his motive for uncovering these sordid details about Henri Lyon?" Babin asked. "I suggest that he wants to destroy Lyon before Lyon destroys him."

"Which doesn't mean he lied," Dumont said defensively.

"No, of course it doesn't," Babin agreed, sitting back in the chair and tracing the curve of his moustache with his index finger. "But maybe his source did."

Dumont was quiet, mentally walking along the path Babin led him.

"What we know," Babin continued, "at least according to Sinclair, is that he paid an unknown source to unearth scandalous information about Henri Lyon."

"Which happens all the time, I assume."

"Ah, again we assume," Babin said. "A word we should best avoid. But what if the man being paid only produced what the man who paid him wanted to hear?"

Dumont thought for a moment, speculating on Babin's statement. "Yes, I suppose that could be true," he admitted.

"But it could also be fact," Babin said. "We only need to determine the truth. Also, not to be overlooked, Lieutenant Dumont, is motive."

"Sinclair's motive for wanting information on Lyon?" Dumont asked.

"No, Lyon's motive for allegedly killing Giselle."

"Maybe he's a psychopath," Dumont offered. "Or there is no motive, only a temper he can't control."

"Or maybe he knew that his mistress, Giselle, and the artist, Jean-Pierre, were lovers."

"Then why send his wife to Jean-Pierre?" Dumont asked.

"To see if Mme. Lyon and Jean-Pierre would become lovers."

Dumont's eyes widened. "That makes no sense at all."

"It does, my dear Lieutenant," Babin said. "But only if you think as a demented man might."

Dumont studied the great detective, baffled by his response.

"I see you don't understand, so I will explain," Babin said. He paused, collecting his thoughts. "What if Lyon's deranged mind found Giselle's murder, and all that led up to it, very satisfying in some depraved way and sought to repeat it?"

"No sane man would do that!" Dumont declared, aghast.

"Exactly!" Babin exclaimed. "Now you are thinking like a true detective. No man in his right mind would ever do that. But a lunatic might."

Chapter Seventy-Seven

Deauville, 1956

"I'm not exactly sure what we're looking for," Marc explained as Anton led him into his cottage. "But I'm hoping this Colonel Fischer left something that leads to the lockbox in the attic. If not the key or combination, maybe a scribbled note or some other reference."

"It's worth conducting the search," Anton said. "My father told me the Gestapo commandeered all three of these cottages during the war."

"The Girards must have been very courageous, part of the Resistance while the Gestapo lived on their property."

"It may not have been as difficult as it seems," Anton said. "The cottages face the street, not Zélie's house. Maybe there was little interaction."

"Still intimidating, just the same."

Anton paused in the parlor. "How shall we do this?"

"I've been looking for a secret compartment, a place where a document or key may have been hidden," Marc said. "But I have no evidence that points to anything specific. I just felt like I had to check."

"I'll look behind the pictures on the walls," Anton offered. "Maybe there's a wall safe."

Marc scanned the cottage layout, which mimicked the other two. "I'll check floorboards and baseboards."

"Forgive the mess," Anton said with a shrug. "Tidiness was never my strong suit."

Marc chuckled. "No problem. I'm not the best housekeeper, either."

They worked together, moving from room to room, inspecting furniture, floors, paintings, mirrors, cabinets and fixtures. They ended their search in the kitchen, Marc watching Anton as he checked through each cabinet.

"Nothing," Anton said as he finished his inspection. "I probably would have noticed anything unusual, anyway."

"At least we looked," Marc said with a sigh of despair. "But it would have been so much easier if we found the key, or at least a note."

Anton shrugged. "It's one less thing to consider. We don't have to wonder what secrets the cottages may hold. Now we know there are none."

"Yes, I suppose you're right," Marc said as he started toward the kitchen door. He turned to leave, but paused, his gaze drawn to a painting hanging on the parlor wall.

"What's the matter?" Anton asked, looking at him strangely.

"I'm not sure," Marc mumbled as he went into the parlor.

"I looked behind the painting," Anton said. "There's nothing there."

Marc eyed the brass label on the frame. "Munich, Germany," he said. "Which happens to be the home of Hans Fischer." He removed the painting and felt along the paper backing, just along the frame. "I think I found something."

Anton watched curiously as Marc took a small pocketknife and gently sliced the paper, fingering a slender object. "What is it?"

Marc looked at him, eyes wide. "It's a key, stapled to the frame. Let me pry it loose."

"Is that what we're looking for?"

"I think so. And there's a paper wrapped around it."

Anton leaned closer as Marc unrolled the paper. "1944," he read. "It's a date."

Marc grinned. "It could be a date. But I think it's the combination. One-nine-forty-four."

Chapter Seventy-Eight

Montmartre, 1874

Andre Sinclair sat in a chair in front of Henri's desk. He was relaxed, hiding a smile, as he eyed Henri with amusement.

Henri was baffled by Sinclair's behavior. Something seemed wrong, but he didn't know what it was. "I don't understand what you're asking."

Sinclair sat back on the chair. "It's an opportunity to amend what was already done."

"Our deal is final," Henri insisted. "The yearling has already been taken to my stables in Deauville."

Sinclair eyed the man before him as if he wondered why he had ever feared him. "I'm in a gracious mood, Henri. The offer I'm about to make will reflect that."

Henri snickered. "I don't think you have an offer to make. I got what I wanted—Golden Cross—and you got what you wanted, an extension on your loan with generous terms. You should be grateful."

Sinclair removed papers from his leather satchel and laid them on the desk. "I did transfer ownership of Golden Cross," he agreed. "But this contract supersedes our original agreement—only because you were so accommodating. If you hadn't been, I would make a different proposal."

Henri was confused. Sinclair acted from strength but was weak. It made no sense. He took the papers and scanned the pages. After a moment, he frowned and glanced up at Sinclair. "This is a mistake."

Sinclair met his gaze, his face firm. "I don't think so."

"I took the yearling in exchange for an extension on your payment due," Henri said. "This contract states that the yearling settles the loan in its entirety. That's a ridiculous proposal. It's only a horse."

"I agree," Sinclair said smugly. "But I've decided it's a fair proposal. And what I want is now most important. You once told me that an asset is only worth what someone will pay for it. I'm sure you'll accept the new contract and cancel the existing one."

Henri looked at him strangely. "Have you gone mad?"

Sinclair chuckled. "No, not at all. You've read my offer. Consider yourself fortunate."

"You've got nerve," Henri declared, the vein in his forehead beginning to bulge. "I could bankrupt you if I chose."

"But you won't."

"I—what do you mean, I won't."

"You won't, Henri," Sinclair said, chuckling. "I know that, and soon you will, too."

"And why is that?" Henri demanded.

"You pretend to be so powerful," Sinclair said, leaning toward him. "But you're not."

"I never said I was powerful. Only stronger than you."

"You could be," Sinclair said. "Except for one flaw. It took me a while to find it, but once I did, I realized you were just a blustering bully."

"You're very brave for a man whose business is collapsing," Henri said. "What is this flaw that you think you've found?"

"I can control myself."

Henri stared at his competitor, the first sign of doubt showing in his eyes, "What's gotten in to you, Andre?"

"Knowledge."

"What does knowledge have to do with anything."

Sinclair laughed lightly. "I can make you uncomfortable by naming a single street."

Henri's brow furrowed. "What street?"

"Rue Brongniart."

A faint flicker of fear flashed across Henri's face, but he masked it quickly. "My apartment? Is that what you're talking about?"

"And the women who share it."

Henri laughed. "Andre, you're a fool. Do you think I'm the only man in Paris who has a mistress?"

"Does Mme. Lyon know you have a mistress?"

"She doesn't have to know," Henri scoffed. "And if she did, she would pretend she didn't. Now get out and stop wasting my time."

"What if she chose to think otherwise?" Sinclair said, showing no fear.

"She thinks, says, and does what I tell her to," Henri said. "That's all you really need to know."

Sinclair started laughing. "Really?" he asked. "Henri, maybe you're the fool. Have you ever thought of that?"

Henri hesitated, wondering what Sinclair knew that he did not. "Andre, are you really that foolish? Do you think I care if you know I have a mistress? Because I don't. You're wasting your time."

Sinclair shrugged. "Maybe I am. Maybe I'm not."

Henri smirked. "You have nothing, Andre. Just a ridiculous proposal propped up with neighborhood gossip."

"Giselle Picard."

Henri glared at him for a moment, his expression vacant, as if the name was not familiar. Then he shrugged. “A prostitute who someone murdered. What does that have to do with me?”

“A woman you enjoyed on multiple occasions.”

Henri laughed. “Nice try, Andre. But that’s a lie, and you know it. I never met the woman.”

“She was strangled to death.”

“Yes, I know,” Henri replied. “I read the newspapers, too.”

“Someone also tried to kill your wife.”

“The police are investigating,” Henri said. “You’re actually a suspect, I might add.”

“He tried to strangle her, too.”

“Maybe the same maniac.”

“Or a jealous lover killed Giselle,” Sinclair suggested. “Followed by a jealous husband attacking his wife.”

Henri laughed loudly. “Absolutely ridiculous. And easily proved untrue.”

“Most scandals are founded in fact,” Sinclair insisted. “As the people of Paris may soon find out.”

“I don’t think so,” Henri retorted. “The people of Paris mind their own business. Just as you should. Giselle Picard means nothing to me. She was a complete stranger.”

Sinclair tried another tactic. “Mme. Jeanette Richelieu.”

Henri shrugged. “We’re friends,” he said. “So what?”

“Does M. Richelieu know you are friends?”

“He doesn’t need to know.”

“What if he found out?” Sinclair asked. “In his private or professional capacity?”

"What if he did?"

"Would his oversight of your company change? Would he seek revenge?"

"M. Richelieu is a sensible man. And you should be, too."

"I am sensible, Henri, as I think you'll agree. Now if you'll sign the papers and cancel my lien, I'll ensure no one ever knows who you really are."

Henri's eyes flashed. "I'm not signing this absurd contract," he insisted, shoving it across the desk.

Sinclair smiled, took the document, and put it in his leather satchel. As he stood to leave, he paused, determined to plant seeds of doubt. "Henri, how long does it take to paint a portrait?"

Henri paused, eyeing him cautiously, his face starting to pale. "You don't know what you're talking about."

Sinclair walked to the door, laughing and shaking his head.

Chapter Seventy-Nine

Deauville, 1956

Zélie poured three glasses of wine and joined Anton and Marc in the parlor. Luc was in bed, fast asleep.

"Luc seems to be doing better," Marc said as Zélie handed him a glass of wine. "I was watching him ride his bike yesterday, and he was having a great time, chatting away about school and Matilda."

"He is doing well," Zélie said, smiling. "He's had no nightmares for almost two weeks, and he has a new friend at school. He lives a few blocks away."

"That's wonderful," Anton said. "Maybe he only needed time, and now he's starting to adjust."

"I sure hope so," Zélie said. She was grateful for all they did, spending time with Luc and expressing an interest in his life—all the interactions that a father figure would provide. "I can't thank the two of you enough for all you do for him. It really helps."

"It's a pleasure to be around him," Marc said.

"He's a smart little boy," Anton added. "I predict a bright future."

Zélie smiled. Luc was her life. He had to be. They only had each other.

They sipped their wine, and, after an awkward pause, Anton came to the purpose for their meeting. "I did speak to my father."

"Did he share his Resistance experiences?" Marc asked.

Anton sighed. "Yes, he did. But very reluctantly."

"What did he say?" Zélie asked, glancing at Marc. "We're both anxious to hear about it."

Anton paused to collect his thoughts. "The network came into existence in 1942 when a British airman appeared on the Chard estate. Marie and Louis Chard had a stone cottage, more of a mansion, actually, just past the racetrack. It's surrounded with acres of woods and pasture."

"I read that they were executed in 1944," Marc said.

Anton nodded. "Yes, along with other members of the network."

"The article I found said that their belongings were confiscated," Marc added.

"They were," Anton replied. "My father claimed everything in their home was removed. But the house was too far from town for the Germans to occupy, so they ransacked it."

"That's such a tragedy," Zélie said, so sad for the many who had given so much. "Did the Chards have children?"

"Two sons that they lost in the war," Anton said.

Marc slowly shook his head. "No family was spared from death or destruction. It's sad what people did to each other."

"Deauville suffered more than most, I suspect," Anton said.

"Was the whole network betrayed?" Zélie asked.

"Apparently," Anton said. "At least the Deauville members were. My father confirmed that the Germans found a safe house filled with Allied airmen. That's when Gaston, Zélie's father-in-law, was killed. But my father wasn't sure if the network had actually been betrayed, or if one of the airmen had been followed by the Gestapo."

"But the network quickly collapsed after that," Marc said. "At least according to the newspapers."

"Yes, it did," Anton said. He looked at Zélie painfully, almost apologetically. "The rest of the story involves Eva."

Zélie had a horrible feeling. She braced herself, sensing that she wouldn't like what she was about to hear. "Please, go on," she said softly.

Anton hesitated, watching her for a moment, and then continued. "Many thought Eva betrayed the network."

"Did they have any proof?" Marc asked. "It must have been chaotic in the days before the Allied invasion. Anyone could have betrayed them."

Anton shook his head. "No proof that I know of. My father said the Gestapo questioned her, but then let her go. Many felt that was an indication of cooperation."

"Did your father know that the colonel in charge of the investigation lived in one of the cottages?" Marc asked. "He would have known Eva well. Maybe that's why she was spared."

Anton shrugged. "Perhaps it was. But he didn't want to talk about it."

Zélie was quiet, absorbing what she heard. It seemed she never really knew her mother-in-law. Eva had only let people see what she had wanted them to see. "Did your father know what happened to the Chards' belongings?"

"No, he didn't."

Marc assessed the information as any trained investigator would. "Did he know if anything of value was taken?"

Anton turned to Zélie, his gaze fixed on hers. "My father said that M. Chard had a valuable coin collection. It was world-renowned, and, before the war, collectors came from around the world to see it."

Zélie shared a glance with Marc. "We know where that is," she said quietly. "It's in the attic."

"What we don't know," Marc said, "is if Eva took it, or it was given to her by the Germans as a reward for betraying the network, or if the Gestapo asked her to hide it. We still have many questions that need to be answered."

Anton shrugged and took a deep breath. "My father also said that the Chards had a collection of paintings that were valuable, which were done by a local artist."

"But Jean-Pierre was from Montmartre," Marc said, referencing the paintings in the attic.

"I know nothing about the artist," Anton admitted, "only the paintings. Mme. Chard inherited them from her grandfather, who lived to an old age, past ninety. He passed just before the war. My father said his name was Claude Dumont."

Chapter Eighty

Montmartre, 1874

"Henri is coming tonight," Elise said as she hurried into the studio, her carriage and coachman just outside the door. "But I'm not sure when."

Jean-Pierre looked at her warily. "Why now? He's never shown any interest before."

"He's suspicious," she warned as she sat in the model's chair. "He's been asking questions about the process and why it's taking so long."

Jean-Pierre sighed and moved behind the easel, studying his creations. "I have three portraits, the poses all different, the shadows cast from different angles. I could finish any of the three."

"Do you have a favorite?" she asked. "Maybe you can complete one and abandon the others."

"Each is an experiment, seeking perfection in a different way. I can't abandon any of them."

"This may be our last session," she said. "Unless something changes drastically. You should finish the painting that needs the least work."

"But I'm not satisfied. I want them perfect."

"If you don't finish, you'll have to explain why. And somehow justify continuing the sessions."

Jean-Pierre was quiet, reflective. "I predict Henri will not even notice. He'll glance at the portraits without seeing what they are."

She smiled. "Regardless of what happens, he'll see a talented artist, a genius in more ways than one."

"I intend to tell him the truth," he said abruptly.

Her eyes widened. "Jean-Pierre, we can't. Not until the time is right."

He smiled. "I meant tell him the truth about the portraits," he clarified. "He must be told that, even though three paintings are almost complete, I like none of them."

She looked at him quizzically. "But why?"

He studied the portraits, slowly shaking his head. "They don't show what I see when I look at you," he said softly. "They're an amateurish attempt to capture beauty—and they fail."

"I'm sure each is perfect," she said, flattered.

"No, you are perfect," he insisted. "The portraits are not. They're paint thrown on a canvas. There is so much more."

"Is that what you'll tell Henri?" she teased, knowing a perfectionist is never satisfied, a romantic never able to love enough.

He grinned. "Maybe I should," he said, walking toward her. "It might open his eyes. But there is so much I want to tell him."

"Like what?" she asked, her heart beginning to race.

"I want to tell him that he has eyes, but he does not see."

"Why is that?" she whispered as he stopped, his lips close to hers.

"He can't see the delicate curve of your earlobe," he whispered, his finger trailing down her cheek. "Or the faint shadows your cheekbones cast, high and defined. Or your lips, full and sensuous, waiting to be kissed."

She leaned toward him, and their lips met, lightly at first and then hungrily. They lingered, and, when she broke the kiss, she pulled him close, feeling his body against hers, putting her head on his shoulder. “I wish it were different,” she whispered.

“Soon, my love,” he said softly. “Very soon.”

She turned, her lips again finding his, a heated desire steaming the room.

A moment later, he reluctantly pulled away. “But for now, you pose, and I paint. We’ll see if Henri comes and what will happen if he does.”

Chapter Eighty-One

Deauville, 1956

Later that evening, Zélie, Anton and Marc stood in the attic, studying the eight paintings that leaned against the wall.

"We still don't know who she is," Zélie mumbled, eyeing the two portraits that featured the dark-haired woman.

"But now we know that Claude Dumont plays a central role in the mystery," Marc offered. "At some point he gained possession of the paintings, left the note claiming they contain valuable clues, and passed them on to his granddaughter. We just don't know how he got them."

"We don't know how Eva got them, either," Zélie said. "Or the coin collection. They're questions we still need to answer."

Anton eyed them cautiously, almost hesitant to speak. "I realize we have no proof of any wrongdoing, but maybe everything was given to Eva."

Zélie knew it was a likely explanation, even if painful to consider. "I'm beginning to think she was the informant, rewarded by the Gestapo for her cooperation."

"But we don't know that for sure," Marc said. "The Gestapo did let her live—that would have been reward enough. I doubt they would have given her paintings and a priceless coin collection."

Anton pursed his lips. "My father has always suspected that Eva was the informant. He knew nothing of the coins or paintings. But he assumed she received something, cash perhaps."

"Let's find out," Zélie said, unable to wait any longer. She led them into the next room, pausing in front of three small wooden crates that sat against the wall. "The first two contain the coin collections. Even a novice can see they're valuable."

Anton eyed the crates and then glanced through the doorway to the paintings leaning against the wall. "I came to know Eva well. We shared a passion for horses but never discussed much else. She was a good person. I loved the woman. I refuse to believe she betrayed anyone, regardless of what my father said. It wasn't like her."

Zélie sighed with despair. "I hate to admit it, because I loved her, too, but it seems the most likely explanation."

"Maybe we'll find more answers," Marc said. "We're guessing right now. We have a mystery, more than one, actually, and we need to solve them. Let's hope Anton's key fits the third crate."

Anton held up the key that was hidden in the painting of Munich that hung on the cottage wall. "We'll soon know."

Marc bent over the third crate, removed the wooden lid, and exposed a metal strongbox snugly wrapped in wood. "Hopefully, we're about to solve another mystery."

Anton handed him the key. "Give it a try."

Marc inserted it in the lock and then fingered the dial. "One," he said, mouthing the suspected combination. "Nine, and forty-four."

The tumblers clicked audibly, and Marc slowly lifted the lid.

"Any traps?" Zélie asked anxiously. "The locksmith warned us."

Marc checked along the mechanisms and gently felt around the edges. "No vials to break, nothing attached to the tumblers, no wires or detonation devices. Just a normal lockbox."

"What's inside?" Anton asked, leaning forward.

Marc fully opened the lid, revealing Nazi currency and Swiss francs, all in large denominations. He whistled softly and looked at the others. "That's a lot of money," he exclaimed. "Although the Nazi bills are probably worthless."

Zélie frowned. "I guess that explains it. Eva was paid off to inform on the network."

"I never would have believed it," Anton said sadly.

"Wait a minute," Marc said, peering at the box. "There's more."

He removed a tightly wrapped stack of bills and withdrew an envelope. He opened it and took out the papers inside.

"What is it?" Zélie asked.

"Personal documents," Marc muttered as he sorted through them. "Colonel Hans Fischer, his wife, three children. Birth certificates and Swiss passports in each of their names."

Zélie looked at him, confused. "I don't understand."

Marc stood, struggling to rise with his stiff leg. "I think this explains everything," he said.

Anton laughed nervously. "Can you please explain it to us?"

Zélie chuckled, too. "Yes, please do. I think you're a few steps ahead."

Marc smiled. "I'll explain," he said. "Fischer was the officer who arrested those in the network. He ran the investigation, conducted the interrogations, and most likely confiscated the Chard's belongings. As any good soldier would have done, he gave everything in the Chard's house to his superiors."

Zélie was starting to understand. "Except the most valuable items."

"Exactly," Marc said. "He gave Eva her freedom but on one condition."

"She had to hide what Fischer stole from the Chards in her attic and never mention it to a single soul," Zélie said.

Marc nodded. "Waiting for the day that Fischer came to claim it."

Chapter Eighty-Two

Montmartre, 1874

Babin sat at an outdoor table in the café at the bottom of the hill and looked skyward. "It'll be dark soon. Less than an hour."

Dumont sipped the last remnants of his coffee. "She's been in there for thirty minutes."

Babin glanced at his pocket watch. "I expect her to remain for thirty more, as we've established as her typical routine."

Dumont's gaze was fixed on Elise's carriage, sitting in front of the studio entrance. "Maybe we should change our location," he suggested, "and watch from the top of the hill."

"Why do that?" Babin asked.

"It might be better if we were closer. Especially as darkness approaches."

Babin studied his underling, his finger tracing the sweeping curve of his moustache. "Do you know something I do not?"

Dumont shrugged. "No, of course not," he said. "But from the café we only observe. We cannot respond. Since one of the attacks on Mme. Lyon occurred after it was dark, and we find ourselves in the same situation, it might be prudent to be closer."

Babin was quiet for a moment, digesting Dumont's logic. "Do you think someone watches us as we watch Elise Lyon?"

"I don't know," Dumont admitted. "But it's possible. The culprit could be anyone. Even her coachman."

"I hardly think so," Babin scoffed. "It is not the coachman, I assure you. If you had connected the dots and formed a line from the beginning of this case to its end, you would know, as I do, the criminal's identity. It's all very clear."

Dumont looked at him, unable to hide his confusion. "Can you please enlighten me, Inspector Babin?"

Babin smiled pompously. "In time even your eyes will see."

Dumont didn't reply. If he was angry, he masked it, studying the studio at the top of the hill. "I still suggest we watch from a vantage point closer to the studio, from the top of the hill by the curve in the road where our coach was parked during the last session."

"And how do you propose to get there?" Babin asked. "Do we walk past Mme. Lyon's coachman, in our police uniforms, or drive past in our police carriage after you've just suggested he could be the man who's trying to kill her?"

Dumont hesitated, not as confident as he once was. "We can walk around the block," he offered.

"And lose sight of the studio? What if the attacker appears? Both attempts on Mme. Lyon's life have been made as she left the studio."

"After she stayed for an hour, sometimes ninety minutes."

"And what if this is the session in which she only stays for thirty?"

"Why not split up?" Dumont asked. "I will go around the block. You wait ten minutes and follow."

Babin eyed his underling closely. "My dear Lieutenant Dumont," he said, his hands resting on his big belly. "For some reason, one that I am unable to explain, I have decided to honor your request. Go, and be quick."

Chapter Eighty-Three

Deauville, 1956

On Saturday morning, Zélie led Marc and Professor Marie Dufour into the attic. The professor carried a leather satchel, a large reference book poking from the top.

"I think I may have some good news for you," Marie said as they climbed the steps. "I've done quite a bit of research on Jean-Pierre."

"We appreciate it so much," Zélie said as they reached the attic, and she led them to the paintings.

"Oh, these are beautiful!" the professor exclaimed. She set her satchel down, removed the book, and took out a large magnifying glass.

"Are they authentic?" Marc asked.

"They seem to be," she muttered. "Let me take a closer look."

Professor Dufour knelt in front of the paintings, examining each with her magnifying glass. "Exquisite," she mumbled. "Oh, look at these. Absolutely unbelievable."

Marc and Zélie didn't disturb her. Marc grabbed three straight-backed chairs and set them in front of the paintings, and he and Zélie sat and watched as Marie moved from one painting to the next. After several minutes she stood and turned to face them.

"Yes, they're definitely authentic," Marie confirmed. "Jean-Pierre had a fondness for various shades of blue, as you can see in some of the paintings—the woman's blouse, for example. His trademark was the use of light and shadows, and their impact on the hues he chose, along with the rich brush work."

Zélie sighed and turned to Marc. "That's one obstacle removed. The paintings are real."

"Now we just have to figure out what each one means," he said.

"I have a better reference book this time, which should help," Marie said. "Most of the paintings are featured. And I recognize a few, now that I've actually seen them."

"We're grateful for any information you can offer," Zélie said. "But I hope you'll let me pay you for your time."

"No, don't be silly," Marie replied. "I enjoy a mystery as much as anyone else. I need something to do anyway. I'm running out of Regency romance novels to read."

Zélie chuckled. "I really do appreciate it," she said. She shifted in her chair, watching the professor work. "We now know where they came from. A private collection owned by the Chards here in Deauville."

Marie knelt on the floor, glancing at her reference book and then back to the paintings. "The Chards aren't referenced in the book. But private collectors often aren't."

"The horse painting still doesn't seem to fit," Marc said. "Except the tie to Sinclair."

"No, it doesn't," Marie agreed. "But it is by Jean-Pierre. I can tell by the signature and brush work."

"But it's not in the book?" Zélie asked.

Professor Dufour shook her head. "No, but I found the others."

Zélie and Marc shared anxious glances as Marie took her reference book and sat in the empty chair.

"Jean-Pierre was born in Deauville," she began. "Not many people realize that because his studio was in

Montmartre. I believe he spent summers here, painting landscapes."

Marc eyed her curiously. "Andre Sinclair had a summer home in Deauville, too."

"And you're certain the paintings are authentic?" Zélie asked, still unable to believe it.

"Absolutely," Marie said. "There's no doubt at all. And my original assessment of a million francs is accurate —a little more, actually."

Zélie looked at Marc in amazement. "That's wonderful," she said, the answer to her financial problems sitting on her attic floor—if only they truly belonged to her. "But the paintings aren't mine. They were taken from the Chards by the Gestapo during the war."

"I can give you information on how to return them," the professor offered. "A government agency has reunited many works of art with their rightful owners—museums and private collectors."

"I would appreciate their contact information, if you have it," Zélie said. "We have some other items that were also stolen from the Chards that we must return—a valuable coin collection."

Professor Dufour glanced through the doorways, scanning the two rooms of the attic. "Some of this is from the same time period as the paintings," she said. "I think those photographs may have some value."

Zélie followed Marie's gaze to a stack of framed photographs she had leaned against the wall beside the doorway. "I'll have to look through those," she said, wondering if any more items belonged to the Chards. "I've been focused on the paintings."

"I can understand why," the professor said as she printed the name, address and phone number of the government agency on a piece of paper and handed it to Zélie. "The Commission for the Recovery of Works of Art. They can help you with everything."

"Thank you so much," Zélie said. "I want to return it all as soon as possible."

"Can you tell us anything else about the paintings?" Marc asked.

"Yes, of course," Marie said, turning the pages in her reference book.

"Can you go down the row and tell us about each one?" Zélie asked. "We arranged them in a certain sequence."

"Sure," Marie said. She looked at the next painting. "Jean-Pierre's studio in Montmartre, which we identified when you came to visit me, and this is the street on which the studio was located."

"We suspect it was also the scene of the crime," Marc added.

"And the two men at the Montmartre police station are Inspector Babin," Marie continued, "who we also discussed previously, and the other man is Claude Dumont, his assistant."

"The woman who owned the paintings was Claude Dumont's granddaughter," Marc said.

Marie's eyes widened. "It does all connect somehow, doesn't it?"

"Just one more question we have to answer," Zélie said. "How did Dumont, a policeman, get the paintings?"

Marie smiled. "I'm sure you'll find out. You're very persistent."

"Can you tell us about the rest?" Marc asked.

"Of course," Marie said, pointing to a Paris scene. "This is titled *The Café.* But no details are listed in any of the reference books I consulted."

Marc pointed at the painting. "Normandy Mines, the building next to the café, was owned by Andre Sinclair, owner of Golden Cross."

Marie chuckled. "It is a jigsaw puzzle, isn't it?"

"We think the blond woman is one of Jean-Pierre's models," Marc continued. "She was murdered on the street where his studio was located. Her name was Giselle Picard."

"The title of the painting is indeed *Giselle,*" Marie said, "so it seems you're correct."

Zélie looked at the paintings aligned in a row. "Now for the last two. The biggest of the mysteries."

"I do have some good news," Marie said. "I recognized the woman with the dark hair as soon as I came in. The title of the portrait is *Elise*, and it seems she may have been one of Jean-Pierre's favorite models. Several works of her still survive, most in private hands."

Zélie paused, pensive. "That's great information, but it doesn't seem like she ties to the crime."

Marie hesitated and then continued. "I think she might. When you came to visit me, you had asked about Henri Lyon, who I was unable to find any information about."

Marc looked at the paintings. "Henri Lyon purchased Golden Cross from Andre Sinclair, but we don't know anything else about him."

The professor was focused on her reference book. "I actually found quite a bit of information about Elise. I think it may answer some of your questions."

Zélie smiled and glanced at Marc. "Please, tell us. We can't wait to hear it."

Marie turned to face them. "Elise was a Deauville native. Her full name was Elise Lyon. She was Henri's wife."

Zélie's eyes widened. "Then she's somehow connected to Golden Cross."

"Wait, there's more," Marie said. "I had told you that Jean-Pierre had never done a self-portrait. But that was incorrect. I found information on this last painting, and it's titled *The Self-Portrait*."

"That's Jean-Pierre?" Marc asked, pointing at the painting.

Marie nodded. "Yes, it is. And apparently, it's the only image we have of him. I suspect this might be the most valuable painting of all."

Zélie looked at Marc, confused. "What is Elise Lyon doing on a Deauville beach with Jean-Pierre?"

Chapter Eighty-Four

Montmartre, 1874

Babin and Dumont were waiting at the top of the hill on a curve in the cobblestone lane, peeking around the corner of a bookshop. A woman sat on her stoop, minding two toddlers. She glanced curiously at the policemen who pretended to look in shop windows.

Dumont studied the road where it wound down the hill, watching a carriage stop across from the corner café that they had just left. Seconds later, the door opened, and Henri Lyon stepped out. He dismissed the driver, waving him on, and the coach continued down the boulevard.

"What is Lyon doing here?" Dumont asked, pointing down the hill.

"A mystery that must be solved," Babin muttered. "He's never come before."

Dumont turned, eyes wide. "I wonder if Elise and Jean-Pierre know he's coming."

Babin cringed, sensing disaster. "They had best be posing and painting, even though we know they are not."

Henri started up the incline, studying the walls that hemmed the road. The light was fading as the day came to a close, and he walked briskly, carrying a cane that tapped the pavement, more for show than support. He paused when he reached the tree limbs sprawling over the wall, scene of Elise's first attack, and eyed the area cautiously, looking in different directions before hurrying along.

"He's coming up to Mme. Lyon's carriage," Babin said. "Maybe we can overhear."

"How long has she been in there?" Henri asked Elise's coachman.

"Almost an hour, sir," the coachman replied. "They should finish shortly. Although sometimes it takes longer."

Babin and Dumont peeked around the corner. "Don't let him see you," Babin hissed.

"Are you going to arrest someone?" the woman across the street asked curiously. "Or are you buying books?"

Babin glared at the woman and held a finger to his lips.

Henri raised his cane, tapping on the door of the studio with the handle. He paused, listening, and rapped on the door again, this time much louder. He turned to the coachman.

"It sometimes takes him a while to answer, sir," the coachman said with a shrug, his voice quivering.

"Take the carriage to the bottom of the hill," Henri snapped. "Wait for me there."

"Yes, sir," the driver replied. He put down his newspaper, sat up in the driver's seat, and rustled the reins. The horse started trotting down the incline, its hooves clicking on the cobblestone.

"He sent the carriage away," Dumont hissed as he turned to Babin.

"Why would he do that?" Babin asked. He was baffled for a moment but was then struck with a terrifying thought. "Unless he has nefarious intentions."

Dumont looked down the lane with a worried expression. "The coachman is parking the carriage at the bottom of the hill."

"There's only one reason to dismiss the carriage," Babin declared. "Lyon does not want a witness for what is about to occur."

"Elise!" Henri shouted, banging harder on the door.

Seconds passed with no reply. Babin eyed Dumont. "This will not be good, Lieutenant. Be prepared to take action."

Henri started pacing along the pavement, muttering, cursing, and shaking his head. He stopped, his eyes lit with rage, standing in front of the door. "Elise!" he bellowed. When he received no reply, he crashed in, splintering the door jamb.

"Hurry!" Babin exclaimed. "We must stop him!"

A hideous scream ripped through the night.

"It's Mme. Lyon!" Babin shouted.

Dumont sprinted across the cobblestone, Babin trailing behind him. The closer they got, the louder the struggle.

"No!" Elise shouted. "Stop!"

Dumont disappeared into the studio. Babin withdrew his pistol, hurrying after him.

Elise screamed again. "Help!"

Babin rushed through the doorway. Jean-Pierre's prone body lay a few feet from the entrance, Dumont on the floor beside him, dazed and holding his head. Elise lay on her back, halfway across the room, the model's chair turned over beside her, askew on the floor. She was choking, gasping for air, as Henri Lyon climbed off her prone body and dashed toward the door.

"No!" Henri shouted at Babin. "It's not what you think!"

Babin pulled the trigger. A bullet burrowed into the chest of Henri Lyon.

Chapter Eighty-Five

Deauville, 1956

At 9 a.m. on Monday morning, Zélie called the phone number Professor Dufour had given her. The Commission for the Recovery of Works of Art was a government organization initiated to recover the many treasures stolen by the Nazis during the war. The Commission had achieved much success in its short tenure, but many thousands of items were still missing.

Zélie was interviewed by a clerk, Mme. Adair, who started with a series of simple questions, including Zélie's name and address and how the works had come into her possession. Mme. Adair then asked for information about the individual items. Zélie described Jean-Pierre's paintings and stated their estimated values, which Professor Dufour had provided. When Mme. Adair had finished recording the information, Zélie described the two crates containing the coin collections. The last series of questions dealt with the original owners. Zélie told her all she knew about the Chards—their Resistance network, their cause of death, and the two sons they had lost during the war.

"Do you have any other items in your possession?" Mme. Adair asked.

Zélie hesitated but decided not to tell her about the lockbox filled with Swiss francs and Nazi currency that belonged to Colonel Fischer—at least not yet.

"Your claim will be assigned to an investigator," Mme. Adair informed her. "You'll be contacted shortly, so she can gather further information and make arrangements to examine the items in your possession."

Zélie hung up the phone, made a pot of coffee, and stepped out the back door, waving to Marc who was in the yard, fiddling with an old bicycle.

"I just got off the phone with the Commission," she called.

"I'll be right over," he said, laying his tools on the ground.

Zélie poured him a cup of coffee, and they sat at the kitchen table. She went through all the details she had given the Commission and told him about the investigator who would be assigned to reconcile it all.

"It's the best way to do it," Marc assured her. "If the Chards have any living relatives, the government will find them."

"I listed Professor Dufour as a reference. Should they need expert information."

"Did they ask for an estimated value?"

Zélie nodded. "I told them a million francs for the paintings, and I guessed at half a million for the coin collections."

"That seems about right," he said, sipping his coffee. "There's also more than a half million in Swiss Francs. And whatever a collector might pay for the Nazi currency."

"Which belonged to Colonel Fischer," she said bitterly. "He probably stole it from innocent people, little by little."

He looked at her, suspecting there was more. "You didn't tell them about the Swiss francs, did you?"

"No," she said firmly and then paused. "At least not yet."

He was quiet for a moment. "What about the colonel's family?"

"If the colonel or his family wanted it, they had twelve years to come and get it."

Marc eyed her curiously. "What if the Colonel is dead, but his family survives?"

"Do you really think the money was his?"

Marc hesitated, and, after a moment had passed, he replied. "No, I don't."

"I promise to tell the Commission about the Swiss francs," Zélie said. "But on my terms, not theirs."

Chapter Eighty-Six

Montmartre, 1874

The Paris Police Prefecture initiated an investigation into Inspector Nicolas Babin's actions in the shooting death of Henri Lyon. To ensure a fair and thorough assessment, since Babin was revered by all for his dedicated service and extraordinary abilities, administrators requested the services of Inspector Bernard Roche from the city of Marseilles.

A husky man with thick gray hair and dark eyes, Roche was familiar with the task required of him, knew the reputation of the man he had been assigned to assess, and was determined to conduct his investigation with the utmost professionalism—a trait that had dominated his lengthy career. He was a serious man conducting a serious investigation.

Roche first visited the three crime scenes: Jean-Pierre's studio, the crooked lane that led up the hill, and the narrow alley where Elise Lyon had been assaulted the second time. He then developed his witness list and arranged for a conference room with a clerk to transcribe testimonies. Before they began, Roche added an expert to his team, Dr. Raymond Cartier, renowned for his intricate knowledge of the workings of the mind.

Witnesses with limited involvement were interviewed first: Elise Lyon's coachman, Pierre Beaufort, Jean-Pierre's neighbor, Mme. Michel, and Henri Lyon's competitor and owner of Normandy Mines, Andre Sinclair. They offered different perspectives into the events that had led to Lyon's death, their testimony captured by the clerk.

Jean-Pierre, the first major witness, was then brought into the conference room.

"I am Inspector Roche, and I will be asking you a few questions," Roche announced.

"Of course, sir," Jean-Pierre replied. "I will tell all that I know."

Roche shuffled through his papers, checked to ensure the clerk was ready, and began. "How long have you had your studio, the one in which Henri Lyon was killed?"

"Almost a year," Jean-Pierre replied.

"Was Giselle your model, the woman murdered several weeks ago?"

"Yes, she was."

"How well did you know her?"

"Fairly well," Jean-Pierre replied. "You could say we were friends."

Roche scribbled a few notes and continued. "Did she ever speak of a lover?"

"Yes, she did. A wealthy man."

"But she was a prostitute, no?"

Jean-Pierre paused. "She was more of a mistress, but with two or three other lovers."

"Did she ever name them?"

"No, she didn't," Jean-Pierre said.

"Did her lover know about the others?"

Jean-Pierre shook his head. "No, she was guarded. She had to be. She said her lover was very jealous and sometimes violent."

Roche eyed the clerk to ensure he had captured the testimony before proceeding. "Did you know that a portrait of Giselle was found in an apartment kept by Henri Lyon?"

"Not until I read it in the newspapers."

"Did he commission you to paint it?"

"No, he did not," Jean-Pierre replied. "But I did paint it."

"Who purchased it from you?"

"Giselle paid for the portrait," Jean-Pierre said. "She said it was for her lover."

Roche remained impassive, jotting down notes. After a moment, he returned to the witness. "You are painting a portrait of Elise Lyon, is that correct?"

"Yes, commissioned by her husband."

"How many sessions have you had with Mme. Lyon?"

Jean-Pierre thought for a moment. "A dozen, maybe more."

"Have you finished her portrait?"

"I've done three—all nearly finished. I will complete the best. That's what I was paid to do."

Roche read through his papers, ensuring he hadn't missed any details. "What happened on the night that Henri Lyon was killed?"

"Mme. Lyon arrived for her session and posed as she normally did. She told me her husband would be coming to observe."

"What occurred when he arrived?"

Jean-Pierre hesitated. "There was a knock on the door, but with daylight fading, I wanted to finish what I was working on—the shadows were just right. I needed only a few more minutes. But M. Lyon became insistent, knocking louder."

Roche eyed the artist warily. "How long was M. Lyon kept waiting?"

Jean-Pierre shrugged. "Not long. Three or four minutes, at most. I was approaching the door when he barged in. His face was contorted with rage."

"Where was Mme. Lyon?"

"Still in the model's chair. But she hurried toward him."

"How did M. Lyon react?"

"He rushed forward, his gaze fixed on a painting of Giselle. He had an angry look in his eyes, and he lunged at Mme. Lyon."

"Did you try to stop him?"

"I did, but he hit me on the side of the head. My last recollection was falling to the floor as blackness overcame me."

Roche paused for a moment, shuffling his papers, and then looked up at the witness. "That is all, sir," he said, nodding to the clerk. "You may go."

The assistant led Jean-Pierre out, and the next witness entered.

"Lieutenant Dumont, I am Inspector Roche, and I will be asking you a few questions."

"I will answer to the best of my ability, Inspector," Dumont promised.

"How long have you been with the Paris Police, acting as Inspector Babin's assistant?"

"Almost two years," Dumont replied. "I came from a police department in Normandy."

"What is your opinion of the Inspector?"

"I have the utmost respect for him. He taught me much about police work."

Roche looked at notes he had collected from a review of Babin's files. "How many times, in the two years you have worked with him, has he drawn his weapon?"

Dumont paused, thinking. "Three times, maybe four."

Roche sat back in the chair, eyeing Dumont closely. "Describe your actions on the night that Henri Lyon was killed."

Dumont nodded and leaned forward. "The Inspector and I were observing the studio from around the corner. We had watched some of Mme. Lyon's prior sessions, ensuring she departed safely with her coachman."

"Did you see Henri Lyon approach?"

"Yes, we did," Dumont replied. "He arrived on foot, walking up the hill, spoke briefly with the coachman and knocked on the door. He waited a moment, knocked again, and directed the coachman to wait down the hill. A moment later, he burst into the studio."

"Did you find his behavior alarming?" Roche asked, scanning his notes.

Dumont hesitated. "Inspector Babin and I had watched Lyon for several weeks. He was impatient and quick to anger—traits that became more pronounced as each day passed."

Roche eyed the witness a moment more. "Why would Lyon crash into the studio? Why not wait for the door to be answered? He knew his wife was inside."

Dumont sat back in his chair. "I don't know what triggered him, but the inspector and I suspected something nefarious would occur, especially when he sent his carriage away. It was almost as if he didn't want witnesses."

Roche took notes and continued. "What actions did you take?"

"I raced into the studio and found Jean-Pierre unconscious. Elise Lyon lay on the floor, Henri astride her, his hands around her neck."

"Did you draw your weapon?"

"No, I lunged for M. Lyon and shoved him to the floor. Mme. Lyon gasped for air, coughing and choking. I very likely saved her life. Her husband fell to the side, and, as I tried to apprehend him, he pummeled me with his fists."

"Why didn't you wait for the inspector?" Roche asked. "Wouldn't that have been safer?"

"I feared for Mme. Lyon's life. The inspector was only paces behind me. I was about to scream for help when M. Lyon scrambled for the door. I then heard the shot. Lyon fell to the floor and made a gurgling sound."

"Thank you, M. Dumont. That will be all."

The assistant led Dumont from the room and brought in Elise Lyon. Roche nodded as she was seated. "Mme. Lyon, I am Inspector Roche. Please accept my sincere condolences for the loss of your husband."

Mme. Lyon nodded meekly. "Thank you, Inspector. It's been difficult."

"Yes, I'm sure," he replied sincerely. He paused, eyed the clerk to ensure he was ready, and then began. "I will be asking you a few questions."

"Yes, I understand."

"Mme. Lyon, how long have you been married?"

"Almost a year."

Roche jotted a note and continued. "Are you from Paris?"

"No, I'm from Deauville, on the coast of Normandy."

"How did you meet M. Lyon?"

"He has a summer cottage in Deauville. We met there. He was a friend of my father's."

"And you married and moved to Paris?"

"Yes, sir."

Roche paused, eyeing the woman who sat before him, young, attractive, seemingly sincere. “Was he a good husband?” he asked quietly.

“He was a good provider.”

“But that isn’t the question I asked,” Roche said politely. “Was he a good husband?”

She hesitated, lips pursed. “He had faults. We all do.”

“What were his faults?”

She sighed, collecting her thoughts. “He was demanding, condescending, and had a quick temper, although it was rarely directed at me. I’d been told he could be violent, but I didn’t believe it until the night at the studio. He was a jealous man—irrationally so, sometimes. But he was also kind and generous, a major patron of the orphanage, which was greatly appreciated.”

“Did he ever harm you?”

She dabbed a tear with a handkerchief. “Only in the studio, on the night he was shot.”

Roche paused, adding more notes. When he’d finished, he looked up, ensured he had everyone’s attention, and then continued. “Who decided you should have your portrait painted?”

“My husband. He wanted to put it over the fireplace in his study.”

“How did he choose the artist, Jean-Pierre?”

She thought for a moment. “He was recommended by a friend of my husband’s, Mme. Jeanette Richelieu.”

“How many sessions have you had?”

She shrugged. “A dozen? Maybe a few more.”

“After one session, you were attacked on the street that goes up the hill leading to the studio. A man tried to strangle you?”

"Yes," she replied, looking away.

"The perpetrator fled when strangers approached."

She nodded, again dabbing her eyes, the memories painful. "A man passing on the boulevard saw the attack. He came to my aid, followed by others."

"A second assault occurred in your carriage after you left a session with Jean-Pierre. A man tried to strangle you, but the attack was interrupted by an observer."

"Yes, an elderly woman approached the carriage."

"Did you see the man who attacked you on either occasion?"

"No, I did not. He was behind me."

Roche glanced at the clerk, waiting until he'd captured all that was said. "Describe the events that occurred on the evening your husband was killed."

"I was expecting Henri to come to the studio, although the session had almost ended when he knocked on the door."

"Was your husband admitted?"

She shook her head. "No, Jean-Pierre wanted to finish while the sunlight was fading. He didn't stop to let him in."

"Your husband knocked a second time, but still the door was not answered."

"No, it was not."

Roche paused, his gaze fixed on Mme. Lyon. "You're absolutely certain that you were posing, and Jean-Pierre was painting."

Her eyes widened at the suggestion of impropriety, but she recovered quickly and answered sternly. "I was posing. He was painting."

Roche eyed her a moment more. "What happened next?"

"As Jean-Pierre approached the door, my husband barged in. He rushed toward me, his face contorted with rage, while Jean-Pierre tried to stop him. Henri started punching Jean-Pierre, and he fell to the floor."

"What triggered his outburst?"

She shrugged. "Waiting for the door to be answered, perhaps. Although he seemed focused on a portrait of Giselle. His eyes lit with rage when he saw it."

Roche hesitated, eyeing her carefully. "What did M. Lyon do next?"

"He shoved me to the floor and climbed on top of me, wrapping his hands around my neck."

"Did his attempt to strangle you feel like the prior attempts—the size and roughness of his hands, the intensity of the grasp?"

She started sobbing. "Yes, it did."

"Seconds later, Lieutenant Dumont arrived and yanked your husband away."

"Yes, but it stopped him only briefly," she said. "Henri hit Lieutenant Dumont repeatedly and then ran for the door."

"What next, Mme. Lyon?"

"I heard a gunshot," she said, still weeping. "And seconds later, Henri was dead."

Chapter Eighty-Seven

Deauville, 1956

Marc Rayne sat in a cluttered room at the Rouen library, studying a microfilm reader with a baffled look on his face.

"It's much easier to use than it looks," the librarian said, a blond woman peeking through black-rimmed glasses.

"It's larger than the machine I used at the Deauville library," he said warily.

The librarian smiled. "This is new, very state of the art. And our newspaper archives are far more extensive."

With only a glance at what was available, the room filled with rows of filing cabinets, Marc realized he would be there for most of the day.

"We also have a reader-printer," the librarian said, continuing her explanation. "If you see an article you want, you can print the screen image from the viewer."

Marc sighed, slightly overwhelmed. "I don't think I understand," he was forced to admit.

The librarian smiled. "I can show you. There is a fee to print the screen image, so if you like, I'll help you when you print the first one. Now, where do you want to begin?"

"Parisian newspapers in the year 1874," Marc said. "Starting in April."

She helped him find the drawer where the reels were kept and then guided him through the process of loading the microfilm. "Now look into the viewer and advance it to the left or right via these knobs."

Marc paid close attention to his instructions. The *Paris Gazette* was displayed on the screen. He was startled by the crisp images.

"Can you see it clearly?" she asked.

"Yes, I can," he said in awe. "What a marvelous machine."

"It's a great research tool," she agreed. "Will you be printing any images?"

He considered the amount of information to review and the tiny notebook he had taken with him. "Yes, I expect to. Several, most likely."

She pointed to a slot on the side of the machine, paper stacked in the opposite end. "You put a coin in the machine and depress the start button. It prints only what's visible in the viewer screen. If it's a long article, it might take several different print attempts to capture it all."

Marc nodded, still bewildered, but not as much. "I think I see how to do it now."

"If you have any problems, just come and get me," she said. "I'll be glad to help."

"I really appreciate it," he said, and he meant it sincerely.

He studied the machine, reviewed the instructions she had given him, and started to examine the microfilm. It took a few minutes before he was comfortable, but eventually he got quite good at operating the equipment.

He located the article he had found in Deauville about the murder of Giselle Picard. As he paged forward, he was surprised to learn of two attempts on the life on Elise Lyon—another prominent figure in the paintings in Zélie's attic. He continued, occasionally printing an article, and read about the investigation, the detectives involved, the different suspects, the perpetrator of the crimes, and the aftermath.

He was absolutely shocked by what he found.

Chapter Eighty-Eight

Montmartre, 1874

When the testimonies were completed, Inspector Roche, Dr. Cartier, and the clerk met to discuss the information gathered.

"Thank you for your assistance in this matter, Dr. Cartier," Inspector Roche said. "It's very much appreciated."

"I only hope I can make a contribution," said Dr. Cartier, a slight man with round spectacles, advanced in age.

"I'm sure you will," Roche assured him. "What was your conclusion?"

Cartier glanced at his notes. "I believe the witnesses are all credible, often substantiating each other's testimony."

"That was my impression, also," Roche said. "Lieutenant Dumont, the artist, and Mme. Lyon, especially."

"I was impressed by the minor details each confirmed," the doctor continued.

Roche hesitated, rubbing his chin and glancing at his notes.

"Is something wrong, Inspector?"

Roche sat back in his chair. "Something doesn't feel right to me though I'm not sure what it is."

"But the witnesses provided very compelling testimony."

"Yes, I know," Roche muttered. "Too compelling." He looked up at Cartier. "Almost coordinated."

Dr. Cartier thought for a moment, glancing over the notes he had scribbled during the testimonies. "Some of the witnesses did use identical phrases."

"I think we might be able to add some clarity by further questioning Mme. Michel."

"The artist's neighbor?" Cartier asked. "She had so little to say."

"Only because we asked so few questions. But sometimes the town gossip sees what others do not."

Cartier nodded. "A few more questions might be helpful."

The clerk summoned Mme. Michel, and a moment later she was seated in the conference room, curiously gazing at Inspector Roche.

"My apologies, Mme. Michel," Roche said. "I know we asked some general questions about Jean-Pierre and his sessions, but it occurred to me that you are, perhaps, the best of the witnesses who gave testimony today."

Mme. Michel leaned forward as if to share a secret. "Not much occurs on my street that I don't know about."

"Yes, I'm sure," Roche said, hiding a smile. "Just a few more questions, and we'll be done."

"I'm more than happy to oblige," she responded.

Roche looked at his notes. "You observed many of the sessions that Jean-Pierre had with Elise Lyon, as you previously testified. Did you ever note improper behavior, or see any evidence that they may have been lovers?"

"I did not," she replied, almost indignant. "If anything like that was going on, I would have known, believe me."

"How about the sessions with Jean-Pierre and Giselle?"

Mme. Michel shook her head. "I don't think Jean-Pierre had any interest in love. He still doesn't."

Roche's eyes widened. "Why would you say that, Mme. Lyon?"

"Jean-Pierre has a broken heart that will never heal."

"From a former lover?"

Mme. Michel nodded. "Although I don't know who it was."

Roche glanced at Cartier and jotted in his notes. "You testified that, on the night Henri Lyon was killed, you heard the gunshot but did not observe the altercation. Is that correct?"

"Yes, it is."

"Did you witness anything else that evening?"

Mme. Michel sat back in her chair, thinking. "I did peek out my door when M. Lyon first arrived. I heard him talking to the coachman."

"And what did you see, Mme. Michel?"

She sighed, hesitated, but then continued. "M. Lyon frowned, pacing in front of the door, and kept glancing at the coachman with a scowl on his face. His eyes then flashed with anger, and he told the coachman to wait at the bottom of the hill."

Roche glanced at Cartier. "That will be all, Mme. Michel. Thank you for your additional testimony."

Mme. Michel rose. "I hope it was helpful," she said as she started for the door.

Roche waited until she was gone and turned to Cartier. "Another example of M. Lyon's temper."

"I agree," Cartier said. "Lieutenant Dumont also provided episodes of his anger, evidenced by a vein throbbing in his forehead. And a business competitor,

Andre Sinclair, claimed Lyon's temper was known to all who had ever dealt with him."

Roche nodded. "What is your assessment of Henri Lyon, Doctor?"

"I believe M. Lyon struggled with three personality flaws, magnified significantly when occurring simultaneously. He was a jealous man, as witnesses have confirmed, had an uncontrollable temper, and was apparently violent, even if Mme. Lyon wasn't aware of it until the fateful night in question. Many suffer from one or more of these shortcomings, but not to the extreme that he apparently did. When these faults converge and a trigger is provided, the results are devastating to those involved."

"Even a novice such as myself can trace the triggers for M. Lyon's outbursts," Roche noted. "Especially those that surfaced through attacks on Mme. Lyon."

Cartier nodded. "I suspect that jealousy ruled his life—both consciously and subconsciously—although he managed to hide it. The attempts on Mme. Lyon's life reflect that, as does information provided by Lieutenant Dumont and Andre Sinclair. Further evidence is revealed by the timeline of events. Each attack on Mme. Lyon occurred after only the slightest hint that she may have formed an emotional attachment to the artist, Jean-Pierre. One can easily conclude that Lyon reacted in a similar fashion, perhaps to a greater degree, when he learned of Giselle Picard's infidelities."

"In your opinion, Doctor, what action would Henri Lyon have taken if Inspector Babin had not shot him?"

The doctor rubbed his chin, contemplating the question. "With the rage that consumed him, I suspect M. Lyon would have beaten Lieutenant Dumont to death."

"Thank you, Doctor," Roche said. "I greatly appreciate your assistance."

Dr. Cartier rose to leave, and Roche motioned to the policemen. A moment later, Inspector Nicolas Babin entered the room, stealing the air with his presence, settling his massive frame in the witness chair.

"Inspector Babin, we finally meet. I am Inspector Bernard Roche from Marseilles, and I have conducted the assessment of your actions on the evening that Henri Lyon was killed."

"Inspector," Babin nodded. "I have heard much about you."

"Likewise, sir, I assure you," Roche said. "Now, if I may ask a few questions, we can conclude this investigation."

"Yes, of course, Inspector," Babin said, sitting back and resting his hands on his belly.

Roche shuffled his papers and then began. "Inspector, what is your assessment of M. Lyon?"

Babin paused, collecting his thoughts. "I believe Lyon was a man who controlled all in life—except himself. At times, he let his rage consume him, acting violently and impulsively, which led to outcomes he couldn't dictate. These episodes were secret to all who knew him, exposed only through diligent detective work on behalf of myself and Lieutenant Dumont."

"Do you think he killed Giselle?"

"Yes, I do," Babin said, fingering the curve of his moustache. "We know he was emotionally attached—her portrait was found in his private apartment. I suspect he found that she had another lover. He then approached her in a jealous rage as she left Jean-Pierre's studio."

"Do you think he attacked Mme. Lyon?"

"I strongly suspect he did, given evidence we gathered and witness testimony—even though unsubstantiated reports claim it was a policeman. Coupled with our hypothesis of what happened to Giselle and similar attacks conducted on Mme. Lyon, we can only conclude that M. Lyon committed each of these crimes. I suspect that, if I had not shot him dead, he might have killed me or anyone else in the artist's studio that evening."

Roche nodded slightly. "I must agree, Inspector," he confided. "The Paris Police Prefecture is honored, I'm sure, by your long and distinguished service. This inquiry is concluded and has determined that you acted appropriately, having only seconds to make a decision that's been proved correct, just as you have done so many times in your illustrious career. Not only do I find your actions satisfactory, but I am recommending you for the highest commendation the city of Paris can offer."

Chapter Eighty-Nine

Deauville, 1956

Mme. Adele Vincent was the representative from the Commission for the Recovery of Works of Art. She was middle-aged, her black and gray hair in a tight bun, and she was plainly dressed in a grey skirt and blouse. She had spent the day with Zélie, more than an hour with Professor Dufour, and the three of them now sat in the parlor with Marc and Anton.

After Zélie made the additional introductions, Mme. Vincent began to speak. "First of all, before we start, I commend you, Zélie, for all you have done and for your cooperation with the Commission."

"Please," Zélie said, embarrassed. "You deserve the thanks, not me. You did all the work. I only made a phone call and spent the day in my attic with you."

Mme. Vincent smiled. "Perhaps we'll agree to disagree," she said, glancing at the other guests. "I'm also impressed by your support network. I'm sure Marc and Anton have been a huge help, in more ways than one, and I'm especially thankful for Professor Dufour's expert assistance during our investigation."

Michelle nodded. "I'm happy I could assist."

"The information you provided on the paintings was invaluable," Mme. Vincent said. "Especially since so little is known of Jean-Pierre."

"I've continued to research the portraits since I was last here," Michelle said. "And I've been able to date when each was painted, if that helps."

"It does," Zélie said, glancing at Marc and Anton. "I would like to know."

"I would, too," Marc added. "It may solve some of our lingering questions."

The professor referred to a notebook she had with her. "All the paintings were completed at various times in 1874." She paused to scan her notes. "With one exception. The self-portrait of Jean-Pierre, the beach scene with Elise Lyon, was painted in early spring of 1873."

Zélie was confused. She looked at Marc and Anton and shrugged, assuming there might be a mistake. The crime, and all that surrounded it, had occurred in 1874. It didn't make sense. Unless there was more to the story, additional mysteries about to evolve.

Marie glanced at the others. "I'm anxious to hear what happens now. Zélie hasn't told me anything."

"She hasn't told us, either," Anton assured her. "We'll be as surprised as you."

"Zélie is very modest," Mme. Vincent said, eyeing her host. "As you know, she contacted us initially to return the coin collections and paintings owned by Marie and Louie Chard. After some research and a few interviews with various collectors, we were able to verify that the items did belong to the Chards. The Nazis took everything from them in 1944. Unfortunately, they have no living relatives."

"What process do you follow then?" Marc asked.

Mme. Vincent shrugged slightly. "Usually, the items would be donated to a museum. That's what we've done in similar situations."

"It's a fabulous collection," Marc said. "Both the paintings and the coins. It would be nice for the public to enjoy them."

"It's also quite valuable," Mme. Vincent added. "Collectively, we valued the coins and paintings at 1.6 million francs."

Anton whistled softly. "That's a lot of money."

"It is," Mme. Vincent agreed. "Zélie also informed us that she found a substantial amount of money, in both Nazi currency and Swiss francs, that probably belonged to Colonel Hans Fischer of the Gestapo. It was given to her mother-in-law, along with the Chards' belongings, for safe-keeping."

"How much money was in the strongbox?" Anton asked.

"The Nazi currency has little value," Mme. Vincent informed them. "Except to a collector, perhaps. But there's over a half a million Swiss francs."

Anton's eyes widened. "That's a small fortune."

Mme. Vincent nodded. "Yes, it is. But unfortunately, Colonel Fischer was killed shortly after the Allied invasion. We were unable to link the money to him and suspect it's most likely stolen, but from a variety of sources."

"Does he have any family?" Anton asked.

"Yes, we did manage to contact his wife," Mme. Vincent said. "She has since remarried and knew nothing about the money or the documentation that was with it. She claims that she and her children all have their official papers and whatever was discovered in the attic is likely forged."

"What happens to the money?" Marc asked, eyebrows knitted.

Mme. Vincent paused for a moment, collecting her thoughts. "Normally, the government would hold the funds, payable to any future claimants. But in this case, there is no proof of where it came from. The money reverts to the holder, who is Zélie Girard."

There was a brief round of applause as all turned to Zélie. "You're a wealthy woman," Anton exclaimed.

"Your financial worries are gone," Marc said, grinning. "Congratulations."

"Actually," Mme. Vincent said, interrupting the brief celebration, "Zélie offered a wonderful compromise—a fabulous solution for where the treasures found in her attic should reside."

The guests fell silent, turning to Zélie and Mme. Vincent.

"Zélie needs the money desperately," Marc said softly. "Her mother-in-law left her deeply in debt. She could lose her house."

Mme. Vincent glanced at Zélie as if they had already discussed her personal situation. After a moment, she continued. "Zélie has agreed to donate all of the money she found but on two conditions."

Marc glanced at Anton and Professor Dufour, a baffled look on his face. "What are the conditions?"

"First," Mme. Vincent continued, "the funds will be used to create a museum here in Deauville which will feature the Chard's coin collections and the works of Jean-Pierre."

"That's fabulous," Marc said, looking at Zélie with complete surprise. "It's just what the town needs."

"What's the second condition?" Anton asked warily, not yet celebrating.

Mme. Vincent smiled. "Professor Dufour shall head the museum, serving in whatever capacity she chooses, from advisor to curator."

"Me?" Marie exclaimed, eyes wide.

"You're the expert," Zélie said, smiling. "We can't have a museum without an expert to oversee it."

"You can advise us on future purchases," Mme. Vincent added. "The central theme of the museum will be the town of Deauville."

"I would love to do it," Marie said, looking at Zélie. "What a fabulous position to have. Thank you so much for thinking of me."

"I wouldn't have it any other way," Zélie said.

Marc looked at Zélie with admiration. "This is a good thing you're doing. You gave up a fortune."

Zélie shrugged and smiled weakly. "I couldn't keep the money, regardless of my financial situation. Not when I knew where it came from. Now something good can come from all of the evil."

Chapter Ninety

Montmartre, 1874

Inspector Nicolas Babin sat in his office at police headquarters. The *Paris Gazette* was sprawled on the desk, competing for space with a large mug of espresso, a plate holding a half-eaten buttered croissant, piles of reports, a box of cigars, and a jar of sweet candies, almost empty. He had enjoyed reading the headlines announcing his commendation to the citizens of Paris and was immersed in an article on the third page when someone knocked on his door.

"Come in," the Inspector called, his eyes trained on the newspaper.

The door opened, and Claude Dumont entered, dressed not in his police uniform but in brown trousers with matching jacket, holding a cap in his hand. "Inspector, I've come to say my goodbyes."

"Ah, Lieutenant Dumont, my brightest pupil," Babin said. "Please, sit for a moment."

Dumont sat in the straight-back chair in front of the desk. "I want to thank you for all you've done for me."

"I was shocked by the news, Lieutenant, I really was. The best man I have ever trained now sits before me, having resigned from the Paris Police Prefecture. What a sorry day for the city of Paris."

"You're too kind, Inspector," Dumont said, blushing. "Nothing means more than your compliments."

"You're a good man, Dumont," Babin continued. "I'm sure you'll establish law and order very quickly in that little town by the sea."

Dumont chuckled. "It was an offer I couldn't refuse —Commissioner of Police."

"I know, I know," Babin interrupted. "You go back to the town in which you were raised. But now you return as a hero and former assistant to the renowned Inspector Nicolas Babin." He pointed to the newspaper. "How flattering, the headlines."

"All well-deserved," Dumont said. "You're a legend, Inspector. I appreciate all that you have taught me."

"It was nothing. You were a good pupil. I may not be so fortunate with my next assistant."

Dumont laughed. "Regardless of who it is, I'm sure you'll train him well."

"Perhaps," Babin said. "Or perhaps not." He laughed loudly and then coughed for a moment more.

"Are you all right, Inspector?"

"Yes, yes, of course," Babin said. He folded the paper and pointed to the headline. "Did you see this? You are not the only one leaving Paris."

Dumont leaned across the desk, trying to read the paper. "Elise Lyon?"

"Yes, although it comes as no surprise," Babin said. "Especially after the merger."

Dumont cocked his head. "What merger is that?"

"Lieutenant Dumont, have you been in a cave?"

Babin scolded him playfully.

Dumont smiled. "I've been making arrangements to relocate. I haven't kept up with the news."

"It seems our friend and former suspect, Andre Sinclair, has done quite well for himself after the unfortunate demise of Henri Lyon."

Dumont still looked confused. "I'm not sure I understand."

Babin rolled his eyes. "I shall read the article," he said. "Mme. Elise Lyon, aged 28, owner of the global conglomerate, Lyon and Sons, announced the merger of her company with Normandy Mines, owned by Andre Sinclair. The combined company will operate under the name of Lyon and Sons and will be run by M. Sinclair. Mme. Lyon will spend most of her time at her summer cottage in Deauville, the town in which she was born and raised. She intends to maintain her Paris townhouse, where she resided for only a year, although her time spent there will be limited."

"I wasn't aware," Dumont said, his expression showing surprise. "But I suppose it does make sense. She's been through a trying ordeal. Why not return to her family and friends?"

Babin leaned forward. "As a very wealthy woman, I might add. And Sinclair now runs one of the most prestigious firms in all of France. It seems those who surrounded Henri Lyon did very well for themselves. Don't you agree?"

Epilogue

Deauville, 1956

Zélie smiled as Luc pushed a metal fire truck with a chrome ladder across the floor under the watchful eye of Marc Rayne.

"Are we going to have macarons and ice cream?" Luc asked, looking up at Marc.

Marc chuckled. "We might," he said. "If you eat all your dinner."

"Thank you so much for watching him," Zélie said. "I appreciate it."

"I'm looking forward to it. Don't worry about a thing. Just enjoy your date."

Zélie laughed. "I wouldn't call it a date, just dinner between friends."

"I don't think so," Marc teased. "Not the way you're smiling. But I do have some news to share with you and Anton when he gets here."

The knock on the front door came a moment later. Zélie left the parlor to answer it. "Come in, Anton."

"Hello, Zélie," Anton said, smiling shyly as he handed her a bouquet of roses.

"Thank you so much," she said. "They're beautiful."

"You're welcome," he replied as his eyes widened. "What a lovely dress. You look fabulous."

She smiled. "Thank you, you're very kind. Go ahead in the parlor while I put these in some water. Marc and Luc are in there."

Zélie filled an amber vase with water, added the roses, and set them on the kitchen table, listening as Luc told Anton about his firetruck. "Would you like a glass of wine before we go," she called into the parlor. "Marc has something to tell us."

"Sure," Anton replied. "I have some news, too."

Zélie poured three glasses of wine and sat in the parlor with Marc and Anton, eyeing Luc as he went into the next room with his truck. She looked at the men expectedly.

Anton glanced at Marc. "I'll go first," he said. "I found someone interested in the cottage, a groundskeeper at the race track."

Zélie was relieved. "Oh, that's wonderful. I can get by if someone rents it. It's still a little tight, but I'm working on it."

"He wants to see it tomorrow morning," Anton said. "I can vouch for his character. He won't cause any problems."

"Perfect," Zélie said. "I hope he likes it."

Marc sipped his wine. "One less thing to worry about," he said and then paused to see if Anton had anything else. "My turn, I suppose. I have some interesting information."

"Really?" Zélie asked. "It must be a day for good news."

"I have copies of several news articles that I found in Rouen," Marc said. "I've managed to piece together what I think is an unbelievable crime."

Zélie glanced at Anton, who shrugged. "We can't wait to hear it."

"Yes, don't keep us in suspense," Anton urged.

Marc opened a manilla folder and removed a stack of papers. "The first is a lengthy article that describes the untimely death of Henri Lyon."

Anton arched his eyebrows. "How did he die?"

"An unexpected altercation, it seems," Marc began. "It started when Henri Lyon barged into Jean-Pierre's studio. His wife Elise was supposedly posing for her portrait, but for some unknown reason, Henri attacked Jean-Pierre and knocked him unconscious."

Zélie's eyes widened. "Maybe she wasn't really posing."

Anton chuckled. "It doesn't seem like she was."

"Wait, it gets better," Marc said. "Lieutenant Dumont entered seconds later and was also attacked by Lyon who had been trying to strangle Elise. Inspector Babin arrived at the scene and shot Henri Lyon, killing him instantly."

"What a tragedy!" Zélie exclaimed. "How could something like that happen?"

Marc shrugged. "It is hard to believe. But Babin was cleared of any wrong-doing and received a commendation for his actions. During the investigation, it was determined that Henri Lyon killed Giselle Picard, a model and known prostitute. She was allegedly his mistress."

Zélie was quiet for a moment, digesting what Marc said. "It's starting to make sense to me now. I think I might know where this all leads."

"Wait, I have more," Marc said. "It seems two attempts were also made on the life of Elise Lyon and, even though a witness claimed the assailant was a policeman, Babin insisted it was Henri Lyon. The attacks on Elise mirrored the murder of Giselle Picard, and the first assault occurred in the exact location of Giselle's murder identified in one of the portraits."

Anton looked at the others, eyes wide. "That's incredible."

"It is," Marc agreed. "For all of Paris, and most of the modern world, that's where the story ended."

Zélie looked at him curiously. "But it isn't the end?"

Marc shook his head, laughing lightly. "I'm not sure why I did it. Instinct, I suppose. Or maybe a lifetime of criminal investigations. But I kept browsing through newspapers, looking for additional information. It's quite easy with the new machines they have at the Rouen library."

"What did you find?" Anton asked. "We can't wait to hear about it."

"One last article ties it all together," Marc continued. "It's rather lengthy, but it's dated February of 1875, and concerns a man arrested for murdering prostitutes. He confessed to the killing of Giselle Picard."

"Then it wasn't Henri Lyon?" Anton asked with disbelief.

"Apparently not," Marc said. "The article states that an exhaustive investigation proved that Lyon didn't even know Giselle Picard. Apparently, someone planted her portrait in his apartment for the police to find, and that was used as evidence."

"Lyon was framed," Zélie said, and she suspected she knew why.

"Exactly," Marc replied. "But we don't know by whom." He then paused, pensive.

"Is there more?" Zélie asked, looking at him curiously.

"I'm not sure," Marc muttered. "But I just had a thought. I was involved in a case in Calais where a witness overheard different conversations that supposedly proved someone's innocence. But it was later determined that the conversations were staged."

"And you think that's what happened here?" Zélie asked.

Marc shrugged. "It's possible. The newspaper articles mention a prominent witness named Mme. Michel who overheard conversations and saw Lyon just before the altercation."

"But how would we know if what she overheard was accurate?" Anton asked. "We're only guessing at this point."

"Yes, I know," Marc replied. "But it seems odd that she was so involved."

Zélie considered all Marc had revealed. "What did Babin say after he was proven wrong?"

"Babin died in December of 1874," Marc explained. "Tuberculosis. He never knew that he killed an innocent man."

Zélie and Anton were quiet, digesting the information. "You were a detective," Anton said. "Did you think Henri Lyon was guilty based on the evidence presented?"

"Yes, it seemed so," Marc said with a shrug. "But I guess we'll never know what really happened."

Zélie eyed the two for a moment, a smile curling her lips. "I know what happened," she said slyly.

Marc looked at her, eyes wide. "You do?"

She nodded. "Yes, I think so."

Anton laughed. "Are you going to tell us?"

She paused, collecting her thoughts. "I actually had suspicions the other day, but what Marc just learned confirmed it," she explained. "Professor Dufour made a few comments that made me realize we might be too focused on the paintings and for the wrong reasons.

Especially when I considered an additional theme that they represent."

Marc glanced at Anton and shrugged. "I don't understand."

Zélie smiled. "I think the town of Deauville is the other clue that the paintings provided."

Marc chuckled. "I still don't get it."

"Deauville is the horseracing capital of France, maybe even Europe," Zélie said.

"The portrait of Golden Cross," Anton guessed.

Zélie nodded. "And what did M. Armand tell us? Andre Sinclair, the original owner of Golden Cross, had a home in Deauville and was probably a resident."

"But he owned Normandy Mines," Marc said. "He was a Parisian businessman."

"He could be both, and apparently he was." She was enjoying herself, watching their expressions as she unraveled the mystery. "What other painting referenced Deauville?"

"The beach scene," Marc stated.

"And don't forget what Professor Dufour told us about that," Zélie continued. "The self portrait of Jean-Pierre and Elise Lyon was painted in early spring of 1873—before she went to Paris."

Anton's eyes widened. "They were lovers!"

"I think so," Zélie said, grinning as she leaned back in the chair. "Professor Dufour did tell us that Jean-Pierre was from Deauville."

"And Elise was a local resident," Marc added. "Henri Lyon had a summer cottage here and was very wealthy, a member of a much different social class."

"An arranged marriage," Anton said triumphantly.

Zélie nodded. "It was common in those days."

"I bet Elise's father owed Henri Lyon in some fashion," Marc suggested, "and he repaid the debt with his daughter's hand in marriage. We all saw her portrait. She was a beautiful woman."

"The three of them must have known each other before the murder in Paris," Anton said. "Elise, Jean-Pierre, and Andre Sinclair."

"Four," Zélie corrected him.

Marc glanced at Anton and shrugged. "You're a step or two ahead of us."

"Claude Dumont's granddaughter lived in Deauville," Zélie said. "And the paintings are in Deauville. We've had the biggest clue from the very beginning. We just didn't see it."

Anton was confused. "What didn't we see?"

"Yes, I don't understand," Marc admitted. "Are you suggesting Dumont knew Elise, Jean-Pierre, and Sinclair?"

"I am," Zélie said. "It was Professor Dufour who prompted me. Do you remember when we were in the attic, and she pointed at the photographs by the door and said they could be valuable, from the same period as the paintings?"

Marc thought for a moment. "I remember her saying that. But those photographs were scenes of Deauville—the race track under construction, the first casino being built."

"Do you remember when we sorted through all the boxes?" Zélie asked. "The day we found the coins?"

Marc's eyes widened. "Photographs," he said. "There were boxes of photographs."

"It seems that one of the boxes must have belonged to the Chards," Zélie said as she walked over to the desk and withdrew two photographs, handing the first to Marc. "I found these."

"A photo of two men," Marc said. "It's a little grainy, hard to see."

"Look at the back," she suggested.

"October 3, 1874," he said, reading a neatly printed description. "Deauville Police Commissioner Claude Dumont greets his closest friend and latest arrival to the city, Jean-Pierre, one of Paris's greatest artists."

"Closest friend," Zélie repeated. "It explains how Dumont and his granddaughter came to possess the paintings."

"You're building a concrete case!" Marc exclaimed. "You would make a great detective."

"I learned from the best," she said, pointing at him.

"Thanks for the compliment, but I never would have figured all of this out."

"One last item," Zélie said, handing it to Marc. "It's a postcard."

Marc looked at the front, reading the caption. "It's the victory celebration for Golden Cross in the 1876 Poule des Produits."

"Read the back," Zélie said.

Marc turned the postcard over. "Four life-long friends celebrate Golden Cross's victory: owner Elise Lyon, former owner Andre Sinclair, the artist Jean-Pierre, and Commissioner of Police Claude Dumont."

"Amazing," Anton said, eyes wide. "They were best friends who all grew up in Deauville. Could this have been a conspiracy?"

Marc paused, pensive. "One of the newspaper articles said a witness claimed the man who assaulted Elise

Lyon wore a police uniform. Were the attacks on Elise staged by Claude Dumont?"

"Think about it," Zélie said. "Everyone got what they wanted. Elise escaped an arranged marriage and was reunited with her lover, Jean-Pierre."

"Dumont was widely recognized for saving Elise Lyon's life and became police commissioner in Deauville," Anton said.

"And Andre Sinclair assumed control of a global conglomerate," Zélie added. She stood and motioned to Anton, ready to leave for their dinner date.

Marc slowly shook his head. "I suppose the question becomes whether or not these four friends framed Henri Lyon, tricking renowned police inspector Nicolas Babin into killing him?"

Zélie shrugged. "It certainly seems like it. But I suppose we'll never know."

"No, I guess we won't," Marc agreed.

"It is closure, if nothing else," Zelie said. "For many different people."

Anton nodded. "Elise reunited with Jean-Pierre."

"Anton Sinclair bested Henri Lyon," Marc said. "Even if he did lose Golden Cross."

Zélie thought about her mother-in-law, the woman she never knew—gambler and Resistance fighter. "Eva's reputation has been restored. Now she can be recognized as the hero she truly was."

"And the valuables she safeguarded have a proper home," Marc said. He glanced in the next room where Luc quietly played with his firetrucks. "Even Luc, overcome with grief when you first arrived, is doing much better."

"He is," Zélie agreed, sighing with relief. "I was so worried about him."

Marc chuckled. "Now he's making friends and riding horses."

"I don't know how to thank you both," Zélie said. "You've done so much to help him."

"Look at all of us," Anton offered. "The Deauville mystery brought us together, and we've become good friends."

"And maybe more," Marc said with a wink.

Zélie playfully smacked Marc's arm and started toward the door. "We won't be long." She turned to Anton and smiled. It felt good. She hadn't smiled that way in a long time.

About the Author

John Anthony Miller writes all things historical—thrillers, mysteries, and romance. He sets his novels in exotic locations spanning all eras of space and time with complex characters forced to face inner conflicts, fighting demons both real and imagined. Each of his novels are unique: a Medieval epic, two Jazz Age mysteries, a Cold-War thriller, a 1970s romance, four WWII thrillers, and the Parisian murder mystery, *A Crime Though Time*. He lives in southern New Jersey.

Other Books by John Anthony Miller

WWII Fiction

To Parts Unknown

In Satan's Shadow

All the King's Soldiers

When Darkness Comes

Historical Mysteries

Honour the Dead

Sinner, Saint or Serpent

The Widow's Walk

Cold War Thriller

For Those Who Dare

Medieval Fiction

Song of Gabrielle

Made in United States
Orlando, FL
20 January 2024

42722729R00231